#1 Steve Dancy

The Shopkeeper

**Center Point
Large Print**

**This Large Print Book carries the
Seal of Approval of N.A.V.H.**

The Shopkeeper

A Steve Dancy Tale

James D. Best

CENTER POINT PUBLISHING
THORNDIKE, MAINE

ISBN: 978-1-60285-573-1

Library of Congress Cataloging-in-Publication Data

Best, James D., 1945-
  The shopkeeper : a Steve Dancy tale / James D. Best.
    p. cm.
  ISBN 978-1-60285-573-1 (lib. bdg. : alk. paper)
  1. Large type books. I. Title.

PS3602.E785S56 2009
813'.6--dc22

2009018868

To Diane

Chapter 1

"Two."

Richard scratched his stubbly chin with ink-stained fingers. "Pass."

I turned to my partner. He passed but not before giving me a sour look.

Everyone stared at Dr. Dooley. He took his time, but we all knew. After forcing us to watch his little drama, he finally said, "Pass," and I immediately responded with, "Hearts."

I caught an uneasy glance from Jeremiah, but I gave my partner a wink and led with the ace of spades. Richard's three of hearts was in mid-flight when a distant gunshot froze everything but the floating card. When I started to speak, Jeremiah halted me with an upraised palm and perked ears.

After a few moments, my companions' rigid expressions suddenly regained life. "Damn," Dooley said.

"Looks like ya might have some work, Doc," Jeremiah said.

"A series of gunshots means a drunk got rowdy, but one or two means somebody probably got himself shot," Richard said.

The explanation was for me, the newly arrived city dweller. The year was 1879, and I had come to the western frontier to explore and find adventure. I had arrived in this Nevada mining settlement only four days before and had soon made friends with the only literate men in this stove-top town.

"Stay here." Dr. Dooley scratched his chair away from the table. "I'll have a look."

"Doc, just hang in and finish the hand," Richard said. "They'll come and get ya if they need ya."

On hot nights, Richard propped the front door ajar with a heavy can of ink. Dooley glanced through the opening to see if any hysterical men were running in our direction.

"They know where ya are," Richard added.

Dooley scooted his chair back up to the table. "All right, let's play."

When I arrived in town, I had gone over to the newspaper office to buy current and back issues of the town paper, a habit I had picked up in my travels. A quick read of four or five issues gave a person a fair grasp of the town and its grand denizens. Pickhandle Gulch seemed to have a penchant for rowdiness, but the newspaper stories concentrated on the silver mines and their monthly production. As best I could tell, people with good claims were growing richer than the paper miners I was familiar with on Wall Street.

When I had entered his print shop four days ago, Richard—reporter, editor, and printer—looked pleased to sell some old copies, but he was absolutely delighted when I answered a casual query in the affirmative: yes, I knew how to play whist. Reverend Cunningham, their fourth, had died a few weeks prior, and the three men had been in a funk ever since.

Thus started our nightly ritual of after-dinner whist. Funny how the little pleasures make life worth living, and life in Pickhandle Gulch needed some diversion beyond the predictable fare at Ruby's whorehouse. I had visited many western towns, but Pickhandle Gulch seemed especially bleak. The discovery of silver had attracted rough-hewn men from all over the continent, and now the settlement had grown to be the largest in southwest Nevada.

"Richard, it's your lead, for God's sake." Jeremiah used an oath I presumed the Reverend Cunningham would have objected to.

Everybody returned their attention to the cards, Richard with a smidgen of glee, and my partner with elevating levels of disgust every time Richard pulled another heart from his hand. Despite my best efforts, the hand played out badly for us, and we went set.

I guessed that my three companions were close to my age, and I had just celebrated my thirty-first birthday. Richard showed the fastidiousness of a printer and was afflicted with a strain of grumpiness that could become endearing once you got to know him. And he was a good whist player short spades during the last hand.

My partner, Jeremiah, ran the general store and

had a good head for numbers and an even better head for cards.

Dr. Dooley wore the crumpled look and grouchy manner of a seasoned physician. I presume he thought this would boost patients' confidence, but I preferred my doctors young and recently educated rather than old and world-weary.

These were three smart men trapped in a dusty, hot town that pined for a wisp of breeze or a cleansing shower. Since I had arrived, neither blessing had interrupted the kilnlike days that invariably melded into flat, windless nights.

As I dealt the next hand, little Jemmy stuck his head in the open door and yelled, "Hey, Doc! Brian Cutler shot Dave Masters!"

"Hurt bad?" Dooley asked.

"Dead."

"Then it's the undertaker's problem, not mine."

"Don't you want to look at the body?"

"Seen dead bodies before. Run along, Jemmy. We got a serious game here."

A serious game was two bits a point, but the size of the bet meant nothing. With the last hand, ol' Doc and Richard led eleven to six, and evidently, no ordinary killing was going to cut short their grab for glory.

I stopped shuffling and asked, "Richard, don't you need to go get the story?"

"Not news. Deal."

"Not news?"

"The Cutlers are a vile bunch," Richard explained. "Two brothers . . . each as mean as a diamondback. They come to town every couple of weeks to get drunk, visit Ruby's, shoot some poor son of a bitch, and get a bath. Pretty much in that order."

I ignored Richard's wave that prompted me to deal the cards. "What about the law?" I asked.

"As long as the Cutlers pay for damages, the sheriff turns a blind eye." He made another hand motion. "Damn it, quit stalling and deal them cards. It's time you took the licking you deserve."

I passed the deck to my right, but Dooley declined to cut. When I continued to hesitate, Richard made another *Hurry up* gesture. I knew the command to deal must hide a larger story, but their faces told me this was all I was going to get, at least tonight. A man killed, but the town newspaperman and the sole doctor barely blink. This was the West, and Pickhandle Gulch was remote and isolated, but my new friends' reaction seemed surprisingly subdued.

I glanced at the other men one more time. No one volunteered to enlighten me, so I shrugged and dealt the cards.

Chapter 2

Other meals I eat for fuel, but I dawdle over break-fast—and Mary cooks a hell of a breakfast. Mary ran the restaurant across the street from my ragtag hotel. It was not a restaurant in a New York sense, but nonetheless it was the best place to eat in Pickhandle Gulch. Her small building, plank floors, and long tables were all made from unfinished lumber, but a few touches like lace curtains had softened the rough appearance. Breakfast for miners usually consisted of biscuits eaten standing up in some stale-smelling saloon. Not fancy, but quick. They needed to get to work. Mary catered to the mine owners, town merchants, and people like myself, who had the time and money to eat a slow, hearty breakfast.

As I entered her tidy café, the aroma pulled the trigger on my appetite. I took my usual seat at a table by the window, and Mary sauntered over with a cup of black coffee that suspended its own little cloud of steam above the rim.

"What'll ya have today, Mr. Dancy?"

"Everything."

"Everything it is—over easy, crispy, and soaked in grease."

"You got it," I said.

As Mary left to prepare my feast, I took a sip of coffee and opened the book I had brought from my room. I prized breakfast, because my lifelong habit was to eat this meal alone. Well, not alone. I always have a good book to keep me company, and I had Captain Ahab as my guest today. Joining the raggedy whist club included membership in an informal lending library. We all owned a few books, and together we had a decent library. I was in a hurry to finish this reading of *Moby Dick*, so I could exchange it with Jeremiah for *The Adventures of Tom Sawyer*, a new book by Mark Twain. I was anxious to get to it, because a few years back, Twain, now a famous writer, had been a newspaper reporter in Virginia City, Nevada.

I was on my second cup of coffee and page 97, when Mary brought over two plates that could feed a family of four. It took me a few minutes to arrange the food the way I like and return to page 97.

"So, you must be the fancy stranger."

"What?" I looked up to see two ugly men. No amount of grooming could make these ruffians presentable, even to a spinster's desperate father. Two identical sets of bulbous noses, prominent chins, and deep-set black eyes hovered over me. The men were not big—scrawny and slump-shouldered, in fact—but they nevertheless spewed menace like a skunk with an uplifted tail.

"Ain't you the one that rented the front room at the Grand Hotel?" This came from the smaller man, but his tone said he was the leader.

"Yep," said the second one, "and I hear ya got a rich man's rig down at Smith's Livery."

"Guilty, but I think the hotel is misnamed." I held out my hand and kept my voice light. "Steve Dancy . . . and you gentlemen?"

"That room costs four bucks a day."

They ignored my proffered hand, so I tried to be nonchalant as I made a dismissive wave. "I got a better deal."

"Where'd ya git yer money?"

I had figured out that these were the infamous Cutler brothers. I wanted to tell the skinny character that where I got my money was none of his business, but the Cutler reputation and mean look prompted caution.

"I'm a shopkeeper."

"A shopkeeper? You musta been a slyboots."

"I ran an honest shop." I tried to look casual as I took another sip of coffee. "But I sold it for a good price."

"Where?"

"New York City."

"New York?" The skinny Cutler spat out the name of my hometown with the kind of disdain sniffy wives reserved for ladies of ill repute. "How'd ya git out here?"

"Train, and then a horse from Denver."

"I meant why. Why'd ya leave New York? Y'ain't thinkin' about musclin' yer way into minin', are ya?"

"No. Sorry, gentlemen, but I know nothing about mining. I just came to see a little of the Wild West."

For some reason, this made the duo laugh. I searched for a way to get back to Captain Ahab, but I came up empty. No use aggravating this dangerous pair. Just be polite and hope they get bored and go away.

The skinny one gave a hail-fellow shove to the one on his right. "This greenhorn wants to see the Wild West, does he? Maybe we should show him a little."

"Well, I—"

The skinny Cutler interrupted me. "Listen, we don't take kindly to strangers tryin' to horn their way into one of these-here mines. Take yer money and git. Got it?"

I couldn't figure out why these two were so concerned about mining rights. Surely they didn't own a claim. I had seen laborers go into the tunnels, and I had seen several overseers, and these two didn't look like either. Later, I would ask Richard about the Cutler brothers, but right now I just wanted to ease their minds.

"Gentlemen, let me assure you that I have no interest in mines or mining. I'm just a tourist in town for a short stay."

"Just out here to see the Wild West, huh? Well, in Nevada, men wear six-shooters. Where's yers?"

I strove to keep my voice light. "Guns can get you in trouble."

"Not wearin' a gun might git ya in more trouble." The smaller Cutler leaned in against me. "Ya better git one, 'cuz ya sure as hell are gonna need it if we catch ya nosin' around our business."

I didn't know how to respond, so I worked to keep my face neutral. I knew that in the West, men wore guns like New Yorkers wore suspenders, but I didn't covet that kind of adventure. Last year, I had decided to sell all my possessions and head for the frontier. For nine months, I had been casually moving in a westerly direction and had been in some rough towns. Never before had I felt a need to carry a sidearm, and I had no inclination to start now. Civilization had come to the West by the late nineteenth century, and despite the dime novels, I found things pretty tame. Until today.

"If your business is mines, I won't need a gun," I said.

The smaller Cutler didn't look convinced. "Either you're lyin' or ya scare easy. Why else would ya be in this goddamn town?"

"Why won't you believe I'm just here to see the sights?"

"'Cuz we been outside, greenhorn. There ain't no sights."

"You're yella." This came from the taller Cutler, who up to now had let his brother do the talking.

This took me by surprise, and before I could stop myself, I blurted out, "No I'm not!"

The taller one grinned. "Then git a gun." He

16

laughed in a way that made me uncomfortable. "'Cuz maybe next time, I'll show ya the sights of mine."

His crude pun actually surprised me. He didn't look intelligent enough to compose a complete sentence. These were dangerous men, and I wanted them to go away. Now.

I tried what I hoped was a disarming smile. "I'll just keep to myself, if you don't mind. No need for gunplay. Noise frightens me."

"Damn, you're yella," the smaller one cackled. With that, he reached over and stuck his finger in my eggs and held my eyes with a challenging leer. When I returned my best attempt at a blank look, he swirled his finger, messed my eggs, and then held a yolk-stained finger in front of my face. "Yep, yella." Heaping on even more provocation, he slowly wiped his finger on my sleeve. "Yer eggs are cold, greenhorn."

I tried another smile and said, "Thank you, I hate cold eggs."

The two men laughed uproariously. As I wondered what additional indignity they could invent, they simply turned and walked to a table in the back. I exhaled in relief, but the echo of the raspy Cutler laugh hurt in an unfamiliar place.

Mary rushed over, clucking like a mother hen, "Oh, Mr. Dancy, let me get you fresh eggs."

Shaking a bit from anger, or perhaps humiliation, I said, "Yes, please, thank you." She started to say something, thought better of it, and whirled before I sputtered out, "Mary, tell those men in back that their breakfast is on me."

"Mr. Dancy, are you—"

"Yes, quite sure."

I didn't like the sad look she gave me as she returned to the kitchen. At least with her departure, wreathed in pity or not, I could get back to the comfort of my morning ritual.

Chapter 3

"That's a mistake."

I thought the Cutlers had finally left me alone. Annoyed, I looked up from my breakfast and book to see a middle-aged, sturdily built man whose face showed the same tatty and frayed history as his workaday garb.

I must have looked puzzled, because he added, "Ya can't buy peace with them Cutlers. They'll just come back until they squeeze the last little spark of manhood outta ya."

I glanced toward the back of the café. "You're probably right. Dumb."

"May I sit a minute?"

I had to find another place for breakfast. "Yes, of course."

The craggy man took a seat across from me and extended his hand. "Jeff Sharp. I understand you're Steve Dancy."

"Yes, I am . . . from New York City."

"A bustlin' place. Too many people for my taste."

"You've been to New York?"

"Twice." Sharp raised a hand to get Mary's attention. Damn; this was not going to be a short interruption.

When Mary arrived, Sharp said, "Mary, dear, could you get a weather-beaten ol' man a cup of hot coffee?"

"With pleasure, Jeffrey."

"I asked you not to call me that." Sharp's tone displayed resigned irritation rather than anger.

Mary winked and scurried off to get the coffee. After watching her retreating backside a while, Sharp returned his attention to me. "The way I see it, ya got two choices. The first is to get a gun, so the odds are a little more even."

"Why not have the Cutlers remove their guns? That'd make things more even."

"Don't suggest that. One of the brothers'll unhook an' invite ya into the street. You'll think you're about to engage in a little fisticuffs, but before ya can say 'Put 'em up,' you'll find a knife in your belly. Seen it before. They'll just gut ya from side to side an' laugh all the while ya bleed to death."

Sharp leaned back and stared at me, so I asked, "What's my second choice?"

"Get out of town."

To buy time, I took a bite of my bacon. After

chewing a bit, I said, "I've never shot at a man, and I'm not going to challenge those boys to a duel."

"Then leave. Right now. Don't finish your meal. Just git up, throw your stuff together, an' ride out before they finish that meal ya so foolishly bought 'em."

"I'm expected for whist this evening."

"I heard about your game. Good men ya sidled up to, but they can't protect ya."

"Who can?"

"Nobody." Sharp leaned over close. "Them Cutlers ain't right in the head." Sharp nodded toward their table. "Inbreedin', I'm a-thinkin'."

"They leave you alone?"

"For now. The Cutlers work for Sean Washburn. He owns the biggest private minin' operation in the state. I own the second biggest." Sharp gave another glance to the back of the room. "Sean lets the Cutlers have their fun, but they won't go against his orders, an' we've had an uneasy truce for years." Sharp shrugged, "Besides, I got ruffians of my own to protect my claims."

The news that Sharp owned mining claims disturbed me. Here I sat, talking to a mine owner, when I had just told the Cutlers I had no interest in mining. Damn. I wanted to look over to see whether they were watching, but I knew that would be a mistake. Should I be rude and noisily send Sharp away? I decided that if the Cutlers had made up their minds, nothing would change them.

Besides, I might learn something from Sharp that could help me out of this mess.

I pushed my plate away. "Listen, I may not be from the West, but I understand that kind of men. I won't let them bait me into something foolish."

"Ya already have. Like a barnyard cat, these boys like to play with their prey before they kill."

"First they'll need to trap me behind a crate. I'll stay in open field."

Sharp looked at me and then shook his head in defeat. "Suit yourself."

After he finished warning me to fight or flee, I had a good talk with Jeff Sharp. I liked the man. While he lacked formal education, he had a different kind of knowledge and the wisdom that comes from having experienced the world. Sharp had been to Europe and South America, worked in mines, driven a stagecoach, bossed a cattle drive, and acted as an agent for a New York importer. He had the savvy of a trader and displayed the confidence of someone who had bossed tough men in the middle of nowhere.

We talked about the pieces of New York that we shared; there were many. The craggy man seemed to crave new experiences and had visited every nook and cranny of the large metropolis. Sharp asked where my shop was located, and he seemed satisfied when I simply said that it was on the outskirts of the city.

At the end of our leisurely conversation, Sharp

looked at me, hesitated, and then said, "There *is* a third way. I could tell Washburn I hired ya. The Cutlers leave my men alone."

"Thanks," I said. "I might consider your offer if things get worse, but for now, I'd just as soon let things settle down on their own."

After I paid the check for both of us, I stood to leave, and Sharp rose with me. Then he did something disconcerting. He extended his hand and said, "Pleasure talking with ya."

I had no choice, so I shook Sharp's hand and stole a glance over his shoulder. Sure enough, the Cutlers were both eying me. Richard had said the brothers came into Pickhandle Gulch every couple of weeks, so maybe I just needed to stay out of sight until they left town.

After I left Mary's, I locked myself in my room to spend a few hours with Melville.

Chapter 4

After reading for a couple of hours, I got tired of being closed in and decided to wander over to Jeremiah's general store for tobacco and some civil conversation.

Pickhandle Gulch nestled between the Silver Peak Range and the Excelsior Mountains. The main road curved up a mild grade toward a stamp mill, an ugly building that pulverized rock and made a nerve-racking noise all day long. About two dozen thrown-together buildings lined either side of a road, and hundreds of hovels scarred the surrounding slopes. Miners built these shelters with rocks because the beige hills that rolled off in every direction were completely barren of trees. For that matter, hardly any foliage reached above a man's boots, and even the valley spread out below presented only a relentless brown landscape spotted with a few rocks and some pale sagebrush. Lumber was the second-dearest commodity in town. Water was the first.

The town did not sit pretty, but the splendor of the countryside grew on you. Its beauty came from its expansiveness. A vast sky canopied sight lines that went on forever, and the russet hills seemed to writhe with the changing light. I liked Nevada, but I sure missed the color green.

Most people lived in outlying areas and came into town to get provisions, visit the saloons, eat a decent meal, and mostly, I supposed, enjoy the hospitality at Ruby's. Wherever they came from and for whatever purpose, few left without spending a goodly sum at Jeremiah's general store.

Jeremiah had migrated from somewhere in Colorado and built a two-story clapboard building to ply his lucrative trade. Behind the building, Jeremiah had buried an ice cellar; every week, he had ice hauled to town from high in the mountains. He made a good profit selling the ice to the town's four saloons, and I blessed him daily for the chilled beer. He lived above his store and, from what I could gather, had few interests besides selling his wares and playing whist. I guessed that Jeremiah was in his thirties, but his prematurely bald pate, pudgy face, and formidable paunch added at least five years to his appearance.

When I entered, Jeremiah gave me a friendly nod and finished with another customer before going into the back room. In a few minutes, he returned with two cups of lukewarm coffee. Handing me one of the cups, he leaned over the counter, pulled out a packet of my favorite pipe tobacco, and tossed it to me. I nodded thanks as he unconsciously reached into a huge cookie jar for a gingersnap. Jeremiah constantly munched gingersnaps as he drank endless cups of truly awful coffee.

I took a sip of the coffee and felt myself grimace. "Jeremiah, you sell decent coffee beans. Why do you drink this swill?"

"I'm runnin' a store here. I don't have time to roast, grind, and boil new coffee all day long. Besides, the higher grades are overrated and over-priced. This tastes just fine."

I waved my coffee cup in the direction of his stock. "Admit it: you're just too cheap to drink your good inventory."

"If it's not to your likin', Mary will sell ya a cup for a nickel."

Something in my face must have revealed my unease at hearing this comment, because Jeremiah looked quizzical and then asked, "What's wrong?"

"I had a bad experience at Mary's this morning."

"Hardly seems likely. She's the best cook hereabouts."

"Not the food. Something else." I motioned toward the center of the store. "Let's sit, and I'll tell you about it."

We settled into a couple of rockers around an unlit potbelly stove, and I stuffed and tapped my pipe until it satisfied me and then took my time lighting it. After a few slow draws, I described my nasty encounter with the Cutlers.

When I finished, Jeremiah gave me a look that reminded me of the pitiful glance Mary had thrown my way earlier. I didn't understand. I knew they considered me a greenhorn, but I had banged around the West for nearly a year and had taken care of myself just fine. Why did everyone worry about a few rowdies with less self-control than a pair of spoiled ten-year-olds?

Sooner or later, everyone had to visit the general store to buy provisions. Most people lingered to trade news and gossip. Women liked to chat as they fingered the dry goods along the back counter, while the men usually shared a smoke around the cast-iron stove that dominated the middle of the store. Jeremiah's sympathetic face invited confidences, so he knew most of the town's secrets and tawdry tales. I needed to figure out how much trouble I was really in, so I started asking my whist partner questions.

Jeremiah told me that dealing with the Cutlers would be dodgy, but the real threat was their boss, Sean Washburn—a pure and simple thug, untainted by even a smidgen of conscience. Washburn's boundless greed and ruthless cunning had built a huge mining operation that extended all over the state, including Virginia City. It was beneath him to actually prospect. He let others sweat it out in the canyon furnaces until they found veins of silver. Then, like a feudal lord, he would jump their claim and append it to his already thriving enterprises. He gave small holders a simple choice: abandon their diggings for a pittance or be buried under their claim. The Cutlers served Washburn as a handy tool to scare the hardscrabble miners—or eliminate them if they refused to scurry away in panic.

Now I understood why the Cutlers seemed so concerned that I might have an interest in mining. They were protecting the interests of their boss.

Jeremiah told me that since I didn't own a stake in a producing mine, Washburn had no professional interest in me. Occasionally, the Cutlers might kill for fun, he said, but most of the time, Washburn pointed them at enough targets to keep them busy. Dave Masters, the man they shot yesterday, had owned a small silver shaft just south of Washburn's main mining operation.

"What can you tell me about Jeff Sharp?"

"How'd ya hear about Sharp?"

"He sat down with me after the Cutlers left, but

they were still inside Mary's and saw us together." Despite my distaste, I swallowed the last of my coffee. "The Cutlers probably think I'm in cahoots with him."

"That's not good. Washburn and Sharp are rivals."

"As I understand it, they have some kind of truce. They leave each other alone."

"When the timin's right, Washburn'll rip up that truce and sic the Cutlers on him."

"Sharp seems a sturdy sort to me. Maybe he can handle them."

"He's a hard man, all right, but he's also generally a good man, and that puts him at a disadvantage." Jeremiah gave a glance toward the gingersnap jar, but he must have decided to wait. "Unlike Washburn, Sharp came by most of his claims legitimately."

"What do you mean *most*?"

"All, I guess." He couldn't resist any longer, so he pretended nonchalance as he walked over to the counter for another cookie. He kept talking to disguise his intemperance. "Recently, a few miners have sold their claims to Jeff . . . at rock-bottom prices. Ya might say ol' Sharp's benefited from Washburn's violent negotiatin' style."

I leaned back and rested my chair against an iron rail that circled the dead stove. "The sheriff?"

"Before Washburn stole his first mine, he bought himself a mayor and a sheriff."

"No other law?"

"Out here? Nope. We got a circuit judge that comes by every few months, but his first duty is to pick up his hush money."

"Why do prospectors keep coming? Surely they don't think they can beat the Washburn machine."

Jeremiah looked a bit scared. "I'm telling ya this because you're smart enough to keep your mouth shut."

"Everyone must already know."

"Locals do, but they don't speak of it. Washburn is *not* a forgiving man."

"So the ignorant miners keep coming on the news of fresh strikes." I tapped down my pipe and relit it. "Why doesn't Richard run an exposé in his newspaper?"

Jeremiah wore a frightened look as his eyes swept the store to make sure it was still empty. When he spoke, it was just above a whisper. "Because he wants to keep living. Washburn orders the Cutlers to kill his enemies."

Chapter 5

We had been sitting around the potbelly stove for about an hour when Jeremiah jumped at the tinkle of a small bell. A striking young woman stepped sideways past the male arm that held the door open. She dazzled me. She looked no more than sixteen, and her clean features beamed wonderment and joy with an openness that suggested unsoiled innocence. Her delicate complexion was set off by emerald green eyes so exciting and excited that you instantly wanted to know her. The man who followed gave the lie to my first impression. A hoary, potbellied lecher, he entered the store and put a possessive hand on the girl's shoulder that said, *This is mine.*

Jeremiah rushed to the door. "Mr. Bolton, good to see ya in town. I have most of your order."

"Not all? Damn it man, I ordered that stuff six weeks ago."

"I'm sorry, sir, but the . . . ah . . . some items must come from Europe."

Bolton's angry glare said he craved those items more than the others. Before he could object, Jeremiah bounded into the back room, emerging a few minutes later with his head peeking around a stack of paper-wrapped parcels piled high in his outstretched arms. He moved behind the counter, bent his knees to lower his load, and slipped his arms from beneath the packages.

The pretty girl squealed with glee and rushed the hidden bounty. As she ripped open one package after another, Bolton gave Jeremiah a sideways nod of his head. The two men went to the end of the counter and bent their heads together in muted whispers. Whatever they were talking about, Jeremiah looked tense.

When the two men broke apart, Bolton moved down the counter to hover over the girl and make sweet noises while she finished opening her presents. As she further examined her treasures, Bolton fired off a series of new orders at Jeremiah for the latest New York fashions in shoes, scarves, and hats. I noticed the young woman lost her gleeful expression and looked resigned when Bolton turned his back to her. Carefully rewrapping each package, she showed no interest in Bolton's excessive and prideful display of generosity.

After the couple left with their bounty, Jeremiah collapsed into his chair and wiped his sweaty brow with a bandana. "Gettin' hot already."

"Yes, indeed," I said.

Jeremiah's look said that he did not like the tone of my voice. I leaned forward, hands clasped, elbows on knees, and pleaded, "Tell me the story."

Despite the lack of a tinkling bell, Jeremiah whipped his head around to assure himself that we were alone. After a moment, he shrugged and said, "John Bolton's got a cattle ranch about a hundred miles north of here. A huge one. He used to be state senator but got beat last election. He still has powerful friends, and rumor has it he's gonna run for governor. Probably why he's spendin' so much time in this part of the state."

"I don't care about that. What's with him and the girl?"

"You scalawag." Jeremiah seemed to relax a little. "That's his wife. They've been married for two years."

"Two years? She looks like a child."

"Fifteen when they wed. Her name's Jenny. She's the only daughter of a dirt-poor sodbuster. Heard the father was glad to be done with her, but he still bartered a bride-price of forty silver dollars. Quite a sum in these parts."

"If he lives a hundred miles north, why doesn't he buy her goodies in Carson City?"

"I presume he does. He probably buys her things in every town he visits, so there's a bundle waitin' for her at every stop. He never fails to order new things every time he's here."

"Good customer."

"Not that good. He refused to pay me for the stuff they walked out with until the rest of the order arrives." I could see Jeremiah calculating in his head. "Damn. That's nearly twenty dollars he owes me."

"Let's see if I can guess what he ordered from Europe . . . French lingerie?"

"Yep." Jeremiah got a wicked grin. "And pissed that he had to pay her douceur without getting fresh wrappings for his plaything."

"I'd take that au naturel."

Jeremiah looked miffed. "Clean your mind of those sinful images, or the devil'll take ya to his bosom."

"You're right." I felt a twinge of shame. With no forethought, I had sullied myself by mentally

31

climbing into Bolton's depraved bed. "She looks like such an ingénue."

"She speaks like a little girl. Must tightly bottle up what happens at night, because I believe her unworldliness genuine."

I glanced at the shop door, closed to the outside. "Unfortunately, the world has a way of intruding."

Chapter 6

"Do ya know how this-here town got its name?"

I jerked in surprise at the question. I had just left Jeremiah's store, and the voice came from behind me, but I recognized it as belonging to the skinny Cutler. Turning around, I saw the two brothers leaning against the sidewall of a building I had just passed. They looked as if they had been waiting for me.

"No idea," I answered.

"Several years ago, a miner used a pick handle to club a poor Chinaman to death."

I tried not to let his smirk bother me. "Interesting," I said as I turned to go.

"There's more, greenhorn."

I stopped. "I thought there might be."

"Ya see, that Chinaman had tried to smuggle silver nuggets out of the miner's claim by hidin' them inside his gums." His weird smile and out-sized facial features reminded me of a *New York Tribune* political cartoon. After he spit a stream of tobacco juice, he added, "That miner first whacked the Chinaman across the mouth . . . then he clubbed him 'til his brains spilled out."

I just stood there and tried not to appear nervous.

The skinny Cutler, still wearing a smirk, pushed himself away from the wall. "Round hereabouts, we don't blame a man for protectin' his claim. Instead, we name the town after his deed."

"I see."

"Do ya?" He took a step toward me. "If ya ain't got yer eye on some silver claim, why'd ya talk to ol' Sharp?"

"When he asked to sit, I didn't know he was a miner. We didn't talk about mining."

"What did ya talk about?"

I couldn't think of a better answer, so I told the truth. "You boys . . . and New York City."

The brothers' baleful laughs increased my unease. "What ol' Sharp tell ya about us boys?"

"He said not to rile you."

"Goddamn." The brothers slapped each other on the shoulder. "That's good advice. Ol' Sharp ought to follow it hisself."

I wanted to know how Sharp had offended the brothers, but I kept that question to myself. "Good talking to you gents. It's a small town, so I'm sure we'll run into—"

"How come ya still ain't wearin' a gun?" the second Cutler demanded.

"No need. I'm not going to interfere with your

business, and I'll do my best not to rile you."

"Ya *already* riled us." The second Cutler took an advancing step toward me. "We told ya, in Nevada a man needs a gun."

"I don't see miners wearing one."

"Ya would if ya visited a saloon after dark, 'stead of playin' old maid with them milksops."

I couldn't think of anything to say that wouldn't make the situation worse. Sharp was right—they were just going to keep coming after me. Without another word, I turned to go. Maybe I should get out of town. It looked like my best choice. Tomorrow I could start riding toward Carson City, my next planned stop and, I hoped, a civilized city.

"Don't rely on ol' Sharp to protect ya. He has his own worries."

I kept walking.

Then I heard the second Cutler yell, "Git a gun, greenhorn. If ya don't, we'll find ourselves a pick handle."

Pickhandle Gulch was indeed a small town. Before I reached my hotel, I spotted the young woman from Jeremiah's sitting on a bench in front of the bank. I tipped my hat and said, "Good afternoon, ma'am."

She barely nodded in return.

"I saw you earlier in the general store," I offered. She looked up with disinterest. "I remember."

"May I sit a moment?" Why did I want to talk to

a married woman?

"My husband's inside the bank."

"That's who I want to talk about, if I may." I brazenly sat beside her on the bench. "Is it true he's running for governor?"

"Why do you ask?"

"Do you know his political platform? I may want to make a contribution."

"I haven't the least idea. Ask him yourself. He's inside the bank."

"Well . . . do you know if he supports stronger law enforcement in this part of the state?"

She turned slightly toward me with a bored expression. "I said he's inside the bank. If you want to talk politics, you'll have no trouble getting his attention."

This line of conversation was going nowhere. I should have left, but despite her indifferent manner, I still found her engaging. I tried another tack. "I've just recently arrived from New York City. Would you like to hear about the latest fashions?"

"Again, you need to talk to my husband. He's the one interested in fashion." She returned her gaze to some point in the middle of the street.

I didn't want to appear a complete fool, so I stood and tipped my hat again. "Excuse me for bothering you, ma'am. Perhaps I can catch your husband at a more opportune time."

As I marched away, my senses registered only the echo of my boots against the boardwalk.

Thankfully, each footfall took me another step away from my embarrassment. Why had I tried to talk to her? I had never approached another man's wife before. And to what purpose? I suddenly realized my clumsy behavior with Mrs. Bolton bothered me a hell of a lot more than my little skirmish with the Cutler brothers.

Then I thought about her behavior. When presented with an armful of gifts, she squealed like a child on Christmas morning, but when Bolton wasn't paying attention to her, she seemed withdrawn and blasé. Which was the act? Why did I care? Damn. This town was full of trouble. If I had had any reservations about leaving in the morning, they had been squashed. It seemed embarrassment drove me to action faster than fear.

Chapter 7

I had bought an apple and a small block of cheese before I left Jeremiah's. This would be my midday meal, which I intended to eat in my room as I worked on my journal. I never tell people I have an arrangement with a publisher, because it makes them ill at ease or causes them to embellish their tales. I already have two full journals, and I was halfway through a third. After I got back to New York, I intended to sift through all my notes and write a rousing novel about the West. I would use some of my notes, put other pages away for the future, and discard the remainder like so many summer flies swatted down in midlife.

I had come west to observe, write my impressions, and become a celebrity in the parlors of the literary set. Sharp's warning about the Cutlers worried me, because I wanted merely to witness the action, not become part of it. I vowed to stay out of the Cutlers' way until I left in the morning.

The Cutlers were right. I had rented the front room on the second floor of the Grand Hotel. My so-called suite included a unique feature, a balcony stretching the width of the building that could be accessed only through a window in my room. On my first day, I had passed a chair through the window, so I could sit on my private perch to jot my notes.

The balcony gave me a bird's-eye view of the town activities, and in the afternoon, the shade from an overhang made my perch the coolest place in town. When I went blank on what to write, I watched the comings and goings until reinspired.

During the day, the hardscrabble path that ran down the center of town was quiet most of the time. The miners were underground, and the heat and glare kept other people inside. The rare individuals who did wander out moved with a poky and listless gait. Nothing aboveground in this woebegone place moved with purpose or speed, except possibly for the occasional swish of a horsetail.

Transients and a get-rich mentality gave

Pickhandle Gulch a bawdy and rowdy temper, but the overriding characteristic of the town was dust. The stamp mill ground perfectly good rocks into a fine sand so the silver could be extracted. Wheels, hooves, and boots kicked up the silt, until a brown dust covered everything and seeped into every crevice and body part. I had been in town for only four days, and I had already taken two baths at the barbershop. Despite folding my clothes and putting them in a drawer every night, I still had to slap off dust in the morning. To keep his print shop clean, Richard must have had to spend more time sweeping and dusting than setting type.

I sliced off pieces of apple and cheese until I had a plateful. This would allow me to unconsciously reach for a bite without lifting my eyes from the paper. With my lunch in hand, I grabbed my journal and ducked through the window and onto the balcony.

I usually read the prior day's notes to make revisions before I started writing about any new adventures. Now I skipped this review, because the Cutler killing last night and my encounters with them today made me anxious to write. Using the flat of my hand, I brushed the dust off the page and prepared to start. They were a nasty pair, and I intended to make them infamous. On second thought, I decided to disguise their identity. I guessed that they would revel in notoriety, and I had no inclination to do them any favors.

I had been writing for nearly an hour when I noticed my little ingénue with her Faustian husband. They were crossing the dirt corridor generously called Main Street. Despite my earlier self-recrimination, I could not take my eyes off her or stop myself from imagining—

"Well, if it ain't our own retired politico and his little whore."

Bolton looked shocked as the Cutlers emerged from the shade of an overhang that protected the building to my left. "Brian Cutler, you apologize to my wife."

"Apologize?" The skinny one chortled. "I was thinkin' of escortin' her over to Ruby's to make an honest woman of her."

The young girl clutched Bolton's arm in fright but tried to put on a lady's look of indignation. Bolton squared his shoulders. "You—"

Brian poked him hard in the middle of the chest. "Don't say it . . . unless you're ready to die."

When Bolton stammered in disbelief, the Cutlers broke into a harmony of cackling. The scene played out in front of me like a stage drama. I sat on my perch, transfixed by this latest episode of Cutler chicanery.

Bolton grabbed his lapels as if he were about to make a political speech. In a basso voice, he said, "I shall speak to Washburn. You boys are off the reservation."

"Don't bluster at me, Senator. Ya ain't nothin' no

more." He leered at Jenny and in a softer, more menacing voice, said, "You're yesterday's news."

The other brother stepped toward the couple. "Yep, just a has-been pompous ass, but ya got a sweet li'l trinket there we might be willin' to buy offa ya."

"This is my wife!" Bolton protested.

"Hell, we heard ya paid forty bucks for the lass. She's used now, so how 'bout ten? Five from each of us."

"Get out of my way!" Bolton tried to walk around the brothers, but they shifted sideways to pen their prey. Whipping around, Bolton sputtered, "When Sean hears of this, I wouldn't want to be in your boots."

"Most likely, he'll wish *he'd* been in our boots."

"That's enough! Goddamn it, move out of our way."

Brian Cutler jerked his gun and jabbed it into Bolton's groin. "How much good will ya do the little lady with no balls?"

Bolton turned ashen. "No—"

"Let's take a walk down to Ruby's. She's got a room free."

The young girl now grabbed her husband's arm with both hands. Bolton's crushed look struck her with terror.

Could this actually be happening, right in front of me? I suddenly realized the Cutlers weren't playing with Bolton. They were serious. Should I do something? Hell, I didn't even know these people. I saw her anguish and started to stand but then remembered I was unarmed. I knew the Cutlers would shoot at any sudden noise.

The smaller Cutler kept his gun on Bolton as he shoved them in the direction of Ruby's. "Don't fret, old man. We'll let you watch."

"Please," Bolton pleaded. "I'll buy you each a girl at Ruby's. Leave my wife alone."

"Had all Ruby's got to offer. We want to taste your piece."

"Listen, we can work—"

Brian rammed the gun harder into Bolton's groin and cocked the hammer. "We don't need your permission."

"Yes, yes. All right. Let's go."

"Now you're bein' smart. The four of us'll have some fun."

I watched them walk away: Bolton with a gun in his side, and his wife escorted by a Cutler on each arm. She didn't fight at first, but after a few steps, she tried to break free. One of the Cutlers tripped her and then slung her around by one arm as he slapped her so hard he broke his grip. I thought she might escape, but the other Cutler grabbed her throat and squeezed any resistance out of her.

As soon as they had walked a few paces, I ducked through the window and quick-stepped across to a beat-up bureau. I hesitated. I kept a gun in the top drawer, but I hadn't worn it since I left

New York. I opened the drawer to expose a single item: a '73 model Colt .45 single-action army revolver. What to do? One of the Cutlers might stand guard outside the room at Ruby's. Could I take care of him without alerting the other brother inside? Probably not. Was this any of my business? A more difficult question.

I paused a long moment . . . and then I slowly slid the drawer closed.

Chapter 8

The sun had started to slip behind the hills, but the scorched air still felt like someone had left a huge oven door open. I spent the afternoon trying to shake off my melancholy and sense of guilt. No luck. I had not ventured out, nor gone to Mary's for dinner. With a shrug of resignation, I decided I could not stay holed up in my room any longer. Besides, it was time for whist.

I stepped off the hotel porch, moving toward Richard's print shop. I felt an uncomfortable sense of malaise when I spotted Bolton and his wife walking down the boardwalk across the street. She looked put together, but the bounce had disappeared, and her inert eyes ripped my heart out. Bolton looked so emotionally beaten that I almost felt sympathy for him. I averted my eyes and gratefully stepped into the print shop to find my three card-mates drinking whiskey around the typesetting table.

Richard kept his newspaper office obsessively neat, with everything always in its place. A press sat in the precise middle of the fair-sized room. Type cases, orderly racks, and a stove lined the walls. The shop possessed another attribute that made it ideal for our after-dark card games: abundant lantern light. I assumed the numerous kerosene lamps allowed Richard to set type into the night, but I had never seen him work after his evening meal.

The men threw me a sad look, and it was obvious I had interrupted a glum conversation. Without a word, Richard lifted the bourbon bottle with a raised eyebrow. I nodded, and he poured a healthy portion into my waiting glass.

After I had taken a deep swallow, Jeremiah said, "Shame about what happened."

"More than a shame," I answered. The whole town must have known, which made her debasement worse, if possible. I suddenly wondered how many had seen me on the balcony. "I saw the Cutlers waylay the Boltons. I should have done something."

"Then we'd be searching for a fourth again," Richard said.

Dooley thumped a type drawer with his boot. "Jenny didn't deserve to get mixed up in this."

I looked at the three men. "Mixed up in what? Something more than utter cruelty?"

Richard glanced at the open door, propped open

43

with the ever-present can of ink. "Washburn supports someone else for governor. He tried to persuade Bolton to drop out, but Bolton refused to lie down, so Washburn had the Cutlers knock him down."

"Why this way?" I asked.

"Because Bolton still has too many powerful friends to kill him outright."

I could not believe it. "Wasn't there an easier way?"

"Easier?" Richard shook his head. "Washburn's clever. Others may whisper, but Bolton has too much pride to ever talk about this or appeal to his friends . . . and it was easy enough for the Cutlers."

"Good God."

"Sometimes I have trouble subscribing to the notion of a good God." Doc sipped his whiskey. "I hope Jenny can escape that buffoon. Bolton keeps her penniless."

"She's got stuff she can sell," Jeremiah interjected.

"What stuff?" My voice was sterner than I meant.

"Things Bolton gave her," Jeremiah answered, with a look that said he meant nothing more. "Clothes and jewelry. She ought to just jump on the stagecoach one mornin'."

"Fat chance," Richard said. "Bolton keeps a careful eye on her."

Dooley kicked the type drawer again. "She's too young and ignorant. Hell, she hasn't been anywhere else. Probably thinks this rotten state is the way of the whole world."

We all stood around feeling embarrassed for a moment, until Richard said, "Let's play cards."

Doc had dealt our third hand. As I tried to focus enough to figure out my bid, Jemmy stuck his head in the door to announce, "There's going to be a gunfight."

"A gunfight?" Richard exclaimed. "Who?"

"The Cutlers have squared off against ol' man Sharp."

All four of us rushed to the window as Jemmy bolted to spread the news of the looming gunfight. Jeff Sharp stood at one end of Main Street with a rifle laid lazily across his arm. The Cutlers stood at the other end, wearing six-shooters and grins.

"Sharp told me he was safe."

"I suppose Washburn grew tired of small stake-holders selling their claims to Sharp. It looks like Washburn decided to tidy up all the loose ends at once." Richard took a swallow of whiskey. "He sure gave those boys a full agenda."

I couldn't believe they were just standing there staring at each other. "What happens now?" I asked, confused.

"The Cutlers will worry Sharp for a few minutes and then split up, run behind some buildings, and ambush Sharp from cover.

"Why doesn't he just use his rifle to shoot them while they're still in the open?"

"Jeff Sharp won't commit murder."

I looked at Doc with incredulity. "That's foolish."

"Yep."

This was not right. I looked at either end of the street and could see another atrocity about to happen. All afternoon I had brooded and chastised myself for doing nothing when these depraved and ugly outlaws had forced themselves on Jenny. This had to end.

I decided. "Jeremiah, watch my cards."

"Where're ya goin'?"

Without answering, I left the print shop and headed for my hotel. I took care to keep an easy stride, just a man crossing the street, oblivious to the threats on either side. I had never been so scared in my life, and it took all my will to keep my pace casual and my eyes straight ahead. With relief, I reached the hotel steps without anyone shooting me. Two paces inside the hotel, I started running as I dug into my pocket for my room key. I took the stairs two at a time, but my shortness of breath came from more than the physical exertion.

Entering my room, I threw open the bureau drawer, but this time I strapped on my gun. After jostling it into position, I drew it, opened the loading gate, and inserted a sixth cartridge. I spun the cylinder before holstering my Colt. The precision movement and perfect holster fit reassured me. I caught a glimpse of myself in the mirror, took two deep breaths, and tried to wipe the frightened look off my face.

When I reached the so-called lobby, I saw no one. Evidently, the hotelkeeper had found a safer place to watch the impending showdown. I glanced out the window. Nothing had changed, except that nobody was in sight but Sharp and the Cutlers.

I casually stepped out of the hotel, and, without pause, nonchalantly strolled toward the Cutlers, giving them a friendly wave.

Big smile. "Howdy." I had safely gotten within five feet. Steady.

"What the hell do you—"

The gun came to my hand as easy as scratching my ear, and my thumb pulled the hammer back without the slightest thought. Two shots fired so quick it sounded like one. Never breaking stride, I continued toward the two contorted men, who now leaked blood into the dirt. I had hit each brother center-chest, but one of the Cutlers gurgled and squirmed for a bit before he finally became still.

This was worse than I had imagined. The dead bodies lay in unnatural positions, and their shirt-fronts smoldered from the close gun flash. Blood had already spread around the bodies like grotesque wings. The pools may have looked like angel wings, but I doubted these two were destined for heaven.

Recovering some of my composure, I kicked their guns free of their holsters. As I scanned my periphery, I opened the loading gate, ejected the spent cartridges, drew two bullets from my gun belt, and reloaded in a smooth, practiced motion. Assuring myself that no additional danger lurked, I holstered my gun.

I paused a moment to tilt my face until I could feel the last rays of a dying sun. Unexpectedly, I felt exhilarated. Was it because I was still alive or because I had assuaged my guilt? Too complicated.

Exhaling slowly, I turned my back on the once-vile Cutler brothers.

I walked the length of the street toward Sharp. Jenny stepped from a building, and I thought I saw the barest of nods, but I could have been mistaken.

Sharp's expression remained fixed as I approached. "I could have handled it," he said.

"I never doubted you could." I glanced back at the Cutlers. "I doubted I could."

Sharp's next words startled me. "Some would say you murdered those boys."

"It was self-defense. They drew on me."

After a long moment, Sharp said, "I can testify to that, if it comes to it."

"So will others."

"Suppose so." He gave me an odd look. "You're a shopkeeper?"

"A gun shop."

Sharp looked a bit startled. "You mean you're a gunsmith?"

"Of sorts. Three smiths worked for me. I mostly dealt with the customers. Played with the new models and tested our repair work."

"You got handy."

"Two, three hours a day'll do that."

Sharp just nodded, so I turned back toward the print shop. I walked slower than normal so my shaky legs would not collapse under me. I had never shot anyone before, and I had trouble figuring out why I felt so elated. The most startling thing was how vivid this dirt-colored town suddenly appeared.

I glanced toward the print shop. Doc, Richard, and Jeremiah stood on the boardwalk looking bewildered. I strode right by them, took my seat at our card table, and fanned out the thirteen cards that sat on the table undisturbed. Slowly the three men followed suit and took their positions.

Jeremiah looked at me as if I should say something. So I did.

"Two."

Chapter 9

"Two?" Dooley looked baffled. "Two Cutlers?"

"No. I bid two."

"To hell with the bid! You jus' killed two men!" Dooley looked frantic.

I snapped the cards together and looked Doc in the eye. "Someone was going to die. Better the Cutlers than Sharp."

"Hell yes. It's just . . . I didn't know you were a

49

gunman."

"I'm not." I opened my cards back up and pretended to study them. "I never shot anyone before in my life."

Jeremiah looked puzzled. "Steve, that was expert gun handlin'."

"I've been around guns all my life . . . since I was a little boy hanging around my father's gun shop."

"Your father's gun shop?" Dooley pulled on his chin. "Is that the shop you sold in New York City?"

"Yes."

"But ya never shot no one before?" Jeremiah still looked perplexed.

"No! What's the problem? I'm not a gunman."

"That's the problem. You're in a mess now." Richard looked like he had lost a good friend. "A big one."

"Won't you stick up for me if there's a trial?"

"Ain't gonna be no trial," Jeremiah said. "Washburn likes to settle these matters in ways that frighten people . . . keep 'em in line for the future."

"What're you talking about? The matter's settled."

"Washburn'll never let this lie." Jeremiah glanced toward the open door. "He doesn't abide anyone triflin' in his affairs. Politics, business, or hired hands." Jeremiah leaned toward me and poked a finger almost in my face. "You did all three."

This made no sense. Just because I had a duel

with the Cutlers did not mean I meant to challenge Washburn. I had done what I had done on impulse; I certainly had not been thinking about Washburn, a man I had never met. I turned to Richard, who seemed the least emotional. "What will he do?"

Richard took a moment. "He's got other bad men, but they're more bodyguards than killers, and none compare with the Cutlers for pure meanness. Ya killed his best weapons." Richard collapsed against the back of his chair and seemed to slouch in defeat. "He may bring in someone special."

"He won't meet me directly?"

That got a nervous laugh. "Washburn surrounds himself with guards armed with rifles and shot-guns. You feel edgy just saying good morning to the man." Richard hesitated a beat. "No, you'll never meet him man-to-man. Not his style."

Richard looked worried. I glanced at Doc and Jeremiah and saw similar expressions of concern. "You all look so grim," I said. "Perhaps I should just leave town before he hears about this." This caused all three men to throw furtive looks at each other. Frustrated that they knew something I did not, I looked at them hard and said, "Tell me."

Dooley looked scared. "Washburn may come after us."

"Why? Because you befriended me?"

Richard shifted in his seat. "Doc and I have a his-tory with Washburn. So far he's only sent us the kind of warnings you can't ignore. Now, he'll assume we encouraged you. If you leave, he'll look for another way to make a statement that'll discourage others from interfering." Richard gave a forlorn look at Dooley. "He'll likely use us for his object lesson."

"You're town elders. Respectable."

"He doesn't care. His ambitions extend far beyond this shabby town."

We sat in silence, and my sudden euphoria dissolved into dread for my newfound friends—and then for myself. There had to be a way out of this mess. Of the three men, Richard had the best grasp of Washburn and his tactics. He edited the newspaper, and he must have run stories about Washburn. My guess was that Richard had been the subject of a stiff lecture, or worse, from Washburn or one of his minions. That would account for him not investigating the Dave Masters shooting. And at some point, Doc had probably classified some dead body as murder. I looked at Jeremiah, and his more relaxed expression told me he had not previously crossed Washburn. I was faced with an ugly dilemma. If I stayed, there was a chance Washburn would confine his revenge to me, but if I ran, he would pick other targets for retribution. From everything I had heard, this man insisted on getting his way.

"I need to get to Washburn," I said.

"You'll never get close."

"I must." I shifted my gaze to capture the eyes of

all three men. "Even if I eliminate another intermediary, he'll just hire another and then another. This beast must be killed at the head. Metaphorically speaking, of course."

Dooley slapped his cards on the table. "Not metaphorically. Kill him . . . if you can." His voice sounded harsh.

"That's quite barbarian, Doc. I thought you were a civilized man."

"I'm a frightened man. And you should be too. It's a hell of a lot easier to thwart two morons than to prevail against a clever villain with the morality of a hungry lion." Dooley pulled on his ear and then shook his head. "This is quite serious. You're far too calm."

I thought I must appear calmer than I felt, but I knew Washburn did not scare me as much as the Cutlers had. I picked up my glass of bourbon and took a small sip, holding it in my mouth a moment. I swallowed hard and then said, "The Cutlers were new to me, but I've dealt with ruthless, ambitious men before."

"To the death?" Jeremiah asked.

"No," I admitted. "Table stakes."

"Washburn plays for keeps," Jeremiah said.

"Perhaps, but I know the game." Their doleful eyes did not encourage. My chair made a harsh scraping noise as I scooted closer to the table. "Tell me everything about the man. I need to know about his mines, his other business interests, political dealings, mistresses, everything."

Richard stared at me. "I'll tell you the only thing you need to know." Richard leaned forward. "Mr. Sean Washburn, Esquire, has ruthlessly built a huge empire on top of innocent and not-so-innocent corpses. He's a scary man, and he's probably already planning to add a few more carcasses to his grotesque pile."

"Then we need to plan as well. Or do you intend to sit here and brood until he makes a visit?"

Dooley began to swirl his bourbon glass through the wet ring it had sweated onto the table. "His empire's big, all right, and we probably don't know the half of it. Nor all the people throughout the state that he's corrupted."

"Tell me what you do know. I'll surmise the rest."

"How?"

"I've seen the type before. He's smart and powerful, but he's vulnerable somewhere."

Richard still looked dubious. "If you attack his business, won't he have more reason to kill you?"

"Goddamn it." I banged my glass on the table. "You say he's already got reason enough. I need to fight him where I can get at him directly. No surrogates."

Jeremiah spoke for the first time in a while. "Makes sense. We can't kill an endless supply of thugs, and we can't just sit here and wait to die."

I was taken aback. "Thank you for the plural pronoun."

"Not as generous as it sounded." Jeremiah gave me an angry look that said this was my fault. "We're all in this thing now, whether we like it or not . . . and I don't."

"I could distance myself from all of you."

"Too late. You've already pulled us in." Jeremiah's expression had not softened.

I didn't make excuses but looked at each man sequentially. Finally, Richard said, "Okay, we'll tell you everything we know."

Chapter 10

I stepped out of the telegraph office, leaving behind a stunned operator. The man had sworn an oath of secrecy, but I feared that this news was far too rich for him to keep my message secret for long. I needed to move fast.

Two nights ago, Richard and the others had told me what they knew about Washburn, and I had used the time to think through the possibilities. Standing under the eave of the telegraph office, I felt myself take a deep breath. Settling on a course of action had lifted my mood. The draft from my New York bank would take several days, but in the meantime, I could do some groundwork around the edges of my plan.

By the time I had left Richard's print shop on that fateful night, the Cutler bodies had magically disappeared, and someone had shoveled unsoiled dirt over the bloodstains. Everyone pretended that nothing had happened, but an ugly tension clung to the townsfolk. When the sheriff failed to seek me out to ask even cursory questions, I knew Washburn had nasty plans for me.

I looked across the street at the bank. Richard had explained how Washburn had slowly seduced Eugene Crown, the president and owner of the only bank in town. At first, he shared a small piece of the action with the banker in exchange for reasonable loans to finance his Pickhandle Gulch ventures. Washburn gradually dragged Crown in so deep that he had no choice but to ride the Washburn wagon wherever it was destined to go. Now the bank made loans to hardly anyone else, because it had committed all its capital behind Washburn's schemes. Richard also suspected that Washburn had ordered Crown not to support anyone else's ambitions.

The town might look ramshackle, but the bank building looked sturdy as a rock. In fact, the bank was actually constructed with stone chiseled into relatively uniform squares. Although the big mines and the stamp mill used their own safes to store bullion, the amount of money pulsing through the town put a lot of cash in the bank. I hoped I had not underestimated what it would take to pull off my little gambit.

As was my habit of late, I carefully scanned both

sides of the street to make sure people were acting normally. Nothing looked threatening. I had also taken to wearing my gun at all times. I found the constant wariness tiresome; I could also feel myself getting used to it. The town might pretend, but I couldn't. Washburn planned my comeuppance sooner or later, and I vowed not to be taken by surprise.

I stepped into the street, intent on setting my own trap for our unsavory feudal lord. A brilliant sun immediately made me squint and tilt my head until my hat brim gave me some relief. The bank had two great steel doors that gave the building the look of a vault. I stepped inside to find a paneled wall interrupted by two iron-barred windows. Inside one of the cages, a tiny man peered at me with apprehensive eyes.

"Good day, sir." When I received no answering salutation, I said, "May I speak to the president?"

After a long pause, he murmured, "He's not presently available."

I may have been an amateur gunman, but I knew how to deal with bankers. With a dismissive tone, I said, "I insist."

"He's busy."

"You don't look busy, Mr. Crown."

"What do you want, Mr. Dancy?" Crown took on a smug look to emphasize that two could play this game.

"Mr. Crown, I am wiring a large draft to this

bank, and I have no intention of discussing it in the open. May we adjourn to your office?"

It was now Crown's turn to speak with disdain. "And what, may I ask, do you consider a large draft?"

I held for two measured beats and then said, "Two hundred thousand." I enjoyed the surprised look on the tiny man's face. When he did not respond, I added, "May we step into the privacy of your office?"

Without comment, Crown disappeared to the right and then reappeared through a door in the wooden wall. He circled around behind me, turned a lock on the front door, and drew the blinds. "Did anyone see you come into the bank?"

I shrugged. It served my purpose for him to worry. Crown gave a little wave with his left hand, and I followed him behind his pinewood fortification. His office was a rolltop desk tucked in a corner out of view of the customers on the other side of the barrier. The tiny man pulled a captain's chair around for me and then did a little hop onto an oversized swivel chair.

"What are your intentions with the money?" he asked.

"Investments."

Crown tried to wipe the look of surprise off his face. "In Pickhandle Gulch?"

"I didn't deposit my money in Denver."

Turning thoughtful, he said, "Mines, ranch

land . . . saloon?"

"I'm open. This is a land of opportunity for those with money and wits." I leaned forward and took on a conspiratorial tone. "What would you suggest?"

Crown leaned back and tried to appear thoughtful. "You're a little late. Washburn and Sharp have gathered up all the profitable mines. Mines that sell stock are for suckers and normally played out. Bolton has grabbed the best ranch land in the state, and the sheriff won't abide competition with his saloons or whorehouses."

"Are you suggesting I take my money elsewhere?"

"No, no." He hesitated, and I hoped his mind was moving along the path I wanted. "There're always opportunities. This is a raw frontier, ready to be ravished by men such as yourself."

I sat rigid in my chair and affected a hard tone. "And what kind of man do you suppose I am?"

Crown looked a little taken aback. "Why, an able man, one willing to use a gun."

"I intend to buy my property."

"Of course you do, sir." He leaned in closer and spoke in a whisper. "But a gun may be necessary to keep it."

I merely nodded. I did not deny I was a gunman, because I wanted Crown to assume I was as ruthless as the other infamous characters in town.

After a few quiet moments, Crown asked,

"You're staying at the Grand?"

"Of course."

"You must see the potential if someone were to put some money into that eyesore." Now Crown used a conspiratorial tone. "I can make some quiet inquiries for you."

"A hotel is not the scale I desire," I said dismissively. I saw the disappointment in Crown's eyes. Richard had warned me that Crown owned half the hotel in a partnership with the sheriff. Washburn divvied up little parcels of his domain so his minions remained beholden to his goodwill. Undoubtedly, the price Crown had in mind would put a grin on both his and the sheriff's face. Besides, they probably assumed they would get it back as soon as someone shot me dead.

"What scale are you looking for?"

"Two hundred thousand dollars is a lot of money, especially out here. In the years to come, this state will boom, and I want to be positioned to profit. I don't need to hurry." I stood to leave. "Put your mind to it and see me at the Grand when you have a serious proposal."

Crown raised his hand to delay my departure. "Mr. Dancy, I have the perfect way for you to profit from all the growth in this state." He pointed the flat of his hand at the chair I had just occupied. "Please, sit, and I'll explain."

Chapter 11

I had just settled into my normal window seat at Mary's when Jeff Sharp slid into the chair across from me. "What're your plans?"

"And good day to you, Mr. Sharp."

"Not for you, I'm afraid." Sharp waved Mary over and held me in suspense while he ordered chops for his midday meal. When she had retreated, Sharp gave me a worried look. "Washburn hired Bill Sprague."

"I'm not familiar with the name."

"Bill Sprague's an assassin. A goddamn deadly one."

"Is he here . . . in town?" I couldn't help but look around.

"No. Probably a few days yet." Sharp accepted a cup of coffee from Mary and then returned his attention to me. "Sprague's in Carson City, where he lives lavishly between jobs."

"You mean there's that much work for him around here?"

Sharp looked irritated. "Meanin' he's engaged in a highly paid profession . . . at least at his level. Rumor has it he takes on only the biggest jobs an' never fails." Sharp's face told me he suddenly realized what he had just said. Embarrassed, he added weakly, "Sorry. I'm about as subtle as an anvil."

"I noticed." I knew the situation was dangerous,

but Sharp's reminder of the stakes jangled my nerves. If I was going to win this battle, I needed to know what Washburn was doing, so I said, "Thanks for telling me straight out, Jeff. What else do you know?"

Sharp tested the temperature of his coffee with a shallow sip. It was scalding, so he took another tentative taste and set it down. "Washburn has never used Sprague before. I suspect he's too expensive for Washburn's miserly tastes. Besides, he had the Cutlers, who worked for a pittance."

"I was told he had other dangerous men on his payroll."

Sharp waved, dismissive. "Brutes, tough enough men, but not indiscriminate murderers. Just take it as a sign of his anger that he's partin' with a goodly amount of cash to see you dead."

I thought a minute. "Actually, that works into my plan."

"You have a plan?" Sharp looked dubious.

"Tell me about this Sprague fellow."

Sharp sipped at his coffee and found that it had cooled, so he gripped the cup with both hands and took a swallow. "I said he was an assassin. A bushwhacker that uses a rifle." Sharp shook his head. "Steve, he hunts his prey from behind cover, an' he's seldom seen by his target . . . or anyone else, for that matter."

No wonder Sharp looked worried. After a moment of reflection, I muttered, mostly to myself,

"Washburn wanted someone who could kill from a distance."

Sharp nodded. "Yep. He's heard about your pistol work." Sharp put his cup down. "Sprague's a sneaky son of a bitch. Hardly anybody'll know he's around until the deed's done."

"Any suggestion?"

Sharp gave me a forlorn look. "None comes to mind."

I noticed he did not advise me to run as before. He had probably come to the same conclusion as our little whist group. I did not blame him. Dooley and the others were friends, and I was just an unknown busybody who had stupidly barged in on a raging little war that was taking place in a remote piece of the frontier.

After a moment of rolling his coffee cup between his two palms, he asked again, "What's your plan?"

I smiled. "I bought Crown's bank."

Sharp looked stunned. "What the hell! Why?"

I shrugged, trying to look nonchalant. "I decided to hang around, so I needed an occupation."

Sharp's face grew wary. "What about Crown?"

"Left town already . . . with his family."

Sharp smoothed his eyebrow and then said, "Crown was also the mayor. Washburn owned him, but he was weak." He seemed to think it over. "Getting rid of the mayor won't dent Washburn's control of this town. I don't see how this helps."

"It helps."

"How?" Sharp said this last in a way that brooked no further temporizing.

"Everyone assumes that Washburn seduced Crown because he was the mayor, but Washburn wanted Crown because he owned the only bank within a hundred miles. Empires, even pilfered empires, require money." I took a sip of my coffee. "By the way, according to my bank's records, you owe me nine thousand dollars."

Sharp recoiled. "My mines are worth tenfold that. Hell, lots more."

"Of course. You run a conservative operation. But then again, you don't aspire to rule everything this side of the Continental Divide."

"I also couldn't get any money outta Crown for the last few years."

"Lucky for you Washburn set a low market price for the diggings you did buy."

Sharp stiffened. "What're ya implyin'?"

"Nothing." Damn, my smugness had offended my only real ally. "My error. I shouldn't have spoken lightly."

Sharp let an uncomfortable silence hang for a long time. I was starting to get concerned, because I needed Sharp, but he finally said in a matter-of-fact voice, "I'm good for my debts."

"Of course. I'm not worried. I guess I was trying to impress you. I actually bought the bank to gain control of Washburn's mortgages."

Sharp sat back and chewed on that one. "Washburn stretched thin?"

I waved my coffee cup in Mary's direction. "Thinner than one of Mary's pancakes. All of Washburn's local mines are mortgaged to the rafters."

Sharp's startled look delighted me. "How much does he owe?"

"More important . . . how far behind are his payments?"

"You intend to foreclose?"

I nodded. "I know how to deal with the courts, but I need muscle to enforce the writs."

Sharp didn't hesitate. "You can't rely on the sheriff. Hire Pinkertons . . . and ya need to hurry." He turned his coffee mug a full circle. "You know, don't ya, that the damned circuit judge is on the Washburn payroll."

"I know, but that only means he can be bought. I just need to establish a new price." I remained quiet while Mary refreshed our cups and then asked, "Where can I get Pinkertons?"

"Denver." Sharp again set his cup aside to let it cool. "The judge won't come over to ya if he doesn't think ya'll be around for his next payday."

"I thought about that. I'm going to set up a trust that will guarantee him his money. How many Pinkertons should I hire?"

"Six or eight." Sharp furrowed his eyebrows. "What's a trust?"

"A pile of money in a Carson City bank that can pay out cash on a regular basis."

Sharp grinned. "You're not playing by Washburn's rules."

"His rules tilt the table. Everything slides to his side." I leaned forward. "How long before the Pinkertons can get here? I'm suddenly in a big hurry."

"About five or six days by train and then by horse . . . if you wire them today."

"Then I'd better get to it." I left for the telegraph office as Mary brought over Sharp's chops. He looked like he was going to enjoy the meal.

Chapter 12

In a few days, I had bought a bank, got rid of Washburn's mayor, ordered Pinkertons by telegraph, and sent what I hoped would be an enticing telegram to the circuit judge. Progress, but Sprague worried me. How long before he got to town, and how could I avoid his sights once he arrived? I needed time to bring my plan to fruition, and that meant I needed a diversion—something to grab Washburn's attention, other than me.

My plan was to break Washburn's lock on the town one piece at a time and put him on the defensive in areas he wouldn't anticipate. Battling business moguls in New York, I had learned to avoid the frontal assault and attack neglected portions of their empires. You had to be careful with this breed of men. When pricked, these carnivorous beasts would instinctively whirl at their tormentors and strike with furious resolve. You had to throw them off balance and make them hesitant, unsure, and disoriented. Next, if possible, you had to deny them their favorite weapons. Washburn's favorite weapons were violence and the threat of violence. Because I had killed the Cutlers, he expected a straightforward contest of arms—his hired hands against my six-gun. I needed his attention elsewhere.

I unlocked the door of my new business and flipped up the shades to signal that the bank had reopened after my lunch break. Walking back to my desk, I started to hand-letter a "Bank Teller Needed" sign, when someone rapped on the wall of my cage.

I put the heel of my boot on my chair leg and leaned my swivel chair back until I could peer through the cage window. What I saw caused me to bolt out of the chair and bound toward the window.

"Mr. Bolton, Mrs. Bolton, how may I help you?"

"Where's Crown?" Bolton demanded.

"Crown found it necessary to return to St. Louis. I bought the bank."

"You? You're a gunman. What do you know of banking? And how'd you get the money?"

"Honestly . . . in New York. And in the process, I learned about banking."

I enjoyed the puzzled look on his face. He was feverishly trying to figure out the implications of this turn of events. I was a Washburn enemy; he was a Washburn victim. At least, I'm sure he saw it that way. Others, including myself, might more appropriately view Jenny as the real victim. I desperately wanted to start a conversation with Mrs. Bolton, but as an aspiring banker, I kept my eye contact with Mr. Bolton.

With so many ramifications flying around inside his head, he finally went to the issue closest to his heart. "My money may not be safe with you."

"My concern as well. After examining the books, I found that Crown had loaned an excessive amount of customer deposits to Washburn."

Bolton sputtered and spewed for a few seconds before he bellowed, "Let me in! I shall not discuss my private affairs in front of the whole town!"

I made a point of gazing around the empty anteroom. "Of course, sir." I stepped over to the door and opened it with a welcoming arm flourish. "Please, step over to my desk." I was disappointed to see Bolton signal Jenny to stay outside, but I was pleased to receive an abbreviated curtsy from her before I closed the door.

Without preamble, Bolton nearly screamed, "Washburn has my money?"

I leaned in close, as if conveying a secret. "I suspect Crown was in cahoots with Washburn. I must admit, I'm concerned about collections. Now I know why Crown dumped the bank and skedaddled out of town."

"You're responsible now. I expect you to make good on my deposits."

I feigned nervousness. "Yes, yes, of course, but I need help. Washburn's not an easy man to deal with." I wiped my brow with the back of my hand. "Perhaps you can help . . . or call on some of your powerful friends."

"It's your bank."

"Yes, regrettably." I pulled down the huge ledger and opened it as if looking for something. "Crown assured me the bank was sound." I shook my head and put on what I hoped looked like a pleading expression. "He left town with all my money."

"What kind of man buys a business without examining the books?"

"Evidently a foolish one. The top numbers looked good. But laying blame doesn't help us out of our predicament."

"*Your* predicament."

"It's your money that Crown loaned to Washburn."

Bolton fumed. Between clenched teeth, he said, "What do you expect me to do?"

"As governor, you could bring the power of the state down on Washburn . . . clean up the judiciary, appoint an honest marshal, prosecute these atrocities."

Bolton slapped the table with his hand. "Goddamn it, I've decided not to run."

"Mr. Bolton, you *must* run. If Washburn's candidate wins, I might as well close up."

"Damn it, man, it would be dangerous for me."

I collapsed into my chair. "Then we both lose."

Bolton sat, contemplative. After a moment, he said, "Some obstacles have been removed. Perhaps I can make a run."

I suppressed a smile at this first reference to the Cutlers. "You can win. I know it. And I can help. If you run, I'll contribute five hundred dollars to your campaign."

"I thought you were broke."

"I have some money left, and this is the only way I can recover my investment in the bank." I leaned forward. "Like it or not, we're in bed together."

"I'm not one to share my bed freely."

I refrained from making a sharp retort. "I can write the check now." He continued to hesitate, so I added, "I've hired Pinkertons. They should arrive any day, and I'll assign several as your personal bodyguards." Still no answer. "Jeff Sharp has also promised support, both financial and security. And Mrs. Bolton can remain at your ranch under the protection of your ranch hands."

I waited. Bolton was a proud man and surely wanted revenge for his humiliation at Washburn's hand, but I had to let him come to his own conclusion.

A long moment passed before Bolton simply said, "All right, I'll run."

After I got the answer I wanted, I ran over to Richard's print shop to find him setting type. "I have a new lead story for you."

"Already got it. It wasn't easy making you look like a banker. People trust their money to solid citizens, not gunfighters."

"Not that story. Bolton has formally announced his candidacy for governor."

Chapter 13

"We need to talk." The burly man took the seat across from me at Mary's.

"Good morning, Sheriff."

I had been reading Richard's stories about my ascendancy as the resident banker and Bolton's aspiration for the governorship. It occurred to me again that I needed to find another place for breakfast. Of course, there was no other place in Pickhandle Gulch, and I was not ready to leave this dismal town.

I had encountered the sheriff many times, but our contacts had been limited to a tip of the hat. Odd, given that I had killed two men in his town. That messy incident probably would not be the subject of this encounter either. The sheriff was a big man, with a belly that rolled out over his gun belt. He had the swarthy look of a bully who demanded petty toadying from anyone he deemed beneath him, which probably included everyone not on the

Washburn payroll. Despite my dispatch of the Cutlers, I assumed he saw me as a lower order of animal. I made a show of folding the newspaper and setting it aside to signal that he had my full attention.

The sheriff scooted his chair so close to the table that the edge gouged into his protruding stomach. "I don't like being in business with you, and our silent partner will be furious."

"What silent partner?"

"Sean Washburn."

"I've read the Grand Hotel contract, and I didn't see his name." Acquiring the bank gave me a 50 percent interest in the Grand Hotel. The sheriff owned the other 50 percent, and I wasn't surprised that he objected to sharing ownership with me.

"That's what silent means."

I leaned back. "What's his interest, Clyde?"

"You call me Sheriff, shithead," he said menacingly. "And he gets 10 percent—off the top."

I shook my head. "No wonder that hotel's so threadbare. Well, I'll not pay another dime until he shows me a contract with his name on it."

"There ain't no contract, shopkeeper. It's a gentlemen's agreement."

"I see no gentlemen."

"Go to hell!" The sheriff pushed back his chair and stared at me. After a while he said, "I never should have sat down with you. You're a dead man."

"Are you going to kill me?"

"No. I'm the law." He put on a bullying smirk. "But you'll be dead soon, just the same."

"Well . . . I'm sure you'll do everything in your power to protect me."

"I won't do shit."

Perhaps the sheriff was more honest than I had supposed. One thing I had learned from this conversation was that he had not yet talked to Washburn or one of his surrogates. I had informed the hotel manager this morning that by acquiring the bank, I was now half-owner of his establishment. When I had asked to see the books, he had gotten nervous and asked for a day or two to get them updated. I let it pass. I didn't really care about the hotel except for its irritation value. It had already irritated the sheriff and, as he said, it would infuriate Washburn.

I kept silent, so the sheriff added, "And don't think you're now the mayor because you bought that damned bank."

"I only bought Crown's commercial interests. The citizenry must elect a new mayor." I smiled. "But it's an interesting thought. It might be fun to be your boss."

"Don't be stupid. Crown was never my boss."

"Was Crown stupid?"

"He wasn't smart to sell out to you. Now he better run fast and far."

I waved my hand, dismissively. "He has the

wherewithal." When the sheriff refused to react, I decided to broach a far more sensitive subject. "I asked because Crown made such bad loans that I question his banking skills."

"I wouldn't know about that." The sheriff acted nonchalant but then intrigued. "I thought most of his dealings were with Washburn."

"Almost exclusively."

The sheriff looked befuddled. "Washburn's the richest man in the state."

"Biggest debtor, you mean. That man owes me a lot of money. Damned if I'll give him cash from that piddling hotel."

Now the sheriff waved his hand. "Doesn't matter. We won't be partners long."

"That's right. I'm executing the buy-out option in the contract." I pulled a piece of paper from my pocket, laid it on the table, and slid it toward him.

"What's that?"

"My offer. Four thousand dollars."

The sheriff made no attempt to pick up the paper. "What the hell are you talking about?"

"I'm offering you four thousand dollars for your interest in the Grand Hotel."

"I'm not selling." His blustering response didn't hide his confusion.

"You said you didn't like being in business with me. Four thousand dollars is a lot of money. Enough to get a new start in a different town . . . a different state, even."

"I'm not looking for a new start, and you can't make me sell."

"But I can." Finally, he looked concerned. "Or I can make you buy me out. It's in the contract."

"I don't read contracts."

"That doesn't make them less binding. If one partner makes an offer to buy, the other partner must sell or purchase the other's share for the same price. Do you have four thousand dollars?"

"That ain't any of your business."

"Unless you've got money stuffed in a mattress somewhere, it is my business." I sat back in my chair and waited a beat. "You have only a little over three hundred dollars deposited at my bank."

"Go to hell."

"You need to enlarge your vocabulary."

"Fuck you." He got up to leave. "We never had this conversation."

"Doesn't matter. I've already mailed the papers to the circuit judge. You have thirty days to decide . . . per our contract."

"Thirty days?" He laughed. "Plenty of time."

"Sheriff, think about my offer. Things are going to get very dangerous around here. You might not want to be around."

He leaned over the table, supporting his weight on two fists. "Are you threatening me?"

"I'm making you a business offer. A good one." I picked the newspaper up and snapped it open. "Have a pleasant day, Clyde."

Seemingly at a loss, he blurted, "I'm riding out to see Washburn."

"Good. The ride will give you time to think. Turn around if you change your mind. The cash will be waiting."

After a few moments of trying to stare me down, the sheriff stormed out without another word.

I didn't believe he would take me up on my offer, but I hoped my display of confidence would tip the balance in my direction. Whether he accepted the four thousand dollars or not, the prospect would at least be another piece to worry Washburn. He could lose both his mayor and his sheriff.

With any luck, Washburn would become so furious, he wouldn't think straight. If his carefully crafted empire began to unravel, he might come out of hiding and give me an opportunity to attack the problem at the source. As I flipped the newspaper out straight, it occurred to me that I might be underestimating my adversary, but I squashed the thought and went back to my reading.

Chapter 14

A couple days later, I wandered over to see Richard at his print shop. Without preamble, he blurted, "Washburn's more powerful than I thought."

"What have you found out?" I asked.

"I received a post from the editor of the *Carson City Tribune*. He said that about two years ago

Washburn started buying up Carson City commerce, judges, and politicians. He doesn't have the town locked, but he's a major influence. This goes far beyond his big mining interests in Virginia City. The man has wedged his dirty fingers into every power hub in this corrupt state."

This news was worrisome. It meant that I had aimed my blows at the periphery of Washburn's empire. "Washburn's candidate for governor?"

"Craig Stevens, president of the assembly. Used to be a Bolton ally when Bolton ran the senate, but I believe he has a short memory." Richard passed the letter to me, so I could read it for myself. "You'll see that he thinks a Bolton-Stevens contest will be a tight race."

I read the letter while sitting in front of Richard's tidy desk. I used my bank office for official business and the print shop for scheming, plotting, and general mischief. After their initial fearful reactions to my gunning down the Cutlers, Richard and Doc had joined my campaign with gusto, especially after they witnessed my first few steps. Jeremiah, unfortunately, had started to put some space between himself and our little cabal, so the card games had ceased, and I had curtailed my lollygagging around his general store. Besides, I had a business to run and a king to unseat.

When I looked up, Richard was bent over a piece of paper, writing a story for his newspaper in longhand. It had been eight days since the Cutler incident, and the town was eerily quiet: no Bolton, no Pinkertons, and no Sprague. At least, no Sprague to my knowledge. Even Sharp had vamoosed a couple of days ago. The sheriff had not returned, nor had I seen any of Washburn's crew to give me a hint what the big man had on his mind. Bolton had returned to his ranch to get his affairs in order for the governor's race and to put Jenny under the guard of his own men. Even Richard's office was quiet, except for the scratching of his pen.

I got up and started pacing. The letter basically said that Washburn was more formidable than I had supposed. In New York, I had kept the political bosses at bay, beat off protection rackets, and handled crooked constables. I had done deals with businessmen so ruthless they ate secretaries for lunch, consumed subordinates over cocktails, and made mincemeat of partners at their snobbish dinner clubs. I had thought that if I fought Washburn my way, I could crush him with tactics honed in the most barbaric and competitive city in the world. After all, this whole sad collection of buildings could hardly equal a single block in my hometown.

But I had misjudged. First, these thrown-together clapboard buildings did not reflect the vast riches being pulled from the earth, and any place where someone could get instantly rich attracted smart men with an edge hard enough to beat back all the other treasure hunters. Washburn had crushed a bunch of little barons to emerge as the preeminent lord over a huge domain.

Second, I had been foolish to assume that Washburn's influence was mainly restricted to the local environs. I was aware that he also had mines in Virginia City and that he had aspirations to control the governorship, but I hadn't anticipated that he had done the preliminary spadework to take control of the entire state. I should have guessed. Feudal tyrants possess insatiable appetites.

I reminded myself that he had a weakness—an impatience that compelled him to reach beyond his financial footing. If the man had unsustainable debts here, he had probably tapped the banks in Carson City as well.

"Richard, what's the largest bank in Carson City?"

"Commerce Bank. But you can't buy it. Not unless you've got a hell of a lot more money. And I mean a hell of a lot more."

"I don't need to buy it; I just want to establish a correspondence relationship."

"A what?"

"A loose partnership. No shared equity, but we coordinate business dealings."

Richard put his pen down. "Are you sure you're approaching this from the right direction? This is a raw frontier, where men attack their enemies straightaway. Washburn solves problems like you by eliminating them."

"Pinkertons are on the way," I said, more irritated than his comment warranted. "I'm willing to employ force if necessary, but I'm not going to start a damned shooting war." I sat back down. "I've got to fight this out the only way I know how."

Richard looked unconvinced. With a resigned shrug, he said, "Commerce is run by the oldest money in the state—older than the silver strikes. They have an upright reputation. They usually don't get mixed up in shady dealings, and they stay out of politics or at least hide their political dealings."

"Would they loan money to Washburn?"

Richard thought about my question. "Probably not. They cater to the cattle, lumber, and railroad interests. Miners need these to run their operations and constantly gripe that the old-money barons extort all their profits. The two sides don't mix easy."

"Then who do you think Washburn might turn to?"

Richard again sat quiet for a minute. "Carson City First. Despite their name, they're fairly new and welcome business with mine owners. The president's a goddamn vulture, gobbling up every Commerce carcass he stumbles across. There's no love lost between the two banks . . . yep, Washburn would go to Carson City First."

"Birds of a feather flock together?"

"Exactly."

I got up and resumed my pacing. After a couple of laps, I stopped in front of Richard's desk. "Then I'll set up a relationship with Commerce."

"I thought you were trying to put the squeeze on Washburn. How can Commerce help?"

"We need an ally in Carson City. Always go with power. Besides, I bet Carson City First would be hard to dislodge from Washburn." I headed for the door. "But in truth, I'm going on instinct. Gotta go."

"Where to?"

"The telegraph office, then the bank. I need more money."

"You got more?"

"Lots more. I need to transfer fifty thousand to Commerce to get their attention. Then I'll write them a letter outlining an ongoing business relationship. I just hope I have enough time."

Richard looked puzzled. "What kind of gun shop did you own?"

"I had more than a gun shop, but it was the source of my good fortune." I was about to leave, but then I stopped and turned back toward Richard. "We catered to the wealthy. Sold mostly expensive shotguns to weekend bird hunters. My dad loved the exquisite machining and craftsmanship of the Italian and English models. Most of them cost more than a constable's annual salary. We made lots of money, and when my dad died, I invested in real estate and railroads. Did pretty well."

"I gather."

I shrugged. "I learned how to deal with men like Washburn."

"Do they shoot opponents in New York?"

"In the seamier districts, but I avoided those. The men I dealt with may not have taken their opponents' lives, but they stole everything else, including their pride."

"Is that why you left New York?"

"Partly. I wanted clarity. But in truth, this Washburn affair is teaching me something—I enjoy the game."

"This is not a game of wits."

I headed toward the door again. "Different stakes, but it's a game nonetheless."

Just as the door swung closed, I heard Richard yell, "You'll need a lot more skill than you've shown at whist."

Chapter 15

"Bolton's dead!"

"What?" I dropped the telegram I had been rereading and leaped to let Richard inside the bank's wood barricade. I hoped I had heard wrong. Bolton dead? That wrecked all my plans. I let Richard pass by me into the inner sanctum, but instead of following, I went into the foyer to lock the door and pull the shade. Damn it. Then it hit me. I had set up Bolton as a diversion. Was this my fault?

Before retaking my seat, I blurted, "What happened?"

"Somebody shot him. He was just sitting peacefully on his porch, smoking a cigar, and the next thing he's dead." Richard looked petrified. "Steve, he was killed at long range."

"Sprague?"

Richard wiped his brow. "That would be my bet."

"How did you hear about it?"

"Telegraph from Carson City. Sent to all the editors in the state."

I sat in thought. The telegram I had been reading came from the circuit judge I had tried to lure to my side with a bigger bribe. He declined to meet with me, pleading that crucial cases would keep him in Carson City for the foreseeable future. The Pinkertons should have arrived two days ago, but I had not seen hide nor hair of them. Last, an emissary from the Washburn empire had delivered checks drawn on a Denver bank that brought his mortgage payments current. When I queried by telegram, the Denver bank responded that they would not confirm the account balances until the checks were presented for settlement. Despite immediately sending a rider, over a week would go by before I discovered if the checks were good.

Washburn had crashed right through my supposed envelopment of his empire. The realization shattered my confidence like a pick slamming into a block of ice. He had moved fast, but the most worrisome part was how easily he had upset my plans. I looked at Richard, and his face showed the fear I felt. "Why do you suppose Sprague went after Bolton instead of me?"

"I don't know, but I sure wouldn't assume that you're off the list."

I thought a minute. "Perhaps I am off the list, at least for the time being. Without Bolton as governor, our power is diminished, and Washburn can deal with us after the election." A new thought struck me. "Damn . . . he'll save a pile of money in an uncontested race."

"Ya think he'll let us live?"

Richard looked hopeful, and I hated to disappoint him. I patted him on the forearm. "Only for a respectable period after the election." I waited a beat. "Unless we make more trouble. Then he might hurry things."

Richard's face regained that frightened look. "What are ya going to do?"

"Make more trouble."

"Steve!" Richard's eyes pleaded. "Is that wise?"

"Listen, Richard, our only chance for a long life is to destroy Washburn, and we need the governor's seat to do that."

"Who could possibly run?"

"That's my question."

Richard took a step back. "Don't look at me."

I laughed at the consternation on Richard's face. "No, not you. You're a good man, but you don't have a big enough reputation to run for governor. We need someone known all over Nevada." I rocked forward, placed both elbows on my knees, and rested my chin on an overlapped fist. "Who can beat Stevens?" As Richard mulled over the question, I had a sudden thought. "Oh my God!"

"What?"

"Jenny's a widow."

Richard gave me an odd look. "Steve, don't—"

"Don't worry. I wouldn't think of intruding on her grief." I said this with such an edge that I was afraid it betrayed my feelings.

"Bradshaw can give Stevens a run." Richard wanted to change the subject. "He's the mayor of Carson City, and he's supported Bolton for years. If he has the courage, he might want to get even with the Washburn crowd."

I pushed Jenny from my mind. "A good man?"

"I thought ya wanted someone who could win."

Richard's answer made me smile. "All right, tell me about him."

"He's a big man in Carson City. He owns the stockyards and supposedly a share of Commerce Bank. He's also president of the Cattlemen's Association."

"Thus his support for Bolton?"

"You got it."

I thought a minute. "Yesterday you said Commerce was a sound bank that stayed out of politics."

"I said they keep a low profile. They don't leave boot prints. Bradshaw and Commerce both prefer the back room to the podium."

"Still, if the bank is upright, it speaks well of him. Do you think he's honest?"

Richard shrugged. "He's a rich man, intent on getting richer."

"Scandals?"

"None that I'm aware of, but I don't pay attention to Carson City doings."

A thought occurred to me. "Does Jeff Sharp?"

"Yep, now that ya mention it. He traipses up there a couple times a year and always seems to have a handle on things."

"Bradshaw?"

"He must know him. Sharp mentions his name occasionally."

My wooden swivel chair had four horizontal legs that splayed out from a central stanchion. I liked to use the toe of my boot to push against one of these legs until I tilted back so far that gravity threatened to upend me. I leaned back into this position and thought through the possibilities.

Finally, I asked, "Have you seen Jeff recently?"

"He just stepped into Jeremiah's store."

"Watch the bank for a few minutes."

"What if a customer comes in?"

"Take their money."

"What if they want money?"

86

I headed for the door. "Don't give 'em any. I'll be back soon."

I bolted through the inner door without a backward glance and nearly ran into the street. I stopped and then backed up till I was just inside the door. Not much protection, but I was not nearly as exposed as I would be in the open street. I thought about getting my rifle, but the news on Bolton's murder was fresh, and Bolton's ranch was a three-day ride. News by telegraph moved faster than a man on horseback, so with any luck, Sprague had not yet arrived in Pickhandle Gulch. I took a deep breath and reminded myself that I could not win this battle by remaining indoors.

Chapter 16

I stepped into the open street, hoping that I was right that Sprague had not had enough time to reset his bearings on me. The threat of being shot without warning scared me more than facing the Cutlers. Just as I started across the street, I spotted six black-clad men riding into town with a demeanor that said *Do not mess with us*. I withdrew back onto the boardwalk and wondered if these men were employed by the Pinkerton National Detective Agency. The riders pulled up their horses in the middle of the street and looked around. After surveying the various people wandering about town, one of the men reined his horse around and walked it in my direction.

Casually resting both hands on the saddle horn, he asked, "Excuse me, sir, but could you direct me to Steve Dancy?"

"You found him."

He tipped his hat. "I'm Captain McAllen, Pinkerton. I believe you engaged my team."

"You were supposed to be here two days ago." My voice sounded harsher than I intended.

"I apologize. We were delayed due to some trouble in Colorado."

"Your office could've sent a telegram. I might've already been killed due to your tardiness."

"Again, I apologize, but we were not in communication with our office. They thought we were on our way."

I considered pushing the matter but simply said, "Would you and your colleagues please follow me into my bank, where we can talk in private?"

Without waiting for a reply, I turned and propped open the door with my back. The captain beckoned his men and swung down from his horse. Each Pinkerton wore a dusty black suit over a once-white shirt now stained with sweat and trail dirt. Their vests provided their only individual touch: one gold, a couple gray, and the rest in a matching black with gold or pearl buttons.

As they dismounted, each man pulled a rifle from his saddle scabbard. The men looked serious, alert, and professional. Without being told, one of them leaned against the exterior wall of my bank and rested his rifle across his arm in an intimidating pose.

After the other five had squeezed by me, I closed the door and led them beyond the wooden barricade. I could hear Richard leap to his feet at the sound of six sets of boots and five pairs of spurs marching toward his sanctuary. We crowded in and remained standing, because my office had only three chairs. Richard looked confused and then relieved when he figured out why I had escorted these tough-looking men into a small space meant for private bank business.

"This is Richard, our local newspaperman. Richard, these gentlemen are Pinkertons."

After handshakes all around, McAllen went right to business. "Tell me about the situation."

After I explained my problem, the only part that seemed to give McAllen pause was Sprague's name. He rubbed his chin and said, "Sprague's a nasty character. Hard to defend against because he works from a distance. I presume we can't keep you indoors."

"No. In fact, I may want two of you to accompany me to Carson City."

"I recommend against traveling."

"I have business in Carson City, business crucial to bringing this troublesome state of affairs to an end."

"In that case, all of us will accompany you."

"No, Sprague's here . . . or coming here. I want four of you to stay and protect my friends."

"Why would he bother your friends? The man works strictly to his contract."

"These men may very well be on his contract list. I can't dismiss the possibility. Besides, I understand he prefers the ambush. If we move with speed, he'll never get set up ahead of us. Two of your men should be enough."

"That's my decision to make, not yours."

"I hired you; I make the decisions."

"Mr. Dancy, I don't work that way. My job is to keep clients from making foolish mistakes. We know Sprague has you as a target. We don't know about your friends. We'll do things my way." McAllen took an intimidating step toward me. "I refuse to break up my team."

"Then please escort me to the telegraph office. I need to wire your head office."

McAllen traded glances with his men, and then he turned a hard look on me. "I'm not comfortable with this. You need to follow my advice. This has escalated far beyond a simple bodyguard engagement."

"I employed you for an open-ended contract . . . for the duration. I can end it only with a trip to Carson City." I tried my own hard look. "You need to be flexible."

"Foolish clients jeopardize my reputation." He made a sideways motion with his head toward the door and said, "If you'll excuse us a moment, I want to talk to my men."

I let them file out, but just before McAllen stepped out, I touched his elbow. "A moment, please . . . alone."

He looked ready to ignore my request but then hesitated in the open doorway. I stepped closer and lowered my voice. "I know this is a difficult assignment; that's why I hired the best. If you see this through, I'll pay each of your men a bonus of one hundred dollars, and two hundred to you."

"And if you're killed?"

"No bonus."

Without a further word, he left to join his men. When I turned around, Richard looked worried. "Steve, what will ya do if they quit?"

"Raise the bonus."

He shook his head. "Then why didn't ya offer more right from the start?"

I thought about that a moment and said, "Habit, I guess."

"Ya need new habits." After I laughed at his quip, he added, "When do ya plan on leaving for Carson City?"

"Today."

"I guess speed is important." Richard sat back down. "Ya might have trouble convincing Bradshaw. Do ya intend to get a letter of introduction from Jeff?"

"I have something better in mind."

Just then, Captain McAllen returned alone. "Will you put the bonus in writing?"

"Of course."

"Then you have your team of Pinkertons."

"Excellent. Would you accompany me over to the general store? I need to talk to someone, and you should hear our conversation."

"First, can we get my men situated in a hotel? We rode hard."

"The man I need to see may leave, but I have three rooms ready for you at the Grand Hotel. Your men can settle in while we talk."

"Are you at the same hotel?"

"There's only one."

"Tell me the layout."

"It's a two-story hotel, and I have the front room on the second floor. Staircase at the rear, with access to the back of the building."

"I want one room on the first floor next to the staircase. Two or three rooms upstairs, with a private one for me, preferably next to yours. Can we board up the rear door?"

"Shouldn't be a problem. I own half the hotel, and the other owner is out of town. One of the three rooms is next to mine, but the hotel is full. If you want a private room, three of your men will need to share."

McAllen made a dismissive gesture. "They're used to that, but I may have further requests after I see the building."

"Fine, but I don't want to miss this man. You and I had best get across the street."

Without a further word, Captain McAllen turned and walked out of the bank. After he had given instructions to his men, he took me by the elbow and said, "Always walk on my left and stay close to me."

With that, he snapped his fingers, and one of the men tossed him a rifle, which he caught effortlessly, checking the breech to make sure a round was chambered.

"Let's go."

Chapter 17

The relief I felt stepping inside Jeremiah's store surprised me. Even with McAllen and another Pinkerton at my sides, I felt my body relax as we moved to the safety of shelter. It occurred to me that my patina of bravery might be thinner than I was ready to admit.

At first glance, I did not see Jeff Sharp, because my attention centered on Jeremiah. He stood at the counter, helping a woman who looked worn out, even though she was probably only in her thirties. I was wondering how I could reestablish my friendship with my old whist partner when, to my surprise, Captain McAllen asked, "Are you here to talk to Jeff Sharp?"

I spotted Jeff sitting on the far side of the potbelly

stove, reading what looked like a legal document. "Yes. Do you know him?"

"We've run into each other a few times."

"Professional or social?"

McAllen lowered the rifle and held it by the stock, close to his thigh. "Both." When he walked directly over to Sharp, I guessed that McAllen's friends did not describe him as a talkative sort.

"Afternoon, Jeff."

Sharp looked up from the papers in which he had been absorbed and immediately smiled. "Joseph." Sharp plopped the document on the next chair and stood to shake hands. "I'm glad to see you pulled this duty." Turning to me, he added, "You're in good hands."

Before thinking, I blurted, "If you knew Captain McAllen, why didn't you suggest him when you recommended Pinkertons?"

"I didn't want ya to wait if he was otherwise employed." Sharp picked up his papers and motioned for us to take a seat. "But providence is on your side. You got the best."

I sat, a little irritated, because I made it a practice to always hire the best, which is difficult enough without friends withholding information. I gave Jeff a discourteous look and then asked, "Have you heard about Bolton?"

"No." I had Sharp's attention.

"He was shot from long range at his ranch."

"Dead?"

"Yes."

Sharp turned toward McAllen. "Washburn hired Sprague. Do ya know him?"

"I've made his acquaintance. Most hired killers have a short career. Sprague has been at his profession for as long as I can remember."

"Which means he's careful an' methodical." Sharp hooked his thumb toward me. "How do ya intend to protect my friend?"

"With difficulty. He's intent on going to Carson City."

This brought Sharp's attention back to me. "Why?"

"We need the power of the governor to thwart Washburn. With Bolton dead, we need another candidate."

"Who?"

"A man I think you know . . . Charles Bradshaw."

Sharp ignored the name. "Why don't ya try for a warrant against Washburn? Accomplice to murder. McAllen an' his men can help arrest him."

"With what evidence?"

Sharp traded glances with each of us. "All right, but travelin' to Carson City is dangerous, even with McAllen's crew to watch over ya." Sharp folded his hands and leaned forward until they rested on his knees. "To get to Washburn, we need to capture Sprague alive an' make him talk."

"You really believe he'd testify against a client?" I asked.

I let Sharp think that one through. Finally, he said, "Bradshaw would be a good choice, but I don't think he'll run. He prefers to buy politicians."

The conversation had come around to where I wanted it faster than I expected. "That's why I want you to come with us. You know Bradshaw; I don't. You might convince him."

Instead of an argument, Sharp simply said, "When do ya leave?"

I thought about that. I had wanted to leave immediately, but we wouldn't make much progress before dark. "First light. Captain McAllen's team needs a night's rest."

"I don't think movin' out into the open is such a good idea, but ya can't sit here an' wait to get shot from a hundred yards away." Sharp picked up his papers and waved them at me. "You're in luck. I need to see my lawyer, an' he's in Carson City." Sharp stood. "Pick me up at my place. I need to pack some gear, an' I'm along the way. I'll have breakfast ready for ya."

I stood as well. "I understand Bolton's place is less than a half-day's ride off the path to Carson City."

"Six to eight hours if you count both ways."

"I want to stop there."

"Why?" Sharp's expression told me he thought he already knew the answer.

"To get the facts straight on his murder." I hesitated. "And I want to see if Jenny needs anything."

Sharp cocked an eyebrow. "Like a bag of sugar?"

"No. Like help with the ranch hands or financial matters." The exchange embarrassed me. "I *am* a banker," I added and immediately regretted the weak excuse.

Sharp grinned at my discomfort. "Sure ya don't want us to ride an extra eight hours just so ya can tip your hat to the pretty lady?"

With a no-nonsense tone, McAllen said, "We ride straight to Carson City."

I looked down on the captain, who had remained seated. "Captain McAllen, as long as you are in my employ, you'll ride in the direction I pull my reins. This entire trip got started on the news that Bolton was murdered. I want to know exactly what happened."

"Steve's right. At least about that," Sharp said. "We need facts before we blow smoke in Carson City. It's not that far outta the way, and if Sprague was involved, he'll not be hangin' around the ranch."

Sharp started to leave, but McAllen stood and put his hand on Sharp's arm to stall his exit. "Mr. Dancy wants only one of my men to join us."

Sharp looked surprised. "How many did you bring?"

"Six, including myself."

"I want Captain McAllen's men to protect Richard and the others," I said. "It's a gamble, but I don't think Sprague will know we left until it's too late to follow."

"I see your point." Sharp folded his papers and stuck them in his pocket. "Steve, I admire your loyalty, but Washburn won't bother your friends. There's already been too much killing to explain away. My advice is to leave just two Pinkertons. Two more should come with us to ride ahead and check out the terrain." Sharp gave me an intense stare. "If Sprague has another target, it's you."

I glanced over at Jeremiah, who was studiously ignoring us. "Two men to protect three seems foolish."

"Doc and Jeremiah are safe. If Washburn wants to quiet anything, it'll be the newspaper."

That made sense, and a couple of trail-savvy Pinkertons could scout ahead of us for places where Sprague might set up an ambush. "All right." I turned to McAllen. "Is that acceptable to you?"

"Barely, but don't tell me my business again, or you'll see my backside as I ride away." He looked me up and down. "Right now, I want you to come over to the hotel and exchange clothes with one of my men."

"You want to disguise me as a Pinkerton? One of your men would do that?"

"They do what I tell 'em."

I did not like someone else possibly taking a bullet for me, but I saw it made sense, at least from Captain McAllen's perspective. Sprague probably had only a rough description of me, and from a distance, he would aim at the rider not dressed in Pinkerton black. I wondered what kind of man would willingly disguise himself as the target of a committed killer. Someone braver than me.

"What about Jeff?" I asked.

"Jeff's bigger and older and known throughout the state. Sprague won't make that mistake. And he may not mistake my man for you. There *is* a risk. To make this masquerade look real, you'll have to ride on the outside of my man."

Jeff jumped into the conversation. "Steve, listen to the captain. This is how he makes his living."

My eyes never left McAllen. "What happens to his bonus if he gets killed?"

"I'll ask him before we leave, but that's not your concern."

"All right." I nodded. "At least for the trip there. We'll discuss this again prior to our return."

"Of course. Our arrangement can be terminated at any time."

Captain McAllen had made his point. I could decide what we did, but he would dictate how it would be done—or he would ride off, taking with him the only protection I could count on within hundreds of miles. I knew I would acquiesce. I had, after all, hired professionals for a reason.

Chapter 18

I had one piece of business to settle before I could leave Pickhandle Gulch. No one had responded to my "Bank Teller Needed" sign, and I needed someone to take care of the bank while I was gone.

During my discussion with Sharp and McAllen, Jeremiah had studiously ignored us and kept himself busy adjusting bolts of cloth that were already perfectly arranged. After Sharp left, I told McAllen I had personal business with the store proprietor and that he should go over to the hotel and take care of his men. He swung his rifle up across his chest and said he and his man would wait for me outside.

When I looked around, I saw Jeremiah on a small ladder, facing his merchandise shelves. I walked noisily over to a point where I was sure he could see me from the corner of his eye, but he continued to pretend to be absorbed in his task.

"Jeremiah?" I said.

Without stopping or turning around, he asked, "What can I do for ya?"

"How about climbing down off that ladder and serving me one of your awful cups of coffee?"

"Steve, I'd like to, but I got a lot to do today. Perhaps another time."

"I need to talk to you."

"Another day."

"The store's empty. Come on down." He hesitated, so I added, "For Christ's sake, Jeremiah, I need your help . . . please."

"With what?" My request must have made him nervous, because his voice pitched up an octave.

"I'm not going to talk to your back, especially not the part you're putting in my face right now."

Jeremiah threw me a wary look and began to climb down. His weight made him clumsy, so even though he had only three rungs to descend, he held onto a shelf to steady his cautious steps. Without hesitation or comment, he disappeared into the back room, reappearing a few moments later with two heavy porcelain coffee cups. We both took our customary chairs around the potbelly stove, and I accepted the proffered cup. The tepid coffee tasted horrible, but I was so grateful for the gesture, I didn't make any of my customary smart-aleck remarks.

Jeremiah looked anxious, so I decided to jump right in and make this as short as possible. "I'm leaving for Carson City in the morning. The trip has to do with bringing this business to a close." Jeremiah gave me a blank expression, so again I went right to the point. "I need someone to watch the bank for me."

"What? You're askin' me? I have a store to run."

"You have Jemmy and that man who comes in on weekends. If you could keep the bank open for an hour or so in the morning and two hours in the late

101

afternoon when the miners get off, that should do it. Maybe put a sign out that says you'll make transactions for fewer than twenty dollars here at the store."

"I can't leave the store for hours at a time. Jemmy only watches things when I go to the privy or sell ice out back."

"What about your weekend man?"

"He's a prospector. He comes in from the field only to keep himself in supplies. He'd never stay in town during the week."

"If he helps you run the store for two weeks, I'll pay him enough to buy three month's worth of supplies."

"How do ya know you'll be gone for only two weeks?" Jeremiah went to the counter for one of his gingersnaps, then grabbed three. He snapped off half a cookie into his mouth and followed it with a big swig of lukewarm coffee. "How do ya know ya won't be gone permanent?"

I ignored the way he'd said *permanent*, as if I might be dead. "I'll find someone to run the bank in Carson City, and I'll dispatch him immediately. Should be here in well under two weeks. In the meantime, I need your help."

Jeremiah looked pained. "I can't."

I forced myself to sip his lousy coffee. "Are you afraid of Washburn?"

"Of course. The two of ya are in a feud. I want no part of it." He gobbled the remainder of his gingersnap and continued to talk with a full mouth. "If Washburn has ya killed, I might get stuck taking care of your damn bank. And for what?"

"I'll make sure you don't get stuck. In case Sprague gets lucky, I'll put in writing that you get full ownership of the bank on my death." I could see that the offer softened his resistance, so I added, "Do you really think Washburn will allow you to continue raking off so much of the mines' profits with this store? That man wants it all, including what's yours."

When Jeremiah just sat there looking worried, I added, "You already pay the sheriff. Soon you'll no longer be a shop owner, just a clerk in someone else's store."

"You know about the payoffs to the sheriff?"

"You do business in this town, don't you?" Actually it had been a reasoned guess.

Jeremiah shook his head. "Ya don't know the half of it. I've sacrificed a lot to do business in this town."

"I know you hide most of your money in the ice-house."

Jeremiah sat bolt upright like a man stuck with a hatpin. "What? How do ya know that? Who else knows?"

"I know your middling bank deposits don't reflect your sales, and you bar and lock that ice-house like it was filled with gold instead of frozen water. It didn't take much to figure out where you hide your money."

"Damn." Jeremiah stood and started pacing. "Damn, damn, damn."

Because of the merchandise stacked everywhere, Jeremiah could only go about two and a half paces in one direction, and then he had to reverse. He reminded me of one of those Swiss clocks with the little wooden characters that every hour just go back and forth lickety-split.

After about three of these aborted laps, Jeremiah muttered, "What am I gonna do?"

"Jeremiah, I won't steal your money. In fact, if you deposit it with the bank, I'll help you protect it. Pay you interest too."

"Ya don't understand." He gave me a forlorn look. "Washburn already owns half this store. Six months ago, he insisted I sell him half for a piddling price, or there would be a fire and I'd lose it all. The Cutlers presented the offer and flipped a lit cigarette into my dry goods to make sure I got the point. What ya warned me might happen in the future has already happened."

"Let me guess . . . you skimmed the money in the icehouse."

He plopped back into his chair, and his slumping body answered my question.

I let him brood a minute and then said, "Watch my bank for me?"

"No. I won't get Washburn heated at me."

I spoke very quietly. "Jeremiah, we've both committed supposed capital offenses against

Washburn. He knows mine. He'll find out about yours." I let him ponder that a moment. "Rejoin our whist group. Working together we can thwart Washburn and save ourselves. Separate, we'll each die, either a little bit each day, or all at once."

"Washburn may not find out. *You* only figured it because ya know my bank deposits."

I just let him think that one through. He dropped his head into both hands. When he looked up, he said, "Ya think Crown already told him."

"Of course. Washburn knows, and as soon as he takes care of other business, he'll come see you for his rightful cut . . . and his pound of flesh."

"I'm doomed." He dropped his head back into his hands and started weeping. I waited. Finally, he looked up with bloodshot eyes. "Tell me what ya want."

"Get Jemmy to watch the store, and we'll go across the street. You've got a good head for figures, so it won't take long to teach you the books."

"I'm scared."

I put my hand on his shoulder. "Tell you what, I'll leave two Pinkertons. No one will mess with you while they're in town."

His face brightened. "Thank you." And then clouded, "But what if the sheriff returns?"

"Give him whatever bribe you normally pay." I pulled a piece of paper from my pocket. "If he wants four thousand dollars, give it to him—after he signs this document."

Chapter 19

Jeff Sharp lived in Belleville, a mining encampment less than twenty miles from Pickhandle Gulch. When we approached, his place surprised me. I should have known better. The man was rich, but his unassuming ways and scruffy dress had led me to expect modest quarters. Instead, as we rounded a craggy ridge, I spotted a great Georgian house built atop a stepstool-like rise at the base of some imposing hills. An expansive porch supported by white columns framed the red-brick structure. The clean lines and symmetry looked out of place in contrast with the surrounding haphazard, raw-lumber outbuildings.

As we rode closer, I became impressed with the size of the operation. The menagerie of outbuildings included a stamp mill, bunkhouses, stables, various smith shops, toolsheds, and what appeared to be a huge cookhouse. I realized that Sharp must keep most of his money in Carson City, because his deposits and loans at my bank did not reflect this size of enterprise. It suddenly struck me that Washburn must do the same. He might have tapped my little bank for money, but he would do his big dealings with big banks.

As we drew closer, I noticed something else: armed guards scattered behind strategic outcroppings. The natural terrain sheltered the cluster of buildings almost as well as a man-made fortress. They evidently expected us, because each layer of guards waved us past. Now we rode as a group, but until a few miles back, two of the Pinkertons had ridden ahead and to the side of our party to investigate likely ambush sites.

My Pinkerton clothes fit reasonably well, but I found the smell of stale sweat off-putting. More bothersome, Captain McAllen had insisted that we exchange horses. I had ridden Chestnut from Denver, and I missed my horse more than my clothes. At least the captain had allowed me my own saddle, which he said looked nondescript from a distance.

An unkempt, bearded man carrying a shotgun met us on the porch of the main house. "Mr. Sharp said you should wait in the parlor. He'll be with you in short order."

Captain McAllen gave his men a perfunctory signal, and they rode over to the bunkhouse. Evidently, they would not have guest privileges in the main house.

At the porch steps, someone had pounded into the dirt a neatly lettered wooden placard that read, "Remove Spurs & Clean Boots." Without discussion, we dismounted, removed our spurs, hung them on the saddle horns, and made a show of scraping our already-clean boots. A hired hand immediately gathered up our reins and led the horses toward the stables.

After I had trudged up the three steps to the porch, I turned to check our approach from the perspective of the house. A picturesque valley fell away from the compound to present a spectacular view. The second thing that struck me was that no one could approach unseen.

Then I noticed an odd smell: the nasal-burning odor of a smelting furnace mixed with the appealing aroma of roasting beef. I walked to the end of the porch and spotted a cow rotating on a spit outside the cookhouse. Sharp's men ate well.

Inside the house, I discovered another surprise. The furnishings were big and comfortable, sized to fit a man. Despite the masculine feeling, the house showed subtle signs of refined taste. Heavy but well-proportioned ranch-style couches and chairs were accented with rich rugs, expensive lighting fixtures, and scattered wooden ceremonial masks that I presumed came from South America. Sharp had used his travel souvenirs to good effect.

Somehow the exterior and interior of the house worked together, and I was sure that a lesser mortal like myself would have made a hash of the whole thing. Despite our numerous conversations, I realized that I still did not know Jeff Sharp very well.

McAllen and I stood in the center of the parlor trying to figure out what to do, when a servant entered and offered us liquor, beer, or coffee. Since the day had already grown hot, and we were thirsty from our ride, we both requested beer, despite the early hour. The servant indicated we should sit and, with deliberate care, placed a coaster in front of each of us. Looking around, I decided the arrangement of couches and chairs created a comfortable seating area that would make any hotel owner proud.

Captain McAllen gave me a quizzical look before saying, "You haven't been here before, have you?"

"No."

"I thought you said you were friends."

"Actually, Jeff was the one who referred to me as a friend. I didn't meet him until this feud started, and I've kept close to town since."

"Well, Jeff didn't build this place. A bigheaded miner erected this monument to his supposed brilliance." McAllen leaned over and lifted the lid from an expensive-looking humidor. The cigar he extracted looked equally expensive. "Unfortunately, the silver didn't run as far as his ambitions."

McAllen sniffed at the cigar before striking a match against his thigh and waving it in front of the tip. He took a long, satisfied draw, leaned his head back, and blew smoke at the ceiling. He was taking far too much pleasure in demonstrating his familiarity with the house.

"If the silver ran out," I asked, "why does Jeff run this huge operation here?"

A voice came from behind me. "I want the men

close so I can direct them, an' I want the ore processed under my nose. We haul ore here from nine different mines spread around these foothills."

I hadn't seen Sharp enter the parlor. He took the armchair at the head of the seating arrangement and reached for the humidor. "Care for a cigar, Steve? They come from Cuba, an' they're as smooth as the inside of a woman's thigh."

I reached into my pocket. "If you don't mind, I'll stick with my pipe." As I went through the ritual of lighting it, I said, "It's hard to believe Washburn's operation's bigger than this."

"Washburn scatters his ventures all over." Sharp enjoyed a puff on his cigar before adding, "He doesn't fear an attack from me, so he has no reason to consolidate his smeltin' operations. I, on the other hand, don't retain a similar confidence in him. I'd rather risk the loss of a single wagon of unprocessed ore than lose a remote outpost."

I nodded because it made sense. "We saw a lot of guards on the way up. Did you add them when this trouble started?"

"Always been there. There's a lot of silver to protect. The guards check people comin' an' goin'."

"Going?"

"The greatest minin' risk is theft, an' refined ore is easy to steal in small quantities. People who work for me know they'll be searched every time they leave." He waved his cigar, leaving a trail of smoke in the air. "Just comes with the job."

"How many people work for you?"

"Over two hundred hereabouts, countin' miners, wranglers, teamsters, guards, engineers, an' the people to take care of them. Washburn has at least double that number, probably more."

The servant entered with a tray loaded with three chilled beers. After an appreciative swallow, I asked, "Who do you bank with in Carson City?"

Sharp took a swallow of his own beer before answering. "You have as much of my business as I intend to keep local."

"I'm not interested in more of your business. I *am* interested in whether you bank with Commerce."

"Why?" He looked surprised.

"My guess is that Washburn uses Carson City First, and I want to apply financial pressure on him. An alliance with Commerce Bank could help."

Sharp studied his beer and then me. "You're right about both our bankin' habits, but I don't see how it matters."

"I don't have it all figured out yet, but it'll matter. Washburn's spread thin, and I'll find a way to leverage that."

"You're thinkin' ya can bankrupt Washburn?" Sharp looked dubious.

"Not enough time, but perhaps I can make him desperate . . . and desperate men fight sloppy."

"Washburn'll just shoot you." McAllen sounded disdainful.

"You mean he'll hire someone to shoot me. Hiring takes money. If I can pinch his purse, I reduce his power. I aim to attack him on the political and business front while he tries to attack me with guns."

Captain McAllen shook his head. "I don't like your chances. You might be long dead before your way can work."

"That's why I hired you, to get me the time I need."

McAllen took a satisfied draw on his cigar. "Time is what I sell."

I laughed. "Please inform your office that you foresee a long engagement."

Chapter 20

The six of us left Sharp's place after a hearty breakfast. I should say four of us, because two of the Pinkertons had left an hour before. It was a three-day ride to the Bolton ranch, but McAllen told me that the first day held the most danger, because the narrow valley we had to pass through provided good cover and a reasonable shot for a marksman.

As we made our way down the center of the tight basin, I occasionally spotted the two Pinkertons riding up on the ridges to either side. By late afternoon, we emerged into a broad valley flanked by distant mountains. McAllen led us off a road that meandered close to the western range and guided us into the middle of the valley. Although this route made the ride more difficult, it put almost a mile between us and any ambush shelter. The expansive sight lines and the absence of trees made me feel more comfortable.

We rode mostly in silence. Jeff Sharp and Captain McAllen stayed in front and barely spoke a word. McAllen evidently thought it unnecessary to introduce me to his men, and they kept a stern, professional demeanor during the ride. The only thing I knew about the man who wore my clothes and had adopted my horse was that his first name was Sam.

Sam spoke to me for the first time, after we emerged from the foothills into the open plain. "Fine horse. What's his name?"

"Chestnut . . . and I'd appreciate it if you returned him unscathed."

Sam gave a short laugh before answering. "I'll do my best. Where'd ya git him?"

"Denver. I traveled from New York to Denver by train, so I needed a rig. The first thing I bought was a horse. Most of my other gear I bought at auction."

"You're a good judge of horseflesh."

"Well, I actually know only eastern riding horses, so I hired a wrangler to help me pick out a good horse for western terrain."

"Really . . . and how'd ya pick your wrangler?"

"That's an odd question."

"Not if ya know Denver. The town's full of hucksters ready to skin some newcomer with more money than sense."

"Well, I watched the horse trading for a couple days to see who bought and at what price. I also wanted to see who would back off and let another buyer take an animal that had outrun its value. After I spotted a savvy buyer, I approached him and asked for his help."

"How much?"

"We agreed on a 10-percent commission."

"He picked the horse on his own?"

"You mean, did he pick the seller?" I had figured out where his questions were leading. "No, I'd heard about buyers and sellers in cahoots. I asked a lot of questions about the animal and the breeder before I authorized haggling."

"Ya did right well by yourself. Chestnut's a fine horse for rough country."

This pleased me more than it should have, because I already knew Chestnut was an exceptional animal; but praise from someone as seasoned as Sam made me feel good.

Just when I thought Sam had relapsed into silence, he asked, "Your saddle doesn't look new."

Now I laughed. "I thought if I bought used gear, I might not look like a greenhorn."

"Guessed as much." Sam adjusted his seat. " 'Twern't to save money."

"Why do you say that?"

"You make decisions like a rich man . . . 'Sides, six Pinkertons don't come cheap." Sam leaned forward and patted Chestnut's neck. After he resettled in his saddle, he asked, "Why'd ya leave the big city?"

"Family matter."

Sam looked intrigued. "What kind of family matter?"

"A private family matter."

"Sorry." He tipped his hat in my direction. "Didn't mean to pry; it's just that a family quarrel drove me outta Missouri."

"Really?" I couldn't help but ask, "What kind of family quarrel?"

"Well now, perhaps mine's private as well."

I chuckled at the expected answer and tipped my own hat. "Sorry. Didn't mean to pry."

"Actually, not private at all. Kinda spread all over the country, for that matter." Sam's expression took on a melancholy hue. "Bad times back home. Despicable Yankees versus true patriots. At least, that's the way my family saw it. Since my sympathies fell with the Union, I became despicable." He sighed. "Almost twenty years ago." He rode a few strides before adding, "Haven't been home since . . . Miss it terrible at times."

That gave me pause. I intended to stay away for a good while, but in the back of my mind, I had thought I would eventually return home. Before I knew it, I found myself saying things out loud that I seldom even said to myself.

"When my father died, his older brother took me under his wing. My uncle showed me how to make money . . . New York style. After a while, I learned why my father had kept his distance from him and the rest of the family's affairs. I was young and naive, but eventually I got tired of his sleazy way of doing business and told him I no longer wanted his help. Made him madder than hell. He secretly got on the other side of a deal of mine so he could teach me a lesson, but I won, and he lost a pile of money . . . family money."

"So ya left?"

"Not right away. But the whole family turned on me, so when I saw they weren't going to forget about it, I sold everything and said goodbye to the big city."

"So you became despicable too."

"Guess we got that in common."

Sam rode awhile before saying, "No offense, but that story kinda backs what my father always said about Yankees and their greed."

"No offense taken. I wish money wasn't so important to my family."

"Not to you?"

"Me? No, money's just the score. A way to keep track of who's winning and who's losing . . . and I like to win."

"There's ways to win that ain't scored with money."

I wanted to change the subject. "Why are you in this line of work?"

"Pride in workin' for a top-notch outfit. Work's interestin', an' we do more good than bad."

"You do bad?"

Sam shrugged. "Men sometimes lie when they hire us."

"Did you ever quit a job when you found out the truth?"

Another shrug. "Not my call."

"You hold with the captain's decision?"

"If I want to ride with Pinkerton, that's just the way it is."

"Suppose so." I stood in my stirrups a minute to relieve my sore buttocks. "Are you comfortable with this engagement?"

Sam looked at me. "Washburn's a bad man. I don't like the trail ya picked much, but I'll stick with it."

I settled back in my saddle. "What would you do differently?"

Sam rode in silence for a long moment. "I'm a direct man who likes simple solutions. Your path meanders, an' I can't see the end point. But . . . that said, other than just walkin' up an' shootin' the man, I don't know what else ya can do."

"Neither do I. I'm trying to figure things out as I go." I pulled my hat brim down against the setting sun. "Also, I'm not eager to be hanged for murder."

"Nope. Seen men hanged. Looks mighty uncomfortable."

When I laughed, Captain McAllen wheeled his horse around and trotted up beside us. "Sam, you keep a good lookout, hear?"

Sam answered in a brisk, no-nonsense tone, "Yes, sir," and directed his eyes across the horizon. I looked around but saw only flat, empty country. I guessed that the captain did not consider levity an admirable trait.

Chapter 21

Two shotgun blasts made me reach for my rifle.

"No alarm," McAllen said. "I sent Sam after dinner. Best birder I ever saw. We'll be eating fresh meat shortly."

We had set up camp in a dry gulch and had just finished brushing down the horses, when the loud reports startled me. Captain McAllen had at least allowed me to groom Chestnut, but I wondered where Sam had run off to when I saw another Pinkerton taking care of the horse I had ridden.

McAllen told his three men to arrange their sleeping gear about fifty yards out from us in different directions, but we kept the horses together and close to where we would bed down. I had left New York to experience the West, but I had soon discovered that I preferred a mattress to the hard ground. These seasoned hands had taught me something: a dry, sandy streambed is more comfortable than the hard pack I normally chose. I just needed to remember to climb out quick if it started to rain.

When I saw one of the men stacking sticks to build a fire, I asked, "Won't a fire draw attention for miles?"

"That's why we stopped before dark," McAllen explained. "Dry wood doesn't smoke much, and we'll put it out at dark. When we're in winter pursuit, we stop even earlier to build up a good supply of embers before nightfall."

After I had left Denver and couldn't find a town for the night, my life outdoors was a haphazard affair. I had the right horse and gear for the range, but I was a raw tenderfoot when it came to living in the open. I did, however, know how to hunt birds. My father's love of shotguns and game birds had rubbed off on me. I would have enjoyed beating the brush with Sam, but I doubted that McAllen would let me out of his sight.

In a few minutes, Sam entered our camp with a smile and two large sage hens. I walked over and held out a hand for one of the birds. "I'll clean 'em," he said, throwing a sideways glance toward McAllen.

"We can each take one," I suggested.

"I can handle 'em."

McAllen didn't approve of his men fraternizing

with clients, and Sam had already received one reprimand. My solution was simple. I reached in my pocket and drew out a silver dollar. "I'll bet you I can dress my bird faster than you."

I heard the men gathering around behind me. I had already discovered that nothing grabbed a westerner's attention faster than a wager pitting one contestant's skill against another's.

A big grin grew on Sam's face as he handed me one of the sage hens. As I took the bird, I said, "Captain, you judge."

"With pleasure. I always enjoy seeing a cowboy separate a rich man from his money."

We picked up canteens and walked over to a pair of knee-high rocks at the side of the wash. Sam knelt, but I remained standing with my legs spread to bring me closer to the surface of my rock. We both laid our birds down, and the captain yelled, "Start!"

Sam's hands moved in a blur as he plucked the hen. I used my knife to deftly cut off the feet and wings. Without hesitation, I stabbed the bird just behind the neck and ripped down the right side of the backbone, all the way to the tail. I repeated the operation on the left side of the backbone, separating the ribs from the spine. Then I held the bird in my left hand and grabbed the head and craw with my right. With a mighty effort, I ripped the spine right out of the bird with all the organs attached. Tossing the guts aside, I worked my fingers under the skin and tore it from the body, feathers and all. Reaching down, I picked up the canteen and rinsed the bird thoroughly. When I turned and handed the hen to Captain McAllen, I estimated that it had taken me just over a minute.

In as casual a voice as I could muster, I said, "Done."

Sam's head whipped around in disbelief, and the other men cheered, slapped my back, and then passed the hen between them for examination. When I turned, Sam smiled as he held out his bird in one hand and a silver dollar in the other. "Do this one. I want to see how ya did that."

After the best meal I had ever eaten on the trail, the Pinkertons positioned themselves in a rough circle around us. The moon was nearly full, so we could see a bit as we sat around the expiring embers and smoked our respective choice of tobacco.

McAllen blew a large cloud of smoke and directed a question at me. "You prefer that new-model Colt?"

The '73 Colt .45 army-model revolver was six years old, so the comment told me something about McAllen's attitude toward things new. I enjoyed talking about guns, but I had learned that westerners could be more than a little animated about their preference in firearms, so I merely said, "It's reliable."

"I prefer the heft of a Smith & Wesson .44 No. 3. A good bludgeon, if one's needed, and faster to reload."

"I wanted something lighter."

"Hell, it's light all right, but you can't hit anything over fifteen yards with that short barrel."

Most men selected the 7.5-inch barrel, but I carried the 5.5-inch model, not for speed of the pull, but because of the reduced weight. I didn't like carrying a huge hog leg at my waist. Although from twenty yards, I could hit a whiskey bottle with my Colt, I only said, "I prefer a rifle for distance."

McAllen glanced at Sharp before saying, "Good idea, if one's close by. But you gunfighters seem to like them short-barreled Colts."

"I'm not a gunfighter."

"But you *are* a man-killer."

"Only once," I protested.

"Twice, I hear."

I did not like the way this conversation was going. "I never shot a man before the Cutlers."

"Well, I hear you're good at it."

"I'm good with a gun, not killing."

McAllen sat quiet a minute and then added, "I been in a few fights and seen more than my share. The man who walks away knows how to keep a cool head. If you took the Cutlers like I hear tell, you're a cold son of a bitch in a gunfight. That's more important than being good with a gun."

I remembered how scared I had been walking into that street, but I decided it would be better to let the conversation die. After another moment, McAllen asked, "Can I see your Colt?"

Without comment I pulled my shooter out and handed it to McAllen butt first, hoping the talk would shift to guns instead of killing. McAllen quickly unloaded the weapon using the ejector rod in a way that showed he was not unfamiliar with the Colt .45. He inspected the barrel, spun the cylinder, and took a couple dry shots.

"Nice, clean feel. What'd you do to it?"

"Started with the pick of the litter, replaced the mainspring with a lighter, tempered one, and filed, polished, and hardened the bents."

"All yourself?"

"I'm a gunsmith."

"Wish I were. Had to go back three times before I got my .44 the way I wanted it."

"Trial and error. That's just the way it is. I probably reworked mine five or six times. Only difference is, I did the work and the testing."

McAllen handed the Colt over to Sharp, who had been sitting quietly, watching our exchange. Sharp turned it in his palm and handed it back. I remembered Sharp in the street with a Winchester and guessed that he had little use for handguns.

After McAllen ran his finger along the barrel, he said, "Filed the sight a mite too."

"That took the most time. I didn't like the fat sight from the factory, so I thinned and shortened it to my liking."

McAllen cocked the hammer in the half position and then in the full-cocked position. After taking a few more dry shots, he handed it back but kept the bullets. After examining one, he said, "Your own loads?"

I nodded. "Forty grains of English powder."

He raised an eyebrow. "Expensive. You use them for practice too?"

"As you said earlier this evening, I'm a rich man."

McAllen poured the cartridges into my out-stretched hand. "You're a rich man, all right, and evidently a good one in a scrape." He picked up his cigar, which he had laid on a rock. "That'll be handy, if we run into trouble."

Chapter 22

I grew increasingly nervous as we drew closer to the Bolton ranch. Jenny was free now, but what did I know of her? She was still a child, uneducated and ignorant of the world. At least, my world. I suppose she would say I was ignorant of her world, and perhaps she would be right.

I tried to figure out what attracted me to her, but my feelings confused me. Sure, she was pretty, but I had known plenty of pretty women. New York was full of them. But Jenny affected me differently than any woman I had ever met. And I had never actually met her—only lusted from a distance. No, that wasn't right. It was more than lust. The attraction had been immediate and powerful. She exuded charm and energy, and her smile had snatched my heart in an instant.

I couldn't make sense of it, so I gave up trying to understand emotions previously unknown to me. Reasoning would not provide the answer. Somehow, some way, I had developed an attachment to her, and no amount of thinking could erase an illogical passion.

Mason Valley presented a welcome sight after the stark landscape we had ridden through. A pretty green valley spread out in front of us, and even as a tenderfoot, I could see it was great cattle country. The open range, green grass, and cottonwood trees made the air feel fresh and the ride seem easier.

We arrived at the Bolton ranch house around noon, and my stomach hoped we would be offered a meal. The main house was a two-story clapboard affair with a large porch that faced an array of smaller, single-story buildings and a huge barn. There were five horses in a largish corral and a single horse surrounded by three cowboys in a breaking pen. I held back with the rest of the men as McAllen approached a lone elderly woman standing on the porch. We were too far back to catch the conversation, but eventually the captain made a slight motion with his hand that bid us forward.

As we approached, the captain said, "This is Mrs. Bolton, and she has kindly invited us to rest our horses and join her hands for the noonday meal."

The title confused me, until I realized that this

must be John Bolton's mother. She was a matronly-looking woman, with a flowered dress draped over her corpulent body. Her flat nose and recessed eyes emphasized a face that looked too large for even her bulky body. Either John had inherited his weight problem, or the Bolton household employed a cook so good it was hard to push the plate away.

I did not want to eat with the ranch hands, so I stepped down from my horse and proceeded directly up the porch. Extending my hand, I said, "Good afternoon, Mrs. Bolton. My name is Steve Dancy. I was saddened to hear of your loss."

Mrs. Bolton looked me up and down and then turned a nasty stare at Sam, who was still dressed in my clothes. When her eyes returned to me, her scorn almost knocked me back a pace. "You have a hell of a lot of nerve showing up here. You're responsible for my son's murder."

I could only stammer, "Excuse me?"

"You're the one who murdered them Cutlers and convinced my boy to reenter the governor's race. He'd be alive today if you'd stayed out of our business."

"I'm sorry you feel that way, but John made his own decision."

"You bribed him!"

"I made a campaign contribution. It was not a bribe."

"Same thing." She turned her back on us and started to enter the house.

"May I speak to Mrs. Bolton?" I asked.

She whirled on me and spoke with venom I had rarely heard. "I'm *Mrs*. Bolton."

"I meant Jenny."

"I threw my son's little whore out of the house."

"She's gone?"

"She's doing what she's fit for. You'll find her in the cookhouse scrubbing dishes . . . among other duties." She turned her back to me but then whirled around once again. "And you're not to take her with you. She has debts to work off."

"What? You can't hold her."

"The hell I can't. And I got twenty ranch hands that say so." Someone punctuated her last sentence with a rifle cock behind us. "She'll stay until she's worked off her debts."

I had never been so angry. "How?"

Now came an ugly sneer. "My foreman'll find ways she can be useful in the bunkhouse."

I forced myself to take a deep breath and get control. I glanced over my left shoulder and saw that my Pinkertons had somehow spread out a bit, and they looked tighter than an obsessively wound pocket watch. Captain McAllen looked as threatening as any man I had ever seen, and his attention seemed riveted on something over my other shoulder. I assumed that the man with the rifle stood behind me to the right and that he was not alone.

After a moment, I asked as casually as possible, "What is the amount of her debt?"

"Forty silver dollars."

"Her bride-price?"

"A loan my son graciously made to her father, which has not been repaid."

"That's ridiculous. Everybody knows that was a bride-price."

"Everyone knows my son gave her father forty dollars . . . and that's all they know."

I could understand the woman being angry at the loss of her son, but this outsized malevolence had to reach further back than three days. "All right, I'll pay the debt," I said, as I reached into my pocket and pulled out my eastern-style wallet.

"You'll not buy your whore with paper money. The debt is forty silver dollars, just as her father insisted on."

I stopped in mid-motion. "Mrs. Bolton, please be reasonable. I'm not carrying forty in coin."

"Then come back when you are." With that she did turn her back on us and enter the house.

After Mrs. Bolton snapped the door shut behind her, I stepped off the porch and gathered up the reins of the horse I had been riding. I tried to make my voice sound casual. "Well, let's see what the cookhouse is serving for the noonday meal."

With my neutral statement, I could feel the tension ease. I walked the horse over to the water trough, and Sharp and the rest of the men dismounted and followed. As the horses drank, I took the opportunity to look around. I was surprised to spot about ten armed hands scattered around, but none of them, at least at the moment, looked ready to cause serious trouble.

When Captain McAllen arrived at the trough, I said, "Let the men clean up. We can handle the horses."

McAllen started to object until he figured out I wanted the three of us to talk in private. The captain nodded to his men and then nonchalantly whispered something into Sam's ear.

As Sam and the others meandered away, I waited to see if any of the Bolton men moved into earshot. After a few moments, I asked, over the noise of the slurping horses, "What did you tell Sam?"

"To act friendly, like nothing happened."

Keeping an eye on our periphery, I turned to Sharp. "Can you explain any of this?"

"Nope." He glanced toward the house. "A mother scorned, I suppose."

I maneuvered to the side of Chestnut and started rubbing his neck. "Guess the history doesn't matter. Either of you gentlemen happen to be carrying a bag of silver?"

"I got three dollars in silver, maybe four if the grand lady will accept two-bit pieces," Sharp said.

"Six," McAllen added.

"That gives us about twelve," I said. "Don't suppose any of your men are riding heavy."

"We'd be lucky to gather up another six," McAllen said.

I looked around. "I could offer her men two dollars paper for every silver dollar."

Sharp nudged one horse away from the trough to give another a chance at the water. "I doubt any of 'em'll defy her."

"Poker?"

"Never happen. Besides, the ranch hands probably don't have twenty silver pieces between them."

We fell silent until Sharp said, "Let's take the horses over to the corral and unsaddle them."

Rather than trying to eavesdrop, the Bolton hands casually moved to keep their distance. They watched, but they did not challenge. Sometimes a reputation with a gun can work to your advantage. We each led two horses over to the corral and silently went about our work.

When we stepped over to the fence to throw the saddles over the rail, Captain McAllen rested his back against one to signal that he had something to say. Once all three of us had taken a similar pose, he said, "Steve, our contract doesn't include saving a damsel in distress."

"We can amend it," I offered.

"No. I can't control this situation."

"Must you?"

"Yes." The abrupt answer told me that McAllen could not be induced with a sweetened pot of money.

I turned to Sharp. "Any ideas?"

"As much as I hate to leave her in this situation, I don't see much alternative that doesn't involve a lot of killing . . . and some of the dead will be in our party."

"You don't think she's bluffing?"

"Nope. Not that woman."

"I think I agree. At least it's not worth the gamble." I pushed myself away from the fence. "Well, let's finish with the horses and get some chow. Maybe I'll think of something."

Chapter 23

We sat down on a bench alongside the cookhouse to eat our pork and beans and biscuits. I had kept an eye open but had not seen Jenny. The beans may have been nourishing, but I could barely find a trace of pork in the soupy concoction. Sharp's men ate better.

I finished the meal in less than five minutes and then lazily wandered toward the bunkhouse with my empty tin plate in the hope of catching Jenny. As I approached the raw-lumber building, a cowhand placed his body in front of the open doorway. He pointed. "Just throw your plate in that bucket."

"Fine meal. Thank you."

"Thank Mrs. Bolton."

"I will. Is Jenny inside?"

"What business is it of yours?"

"I'd like to offer her my condolences."

"She don't look to be grievin'. Besides, she's busy."

"It'll only take a moment. I had business dealings with her husband."

"You can see her after Mrs. Bolton gives the go-ahead."

Obviously, I was not going to gain entry without a confrontation, so I flung my plate into the wooden bucket with a loud clank and turned toward the ranch house. As I turned, I noticed that a few men had spread out behind me, but McAllen and the others kept them in check with postures and expressions that told them to be careful. I felt a little more confident knowing someone watched my back.

I tried to figure out Mrs. Bolton's motivation. It had to be more than personal animosity. My mind raced as I marched toward the ranch house, but I came up with no solution that did not involve gun-play. And I could not be sure McAllen and his men would back me up, damsels in distress being out-side our contract and all.

"May I have a word?" I turned to see McAllen striding in my direction. I slowed my pace to let him catch up, but I did not quit walking. He put a hand on my elbow to stop my progress. "What are your intentions?"

"I'm going to see that fat witch."

"Don't rile these men."

"I'm going to negotiate with her, not shoot her."

"What if she won't answer the door?"

I suddenly knew my strategy. "She'll talk to me."

McAllen looked at me a long moment and then said, "My obligations go only so far."

"I understand. There'll be no trouble."

With no further comment, McAllen walked away, but he still made a show of pointing to his men and giving them some type of hand signal. The Pinkertons casually moved to all points of the compass. His obligations may have gone only so far, but he seemed to be still on the job. On second thought, he may have been concerned only about the safety of his own men in case I had misled him about not causing trouble.

As I approached the house, a ranch hand armed with a rifle got up from a chair and stood in front of the door. Without stepping up to the porch, I said, "Tell Mrs. Bolton she needs to talk to me if she wants to retain ownership of this ranch."

"She asked not to be disturbed."

"Disturb her. This is not about Jenny. It's about business I had with her son."

He looked puzzled but turned and entered the house without knocking. After a few minutes, he returned and waved me in with his rifle. "I'm to accompany you."

Without comment, I mounted the steps and entered the house. Her man walked so close behind me that I thought he was going to poke me in the back with his rifle barrel. I hesitated in the central hall, and he said, "To the left."

The sitting room was obviously decorated by a woman. The flowery fabrics were accented with more knickknacks than could comfortably fit on the flat surfaces. Mrs. Bolton sat in an overstuffed easy chair, holding a china teacup and saucer with both hands. Her bulk seemed to overwhelm the dainty room. She took a purposeful sip and then indicated a straight-backed ladder chair to her right.

I sat with the full knowledge that no refreshment would be offered. "Thank you for seeing me."

"Get to your business. My hands have work to do."

I bet that she was highly displeased that her men had just stood around looking threatening since our arrival. "I apologize for the intrusion, ma'am. We'll be on our way soon." I jerked a thumb over my shoulder at the rifle-bearing overseer. "Do you have complete confidence in this man?"

Holding the teacup by the saucer, she ordered, "Speak your mind."

"I want to talk about John's last will and testament."

The rattle of the cup in the saucer told me I had hit the mark. "What will?"

"John filed a will in Carson City leaving his possessions to Jenny."

Another rattle. "This was my husband's homestead. I built this ranch while John played politics in Carson City. That bitch ain't taking it away from me."

"She has the law on her side." I shrugged. "John seems to have been smitten with the girl."

She waved her man away and did not speak again until after she heard the front door close. "I don't believe you."

"That he was smitten or that there's a will?"

She set her teacup down on a doily-covered side table. "My son and I had words about that little harlot, but I don't believe he'd spite me like this. I'm his *mother* for Christ's sake."

"Lust drives men to do foolish things. You know that John considered Jenny his most prized possession."

"Possession, not heir." She threw the words back at me like they were bullets.

"Nonetheless, he decided to bequeath everything to her. Perhaps his anger with you was greater than you knew."

"Oh, I knew. That slut ruined my life." She grew quiet, and I could see her mind working. "You said you could save the ranch for me."

"For a price."

"Spit it out."

"I'll trade you John's last will and testament for Jenny and some money."

"How much money?"

"Don't know yet. Depends on how much I need to bribe the lawyer. He'll be breaking the law, so I don't suppose it'll come cheap . . . probably about a thousand dollars for him and another thousand for my troubles."

"If you want Jenny so bad, you cover the bribe."

"I don't want Jenny; I just want to see her clear of this place."

"You're a liar. You want her to come with you, and you don't want no ranch weighing her down."

I decided her accusation worked to my advantage, so I let it go. "Let me make this clear: I do the work; you pay. But it's got to be done fast, before the will gets filed in front of a judge in Carson City."

She thought about it a minute. "You bring me a last will and testament with my son's signature, like you say, and I'll pay one thousand dollars. You cover anything more."

I pretended to think a minute. "One other condition: you bring Jenny back into the house until my return."

"I figured that, but if you're lying, Jenny will regret the day she was born."

"Have the thousand dollars ready on my return in a couple of days." I waited a couple of beats. "I won't insist on silver."

She suddenly looked smug. "I'll write a draft against your own bank."

"No." I couldn't let her get the upper hand. "On second thought, give me a draft now against your son's Carson City bank. I'll need it for the lawyer."

For some reason, my request caused her to laugh uproariously. When she quieted, she said, "You've got to be mad if you think I'd trust a thousand dollars in your hands before I get the will." She smiled and picked up her tea again. "The draft will be against your bank and only after you bring me the will . . . or no deal."

Knowing she had to believe she outfoxed me, I said, "Agreed. Now I want to see Jenny."

"Why?"

"I want her to know about our arrangement."

"She's not to know about the will."

"I'll just tell her I'm conducting some business for you."

"'Fraid I'll throw her back in the bunkhouse as soon as you leave?"

"Yes."

This incited another laughing spell. "Very well. Tell my man to fetch her."

Chapter 24

I rose from my chair as Jenny entered the room and almost gasped. She wore a filthy calico dress with a torn collar that showed sweat stains, and her matted hair looked like it hadn't been washed in months. She wore no shoes, and it appeared from the drape of her dress that she also wore no under-clothing. She did wear a pained expression caused by the tight grip on her upper arm.

I caught the eye of Mrs. Bolton's man and said, "Let her go."

The man shifted his gaze to Mrs. Bolton and evidently received a signal, because he let go of her.

As Jenny rubbed her arm, her pained expression was replaced with a look of defiance.

"You may go," Mrs. Bolton said, and the man backed out of the room.

Since there were no other chairs close by, I stood and said, "Please take a seat."

Jenny straightened her posture and said, "I'd rather stand."

I was not going to argue, so I remained standing as well. "Mrs. Bolton has some business she would like me to conduct for her in Carson City. I agreed on the condition that you are allowed back into the house."

Jenny shifted her gaze from me to Mrs. Bolton. "No, thank you. The company's better in the bunkhouse."

Her answer shocked me. "No one will bother you here."

"No one bothers me none in the bunkhouse." She lifted her chin and threw a nasty stare at both of us. "I get along just fine with the hands."

Mrs. Bolton started laughing again. "My dear, I'm heartened to hear that you get on so well with the boys."

Jenny took a half-step toward Mrs. Bolton and checked herself. I was caught between two hellions determined to give no quarter. What a history this house must have witnessed. Now I understood why Bolton took Jenny with him whenever he left the ranch—not only for her company but to shield her from his mother's talons. If he had left her at the ranch, there was no telling what he would have found on his return.

I racked my brain to think of a way to negotiate a truce, but I could think of nothing that would move either of the women. Finally, I turned to Mrs. Bolton and asked, "May I see Jenny alone?"

"You may not," Mrs. Bolton said.

Jenny turned a scornful look at me. "Have you come to rescue me?" She used a mocking tone that made me feel stupid.

"I came to discover the facts around John Bolton's murder. I understand you witnessed it."

"Yes, but there's nothing to tell, really. I was standing about five feet from him when his brains got spattered all over the ranch house wall. I didn't even hear the shot until after."

"Did you see who shot him?"

"Were you not listening? I said I didn't hear the shot until afterwards. The killer was far away."

She made me feel stupid again, so I pressed on in a different direction. "Was Mr. Bolton on the front porch?"

"Yes. My *husband* was enjoying a cigar and a recess from his mother's henpecking."

Mrs. Bolton smiled sweetly. "Tell Mr. Dancy what we were arguing about, dear."

Her comment started an unsightly staring contest. Jenny looked like a hellcat ready to pounce, while Mrs. Bolton just stared back like an ill-tempered Caesar. I watched the competition for a minute and then said, "Can I trust you two ladies alone for a minute? I need to talk to Captain McAllen."

Mrs. Bolton broke the duel and gave me her too-cute smile. "We'll both be right here upon your return . . . but don't dally."

I walked quickly outside and found McAllen and Sharp still at the bench where we had eaten our lavish meal. Walking over to them, I noticed my admittance to the house had lessened tensions considerably. Men on both sides stood wary, but their relaxed postures told me that they thought a peaceful settlement was in the offing.

McAllen and Sharp stood as I approached. "Bolton was on the front porch when he was shot. The rifle report took over a second to reach the house."

Both men took a sight line from the porch to the horizon. McAllen said, "Things look calm. I'll take a look, but Sprague's careful. Probably picks up his cartridge casing."

"Have you talked to Bolton's men about the shooting?"

"They didn't look none too friendly," Sharp said.

I waved over the man who had let me into the house. He hesitated a second but then approached us. As he walked over, he raised a hand, telling the other men to stay put.

"Yep?" He worked hard to appear unruffled.

"I assume you're the foreman," I said.

"I am."

"Did you or any of your men see Mr. Bolton get shot?"

"Nope."

"Did you search over there?" I waved my hand in the general direction where the shot must have come from.

"I took a look. Found an impression in a swale where the killer laid down. Over a hundred and fifty yards. Damn fine shot, if you'll excuse me for sayin' so."

"Any cartridge casings?" Captain McAllen asked.

"Didn't see any, but I coulda missed somethin'. Why's that important?"

"Sprague carries a Remington Creedmoor, which uses a .44-100 cartridge. Odd casing and not common hereabouts."

"Sprague?" The foreman took off his hat and wiped his brow. "Goddamn."

"Not sure, but a cartridge would sure help us figure out what we're dealing with."

"Well, hell. Come along, and I'll show ya where he was shot from. Maybe we can find somethin'."

"Much obliged, but could I have a word with Mr. Dancy first?" McAllen jerked his thumb in my direction.

"I'll be over there, keepin' an eye on the both of ya." The comradeship that had evolved during our conversation seemed suddenly revoked.

After the foreman had retaken his position on the porch, McAllen asked, "What's going on in there?"

I grinned. "A catfight."

"The two gentlewomen givin' ya a bit of trouble, are they?" Sharp seemed amused.

"Jenny says she'd rather service the whole bunkhouse than stay a single night with the resident witch."

"You got her back into the house?" McAllen asked, incredulous.

"I got Mrs. Bolton's permission for her to return, but Jenny's acting as defiant as a mule. I left to give her time to think through the alternatives."

"How'd you get the old battleaxe to change her tune?" McAllen asked.

"With a less-than-truthful bluff. But let's leave that for the trail. I want to get back inside to see if Jenny's come to her senses."

"What if she hasn't?"

"Then I guess we ride hard and get back as soon as we can."

Sharp asked, "Do ya think things are settled down enough for me to accompany McAllen an' the foreman?"

McAllen answered. "If there's a cartridge out there, I'll find it."

"I'm a miner. I know how to spot things in rocks."

McAllen looked around. "All right. I think we've passed any crisis here. I also want to find the spot where he tethered his horse. Might not have been as careful there." McAllen returned his attention to me. "We might be awhile."

"Don't be too long," I said. "I want to make headway toward Carson City before dark."

With our tasks defined, we went our separate ways. I hoped Jenny had softened her attitude, because I hated to think of her in the bunkhouse for several more nights. As I reentered the frilly parlor, both women were seated with their hands folded in their laps. A good sign, I hoped.

"Your foreman volunteered to show Captain McAllen the spot where the assassin positioned himself for the shot. We want to search the area for the cartridge casing. That'll help prove who killed him."

In a tone that did not invite debate, the senior Mrs. Bolton said, "Sean Washburn killed my son."

"No doubt he hired the man who did it, but we need proof to call in the law."

She gave me one of her *I'm not evil* smiles. "You're handy with a gun. If you're so interested in playing the champion, revenge my son."

"Mrs. Bolton, if I get the opportunity, I will. But so far, I've never even met Washburn."

"He's a huge, pompous brute with flowing gray hair. You can't mistake him."

"Gray hair?" I had assumed he was younger.

"He turned gray early and decided to make it an asset. He likes his hair to billow out behind him when he rides."

"Sounds vain."

"A vainer man you cannot find. He wears gray suits and rides a gray horse that stands at least fifteen hands. He makes quite a picture."

"I shall keep an eye out for him." I turned to Jenny. "Have you reconsidered?"

"Yes. Mrs. Bolton bribed me."

I was suddenly wary. "With what?"

"A hot bath, my personal effects, and a promise that you'll take me to a stagecoach stop on your return."

I looked at the matron, and she actually winked at me. I supposed she had decided to treat Jenny with a little deference because my mission in Carson City might fail. If Jenny got hold of the ranch, Mrs. Bolton would probably find the bunkhouse under-decorated. I tried to make my voice firm when I said, "I think she should add travel money to the offer."

"My personal effects include a few items that will bring a good price. I don't want her money. Only what's mine."

"Very well. I'll tell the men to saddle up, and we'll be on our way."

I started to leave, but Jenny stopped me with a question. "What do you want for your heroic efforts?"

This surprised me, and I could only stammer, "Nothing. What do you mean?"

"I see the way you look at me. I'm beholden, but you may only lie with me once."

"That's. . . you've misunderstood my intentions."

"Don't act so innocent. I know why you did this. When I get to Carson City, I'm starting a new life, and I'll not be leaving behind debts."

I was flabbergasted. She spoke so casually about something so intimate. Then I realized she had probably never experienced intimacy. "You are not in my debt, and if you were, I wouldn't accept payment in that fashion."

Jenny's posture stiffened. "One fuck. That's it. I won't allow you to keep me as your whore. When I leave here, it'll be as a free woman. No man'll ever buy my favors. If that's not good enough for you, ride out and don't come back."

I glanced at Mrs. Bolton, and she looked unusually pleased with the exchange. I bowed my head and said, "Good day, ladies. I shall return, and Mrs. Bolton's conditions are completely satisfactory. I need no further remuneration." I started to leave, but my anger got the better of me. "And you may keep your favors for someone you fancy." I snuggled my hat back on my head. "Besides, a fuck at Ruby's only costs two dollars."

I exited the house to the sound of my own boots and Mrs. Bolton's laughter.

Chapter 25

After we left the ranch, I rode for nearly an hour in utter turmoil and dejection. Turning aside any attempt at conversation, I tried to think things through but could not get a grasp on my feelings. Why was I so infatuated with this girl, and why did her dismissive remarks bother me so much? She was an ignorant and sullied farm girl nearly half my age. Not exactly the type of woman I could show off to New York society. What did I expect? An affair? I certainly would never marry the girl.

My infatuation had started the first time I saw her in Jeremiah's general store. She was vibrant and fetching, and her personality effortlessly filled a room. But that was before the Cutlers and the bunkhouse. She had also closely witnessed her husband's gruesome murder. No wonder she no longer radiated joy and innocence. Now she proudly displayed a hard disposition and a tart tongue, a tongue she had doubtless learned to wield from the mistress of the house.

As I thought about it, I had to admit that my initial image of Jenny might have been false from the start. On the other hand, if it had been accurate, then her guileless and charming nature probably had been doused, perhaps beyond rekindling.

Calming a bit, I realized she had spoken with an elocution that belied her lack of education. She must be smart—and certainly strong-willed. Her defiance of Mrs. Bolton, although shocking in its consequences, made me admire her all the more. It made no sense, but Jenny Bolton still held a grip on me, and there was no way I could shake it loose.

Riders became more numerous, along with an occasional wagon and even soldiers. McAllen became concerned because the cramped terrain provided hiding spots, so he positioned one of his men on the far side of the river, and I could hear another thrashing through the brush to our right. McAllen feared our little detour gave Sprague plenty of time to catch up if he chose to chase us down.

Looking around, I became aware of my surroundings and realized I had been so preoccupied with my thoughts that I had forgotten to be scared. Bless Jenny for small favors.

Our route ran along a river bordered by picturesque pastures and meadows. Sam must have sensed that I had returned my attention to the trail, because he said, "That's the Carson River."

"Pretty," was all I could muster.

"This here's called the Kit Carson Trail. Blazed by the great scout himself." When I didn't respond, Sam added. "Ya know, the Pony Express used this route."

"How long ago?" I asked to be polite.

"Almost twenty years. Telegraph put 'em out of business."

"Would you have wanted to be a rider?'

"Hell, yes. I'll take any job where they pay me to ride fast. That horse you're on may not be as sure-footed as Chestnut, but he runs like the wind." Sam laughed. "I love to give chase to outlaws. Most times, we gotta walk, but on occasion, I can cut him loose and ride hell for leather."

"I'm afraid you're a bit large to have ridden for the Pony Express."

"Yep, they liked little men. But, damn, it musta been fun."

I like to ride a horse at full gallop and even jump, but riding all day at breakneck speed didn't sound like fun to me. The path grew a bit broader, so I gave my horse a nudge and trotted up beside McAllen. Sam immediately moved up as well and took a position on my outside.

"Did you find anything at the shooting site?" I asked.

McAllen answered while keeping his eyes roving. "Wondered if you'd ever ask. Nothing at the shooting site. We found where he tethered his horse about three hundred yards further out, but he had swept it clean as well."

"Nothing then?"

"Oh, we picked up his trail out a ways. Good hoofprints. The horse is missing a nail in the right rear shoe."

"But no casing?"

"No." McAllen reached into his pocket and

handed over a piece of paper. "That's a drawing of the hoofprint, signed by the three of us as witnesses."

"Doesn't seem like much," I said.

"It's not—not by itself, anyway. But maybe we got something else. Sharp found a cigarette butt off to the side of the trail."

"Can that help?"

"Possibly," McAllen said. "The paper's white, and Sharp says there's a fancy tobacco shop in Carson City. If the tobacconist can testify that the butt is the brand Sprague uses, it'll help corroborate his presence."

I knew white cigarette paper was more expensive, and thus less common than brown, but it seemed awful thin.

Sharp added from the other side of McAllen, "Considerin' his reputation, if we can tie both the horse an' the butt to Sprague, a reasonable judge might let it go to trial."

"I'll bet he'd be acquitted," I said.

"Probably . . . but while he was in court, my job'd be a sight easier," McAllen said.

I matched McAllen's light tone. "Well then, by all means, let's find ourselves a reasonable judge."

"In Nevada?" Sharp said. "That'll be harder to spot than a lonely butt tossed six feet off a trail. On second thought, we need more."

A thought struck me. "We might have more. Jenny said the shot blew Bolton's brains against the wall. The shot must have passed through. The bullet can at least confirm a .44."

"Depends on how bad it's mashed up. Rather have the casing, but three tiny pieces of evidence is better than two." McAllen sounded almost hopeful.

Sharp nudged his horse forward so he could see me around McAllen. "What happened in that house?"

After I explained my ruse with the fake will, Sharp asked, "How're ya gonna come up with this will?"

"Got a couple days to figure that out. In the meantime, Jenny's back in her own bed."

"You could use a forger. There's plenty in Carson City with all the false claims."

"Maybe, but I've been thinking. Mrs. Bolton went for my line too easy. She must suspect there's a real will and that John did give Jenny his holdings."

Sharp rode a ways before he said, "Did ya see that horse in the barn?"

"No." I turned toward Sharp. "Why?"

"All the other horses were in the corrals. The one in the barn was small. Coulda been Jenny's."

"What are you driving at?"

"I think Mrs. Bolton was tryin' to scare Jenny into runnin'. She could sneak into the barn, saddle up, an' be gone easy enough, then sell the horse in town an' jump the next stage for who knows where." Sharp wiped his forehead with the edge of the bandanna he had tied around his neck. "Yep, if Mrs. Bolton thought Jenny might have a legitimate claim on the ranch, she'd sure as hell want her to disappear. Could explain her meanness."

"Her meanness, as you call it, goes beyond trying to chase her away. That was as nasty a piece of business as I've ever encountered."

"No use tryin' to figure out a woman's hates. I think some just hate for the pure joy of it." When I did not respond, Sharp added, "Jenny's little more than a child, but if the ranch is really hers, ya should stay out of it, despite what ya promised that ol' hag."

"If Bolton willed Jenny the ranch or put her name on the deed, then I'll help evict that old shrew. If Jenny has no claim, then I'll fake one and trade it for her freedom. Either way, I'm already in it up to my boot tops."

McAllen turned the conversation in a direction that made me uncomfortable. "You got that pretty lady out of the bunkhouse, so what's put you in such a funk?"

"Nothing. I'm just worried about how to pull it off."

"Nothing, my ass. What happened? The little girl reject your advances?"

"No!" That came back too strong. "I mean, I made no advances."

"Well, something put you in the dumps."

I turned in my saddle and glared at McAllen.

151

After a moment, he said, "I apologize. None of my business. But your safety is. Get back in position."

I reined my horse around and fell in with Sam behind Sharp and McAllen. It took a few minutes for my temper to abate, but I knew it was embarrassment, not McAllen's nosiness, that got my ire. I was tired and sore from riding, and I wanted my own clothes and my own horse back. In fact, I wanted this whole damned affair over with. How had I gotten so deeply involved with these hardtack men?

Then I remembered that day in the street with the Cutlers. What had I been thinking? I hadn't been thinking. I had let emotions rule me, just as I was letting an obsession with a young girl dictate my actions now. Jenny was not important. I barely knew her. In fact, I'd had only one real conversation with her and that had been rather unpleasant.

I told myself that I should be concerned only with getting out of this mess. As I thought through my tasks in Carson City, I felt myself relax, and I was finally able to ride comfortably in the saddle.

More soldiers passed us on the road, and I saw a fort ahead. I was trying to think how the cavalry might be useful, when Sharp interrupted my thoughts. "Fort Churchill. Built durin' the supposed Indian troubles about ten years ago."

"Any trouble nowadays?"

Sharp sighed. "Yep, but of a different nature. The Indians have a tent encampment in Carson City. Sits right close to Chinatown. Now you're more likely to meet a drunk Indian than one on the warpath."

"You sound disappointed."

"I don't go for that noble-savage crap you easterners peddle. I've known too many Indians close up. Same faults as us. But it makes me sad when I think about what we lost."

"You mean the Indian way of life?"

"No. I mean fightin' a worthy enemy."

Chapter 26

Carson City disappointed me. It looked like all the other collections of slapdash buildings that Nevada called towns. I had always believed that if Abraham Lincoln had not needed another free state to shore up the North during the late war, Nevada would still be a remote and ignored territory.

Carson City had been settled as a trading post less than thirty years earlier, so I should not have expected the sophistication of Denver or St. Louis. I had visited both cities, and neither was the primitive hinterland a New Yorker might expect. Carson City, on the other hand, lived up to the image of a new-made town populated by people who had nothing but wanted everything.

After we passed the railroad station and approached the statehouse, the town began to look a bit more established. The main thoroughfare was crowded with wagons, horses, and people bustling about with purpose. Although the commercial district had the same disheveled look as most of the other towns in the West, the residences along the side avenues set Carson City apart. Radiating off the central artery were numerous tree-lined lanes with houses substantial enough to indicate that people intended to stay awhile. In fact, some of these homes were large and well designed.

"Do they mine hereabouts?" I asked Sharp.

"Nope, but Virginia City is only about twenty miles away."

I glanced up another side lane with nice homes set back from the street. "Looks like there's some money in Carson City. Settled money."

"For a mine to prosper, you need two things: lumber to shore up the shafts an' a way to transport your bullion to market. Trees an' trains. Carson City has a lock on both. Sometimes I think we miners just toil for a bunch of shysters in starched collars."

"Which reminds me, I want to buy some clothes while we're here."

Sharp pointed ahead. "That's the new state capitol building. Wherever ya find politicians, ya'll find haberdasheries."

The stately capitol building looked sturdy and permanent, as befitted the only pretense to law and order in a society struggling against anarchy. The structure sat in the center of a city block, surrounded by a pleasant park with footpaths, trees, and neatly groomed grass. A white cupola with a silver roof capped the two-story sandstone building, giving it a Federal-style appearance that I had seldom seen west of the Continental Divide.

"Looks impressive."

"Looks deceive." Sharp spit. "A more corrupt state government you will not find."

We wove through the traffic clogging the street and made our way to the St. Charles Hotel. As we dismounted, a liveryman ran up and offered to take our horses to the stable. Perhaps Carson City had some sophistication after all. I gave the boy two bits and looked around. New construction seemed to be going on everywhere, filling the street with the noise of hammering, yelling, and an occasional curse.

When we checked into the hotel, McAllen insisted on rooms next to each other. I noticed that he did not ask to nail the back door shut. The hotel must have been one of the best in town, because I was able to get a two-room suite, and the hotel-keeper informed us that there would be daily maid service and hot baths with fresh water for every guest. In Pickhandle Gulch, I paid extra for water that miners hadn't already turned to mud.

After we had climbed the stairs, McAllen stopped us on the landing. "This is Sprague's home base, so I don't expect trouble, but don't go any-where without one of my men." He nodded toward Sharp. "Not even with just Jeff."

"I have sensitive business to conduct."

"One of us will accompany you, but we'll stay out of earshot."

I turned to Sharp. "What's the best restaurant in town?"

"Right here in the hotel. Not in a class with New York but good nonetheless."

"Would Bradshaw accept a dinner invitation with you and me?"

"I'll see."

"Good. I'm going to order a bath. Let me know when you get an answer."

The hotel bathroom had four tubs separated by folding screens. An attendant drained the dirty water between guests and even made a rough attempt to scrub the tub before pouring in fresh water. In the Pickhandle Gulch barbershop, I had paid six bits for a fresh bath, but the hotel charge of two dollars still seemed like a bargain.

I had just had my bath freshened with a bucket of hot water, when Sharp came in and swung a stool around next to me. "Bradshaw meets us for supper at seven."

"How do we approach him?"

"Straightaway. Bradshaw isn't given to political blather."

"But he *is* a politician." I sunk down until the water touched my chin. "He's mayor, and he has his fingers in everything else."

"He's a businessman first. Bein' mayor requires only his pinkie."

"You don't think he'll bite, do you?"

"I've thought about it, an' I can't figure an angle that would get him into the race."

"I have."

Sharp looked dubious. "What?"

"Washburn wants to be the most powerful man in Nevada. I don't think Bradshaw's ready to relinquish the title."

"Stomp the pretender before he gets a toehold?" Sharp signaled the attendant and started to pull off his boots. "Bradshaw'll look for a way to do that without gettin' hobbled by the governor's job."

The attendant filled the tub next to me and folded back the screen so we could see each other. Sharp started to hand two dollars to the attendant, but he waved it away. "Mr. Dancy bought all four tubs."

Sharp laughed and then said, "Ya do things in a big way, don't ya?"

"I like privacy when I bathe."

Sharp stopped just as he was about to step out of his drawers. "Sorry. I just—"

"Jeff, I meant strangers. Hell, get that trail dust off you."

Sharp finished undressing and slid into the water, giving a long sigh of pleasure. I allowed him to enjoy the moment before I said, "Bradshaw has controlled the governor up to now. He knows how useful it is to have the state chief executive in his pocket."

"Let me tell ya somethin' about Bradshaw. I like the man, but he's a master at corruptin' people. He knows Craig Stevens, dealt with him as head of the Assembly, an' he'll be confident he can seduce him after the election—Washburn or no Washburn. Might already have him in his pocket an' suckered Washburn into payin' for his campaign."

I thought about it a minute. "I don't think so. From what I've seen, Washburn's a smart operator. He'll have something on Stevens to keep him in line." I dunked my head and wiped the water away from my eyes with the fingers of both hands. "I need to persuade Bradshaw to run. Everything depends on it."

Chapter 27

Bradshaw was older than I had expected. I guessed he was in his mid-fifties, which looked out of place in a town populated with people twenty to thirty years younger.

His age was not the only thing that made him stand out. A few scattered couples in the hotel restaurant were dressed well, but for the most part, customers were dressed in a rough type of attire more appropriate to a saloon. Bradshaw set off his tall, thin stature with a charcoal suit that looked as if it had been tailored in the East. His short hair and neatly trimmed beard projected an image of power and money. I was glad I had brought along one of my own New York suits and had it brushed and pressed for this appointment.

We stood as Sharp made the introductions. Captain McAllen and one of his men watched the exchange from another table, but Bradshaw did not seem to notice. After we had retaken our seats, Bradshaw said, "So you're the famous shop-keeper."

"Guilty, I suppose, but I'd rather be clear of this mess."

"And what mess would that be?"

"I seem to have made an enemy of Sean Washburn."

"So I hear." Bradshaw laid his napkin carefully across his lap. "I accepted this invitation because after all the talk, I wanted to meet you. I, however, am not the subject of widespread gossip, so why did you want to meet with me?"

Sharp had been right. Bradshaw didn't blather about politics—nor anything else, I imagined. I didn't want to jump right into my purpose for this dinner, so I suggested we get drinks and order our meal first. Bradshaw gave me an appraising look and then assented with a nod.

When the waiter arrived, Sharp ordered a bottle of French wine and suggested that I try the trout. Since I hadn't had decent fish since Denver, I gladly agreed.

With our orders placed, Bradshaw's next question indicated that he was not a patient man. "Why did you make a large deposit in Commerce Bank?"

"You've probably heard I bought the bank in Pickhandle Gulch. I want a correspondence relationship with Commerce."

"Is that why you asked me to dinner?"

"No. I know you're a board member, but I'll handle the bank arrangements tomorrow. Tonight I want to discuss a political matter."

"I'm listening."

He looked wary, so I decided I might as well plunge in. "Washburn is supporting Stevens for governor. You supported Bolton, but he was killed a few days ago. We need another candidate."

"We?"

"Jeff and I also backed Bolton."

"Well, what do *we* suggest?"

I hesitated but decided not to irritate the man. "That you run."

Bradshaw sipped his wine and nodded approval of Sharp's choice. After another swallow, larger this time, he looked at me. "I suspected as much. The answer is no. An emphatic no." He held up his wineglass in salute. "Now, with that settled, we can enjoy the evening."

This was not the way I wanted the discussion to go. I had intended to present the arguments for a strong candidate and then softly broach the idea of Bradshaw himself running. Now I had an answer before the first course had even been served. To give myself a moment to think, I also tested the wine. It was excellent, and I turned the bottle to read the label. "Nice choice," I said to Sharp.

Sharp gave me a wicked smile. "Since you're payin', I ordered their finest bottle."

"Then I shall be sure to enjoy it." I turned to Bradshaw. "May I ask why you won't run?"

He looked as if he might say no, but then he must have decided it was better to explain. "Politics is for men who have no other route to power."

"But you're the mayor."

"A mostly ceremonial position." He gave a dismissive wave. "It doesn't take much time."

"Your interests will be threatened by a hostile governor."

Bradshaw laughed as if I had just told an amusing story. "Stevens?" He laughed some more. "The man's an incompetent buffoon. He's no threat."

"Washburn will tell him what to do."

Bradshaw stopped laughing. "Washburn can have the governor; I have the legislature. We'll see who knows how to get things done in this state."

My plan appeared dead. "Can you think of anyone else who could run and win?"

"The election's only six weeks away. Too late, I'm afraid. Stevens will get the office. We'll see what he can do with it." Bradshaw gave me a direct look and then straightened his posture to show me that he meant what he said next. "Gentlemen, let me make myself clear." He waited a beat. "My continued presence this evening depends on a different subject for our dinner conversation."

I took another sip of wine and then said as sociably as possible, "How's the price of cattle holding up?"

Chapter 28

Dinner had been exceptional, but when I received the check, I saw that it had not been a bargain. The Comstock Lode had made money plentiful and prices dear.

Sharp and Bradshaw were good dinner companions, and if I had not been so disappointed about Bradshaw's refusal to run for governor, I would have enjoyed the evening. Bradshaw knew more stories about the West than anyone I had ever met. And not just Nevada stories. He told fascinating tales about Kansas cow towns and the California Gold Rush. If my mind had been on my journal, I would have felt like I had struck pay dirt.

We were ready to call it an evening, when I felt someone approach from behind me. I heard McAllen's chair scrape the floor, and Sharp quit talking in the middle of a sentence. When I dressed in a suit, I carried a Remington .38 pocket pistol under my arm in a shoulder holster of my own design. I raised my hand slightly and turned toward the intruder. What I saw almost made me bolt to my feet.

"Take it easy, Dancy. I only came over to say hello."

The man behind me wore an expensive gray suit, a great mane of obsessively groomed gray hair, and a taunting sneer. He also wore two nickel-plated revolvers in a cross-draw configuration. Two menacing bodyguards stood one step behind him at either shoulder, like dreadnoughts protecting a cargo steamer. When I glanced back at my Pinkertons and then at our table, the only person seemingly not on edge was Bradshaw.

I cleared my throat and slowly rose to my feet. "Mr. Washburn, I'm afraid I cannot accept your apology for your shabby behavior. Shall we step outside and make a fair fight of it?"

The sneer lifted, to be replaced by a look of such rage that I thought I might get my duel. Instead, Washburn said dismissively, "You're not worth the effort. I never deal with little men. Sit. It's not polite to stand in front of your dinner guests."

Disappointed that he had deflected my challenge, I slid back into my seat. It would have been so much simpler if we could have just shot it out, but I knew a quick solution had little chance with this man. Brave men don't travel with bodyguards. Then I remembered my Pinkertons. Well, maybe I wasn't that brave either.

Washburn's attention turned to Bradshaw. "Mr. Bradshaw, I'm disappointed in the company you keep these days. In case you didn't know, this man is a notorious killer."

Bradshaw continued to look at ease. "Mr. Washburn, who I dine with is none of your business."

"None of my business?" Washburn glanced left and right at his two guards and then grinned. "Everything in this state is my business or soon will be. What I don't own today, I'll own tomorrow."

"You've elbowed your way into the game, Sean, but you're an interloper. You may know how to scare ignorant prospectors in the hills, but you don't understand how the game is played here in the capital. The stakes are higher here."

"You old fool. I play the game my way. Make my own rules. And as for the stakes, they may very well include your continued health." Washburn put his hand on our table and leaned in toward Bradshaw. "I suggest you cash in your chips and leave the game to your betters."

Bradshaw seemed to grow even more relaxed. "This isn't Virginia City or Pickhandle Gulch. Men here compete with brains, not guns."

Washburn straightened as if he had been struck. "You sayin' you're smarter than me?" His face went through a series of emotions, none attractive. "You old fool. Hell, that's supposin' you still got some brains left inside that numskull of yours."

Bradshaw folded his hands on the table and

crossed his legs. "Bully tactics are a sure sign of weakness."

"Weakness! Goddamn you. In three months, you'll be poor as a church mouse and wondering how it all happened." Washburn arrogantly tossed his mane of hair, but the gesture came across as effeminate. Then he leaned on the table with his knuckles and shifted his head until it was close to mine. "Mr. Dancy, I have one word of advice for you." He leaned in even closer. "Git!"

I ignored his spittle on my face and tried for my own casual pose. "Do you think growing long hair and wearing two pistols makes you Bill Hickok?" I reveled in the instant look of anger. I took the last sip of my wine and said, "I always figured that if a man wore someone else's character, he didn't much like himself."

Washburn straightened and visibly worked to control himself. "On second thought, don't git. After I squash Bradshaw here, I'll need some new entertainment." With that he marched out of the restaurant, his two ruffians in tow.

After Washburn left, no one spoke. I glanced at Captain McAllen and his man, but they were both staring at the door, I suppose to make sure the threat stayed gone. I kept my eye on McAllen because I wanted to call him over.

I was still looking the other way when Bradshaw's fist smashed the table and rattled the dishes. I heard him exclaim, "Goddamn it!" I whipped around to look at him. "That son of a bitch!" His face was redder than our waiter's vest, and he breathed hard for a moment before adding, "You've got your candidate for governor."

"You'll run?"

"Hell, yes. I'm gonna wring that strutting peacock's neck."

Chapter 29

Bradshaw's outburst had drawn McAllen's attention back to our table.

I gave him a wave, and he immediately walked over.

"Can your man follow them and find out where he's staying?"

"I already know where Washburn stays," Bradshaw interjected. "He bought a house on West Musser Street last month. A big one, with servants and all. I gather he wants to make his presence known in Carson City."

"Paint it gray?"

"What?" McAllen looked puzzled, but Bradshaw laughed.

"Never mind," I said to McAllen and then turned to Bradshaw. He seemed to have regained most of his composure. "May I introduce Captain McAllen of the Pinkertons? The captain and his men are working with me."

Bradshaw stood to shake McAllen's hand. "Pleased to meet you. How many in your crew?"

"I have three men with me."

"That should do. I don't expect Washburn to bring his rougher ways of doing business into Carson City. He seems intent on building a respectable front here."

When Bradshaw was seated again, I asked, "Where can we talk in private?"

Bradshaw looked around. Most of the tables had emptied, so he said, "Right here's as good a place as any. Order some brandy."

I gestured for McAllen to sit at the remaining place at the table. Before I could look around, the waiter appeared at my elbow, and I ordered a good cognac. When I resumed the conversation, I kept my voice low. "How can we use Commerce Bank to put pressure on Washburn?"

Bradshaw looked at me with renewed interest. "Brains, not guns?"

"We might need both, I'm afraid. That's why I asked Captain McAllen to join us."

Bradshaw looked at McAllen. "How long have you been with Pinkerton?"

"Twelve years, sir," he answered.

"He's the best they got," Sharp added.

Bradshaw returned his attention to me. "In answer to your question, we attack Carson City First. They hold Washburn's debt."

"Not all of it. I picked up a share when I bought

the Pickhandle Gulch Bank. I started foreclosure on his mines down south, but he delayed court action with a draft against a Denver bank. I'll know in a few days if the draft is honored."

Bradshaw looked at me as if he saw me for the first time. "What's in this for you?"

"Victory over Washburn—plus some smaller stuff, like my life and the lives of my friends."

He looked at Sharp, who gave him a reassuring nod. Bradshaw tapped the table a moment and then said, "By the end of the week, Carson City First's charter will be revoked."

His comment startled me. "You can do that?"

"I didn't say I'd try."

"Under what pretense?" I could not believe it could be this easy.

"Filing false claims. The bank recorded some mining claims on behalf of their shareholders and big clients. A few were questionable. They intend to tie the matter up in court for months, but I'll paint it as just the surface of a major corruption scandal. The scathing speeches from the senate floor will hint at other nefarious deeds. Newspaper stories will demand that the officers be indicted. Within the next couple of days, the governor will rise up in righteous indignation and revoke the bank's charter in the name of responsible government and protecting the public interest."

"That's remarkable. In New York, that would take months . . . years perhaps."

"Advantages of a small town. Not that many people to get on board."

"How much will this hurt Washburn?" Sharp asked.

Bradshaw scratched his whiskered chin. "Only six weeks until the election—that's not much time. Even if he's in arrears, we can't foreclose his loans in time to do much good, but we can dry up any new funds."

Bradshaw appeared to have a new thought. "We'll use the scandal to hurt Stevens in his campaign. By the end of the week, I'll tie him *and* Washburn to the biggest scandal in Nevada history. They're both so tight with Carson City First that everyone will believe they're culpable, and six weeks won't give them enough time to defend themselves in court. We'll also hit 'em with so much legal crap, they'll think they went wading in an outhouse."

"Can you destroy Stevens before the election?" I asked.

"Hopefully, in the next few weeks." Bradshaw switched his attention from me to Captain McAllen. "Your Pinkertons can help. Will you put two of your men at my disposal?"

After I nodded, McAllen turned a hard look on me. "They aren't your men."

"You're all under my employ," I answered.

McAllen aimed his hard stare at Bradshaw. "What kind of work?"

"Investigative."

McAllen waited about three beats and then said, "I can approve a short assignment."

"Good. I'll have them made officers of the governor's office and point them at people who frighten easily. A few of the right questions will get this town buzzing." Bradshaw gave me a direct look. "We'll also need a demonstration of violence. People need to know we can handle Washburn and his hired gunmen, or they won't come to our side."

"You want me to shoot somebody?" I asked mockingly. "Should I pick a victim at random, or do you have someone specific in mind?"

I heard Sharp laugh quietly to the side of me, but Bradshaw remained serious. "Don't be ridiculous. But at the same time, we can't ever be seen to back down from a physical threat. If the opportunity comes, shoot one of his men. Better yet, goad Washburn into a fight. I'll protect you legally."

People who have never killed find it easy to act casual about violence, but Bradshaw was right. Still, though I had tried to get Washburn into the street just a few minutes ago, I didn't like somebody else telling me to shoot someone. I decided to direct the scheme along a more benign path. "We'd like to indict Washburn for conspiracy to murder Bolton."

I asked Captain McAllen to describe our scanty evidence. When he finished, I asked Bradshaw, "Enough?"

"Well . . . I can probably engineer an indictment as long as the arraignment date is set for after the election. But if you don't get any more evidence, the case will be quietly dropped a day or two in advance of the hearing. In the meantime, it should give Mr. Washburn something else to worry about."

I felt it was time to bring up another subject. "I want to see the circuit judge. He telegraphed me that he was tied up in Carson City. Where can I find him?"

"What the hell for? He's useless."

"He's in Washburn's pocket, and I want him in mine."

"Judge Wilson's a twitchy little man, and Washburn's an accomplished scaremonger. I doubt you'll be successful."

"I still want to give it a try."

Bradshaw just pointed to a meager man at a corner table with a beautiful woman.

"Wife or prostitute?" I asked.

"Neither. That's the widow Clark; Judge Wilson is courting her. I don't know if she's serious about his advances or just likes the food here."

After a few minutes of sizing up the little man, I described a rough plan to McAllen. He thought about it a moment and then said, "Let's do it."

Chapter 30

McAllen and I walked over to Wilson's table and glared down at the couple. Wilson was so enthralled by the widow Clark's cooing that he didn't notice us, but she broke his trance by glancing up in annoyance.

"I understand you know the Cutler brothers," I said, without introduction.

"Excuse me?"

"The Cutler brothers. Pickhandle Gulch."

"Do I know you?"

"You're about to."

"Get out of here."

I slammed the table. "Get out of here? Would you tell the Cutlers to get out of here? Hell, no!" I did my best to appear mad as a March hare. "I'm the one who killed those sons of bitches. Now tell the lady to make herself scarce. We got business."

The man literally trembled in fear, but he managed to sputter, "I'm an officer of the court."

"Who gives a shit?" I said.

McAllen stepped behind the widow and stood uncomfortably close to her. She looked at the two of us and said, "I really need to visit the room out back anyway. I'll just be a few minutes." Without waiting for permission, she scurried away.

I slid into her seat as McAllen shifted sideways

to block Wilson from standing up. "You ignored my telegram."

"You're Steve Dancy," Wilson said in a shaky voice. Glancing at the stolid McAllen, he asked, "Who's this?"

"Someone who does dirty work for me. He's quite good."

Wilson tried to gather himself up and spoke in his courtroom voice. "What do you want?"

I let a long silence ensue before I said, "I want you off Washburn's payroll . . . and on mine. I'll set up an assured payment system for three years."

"I'm paid by the Nevada courts, not Washburn."

"Break two of his fingers," I said to McAllen, nonchalantly.

McAllen immediately grabbed the little man's hand.

"What?" Wilson looked up into McAllen's narrowed eyes. "No, stop!"

McAllen squeezed for a long moment and then let go of Wilson's scrawny hand. He then made a show of slowly withdrawing his own hand to let it rest against the butt of his gun.

Wilson's nervous eyes flitted around the room looking for help. "What if, for sake of argument only, I said that Washburn and I had some mutual business dealings? Why would I discontinue involvement with profitable enterprises?"

"I'll pay more—and you'll end up dead if you don't."

Wilson looked dubious for the first time. "You wouldn't murder me."

"But you believe Washburn would?"

This made him visibly more nervous. He scanned the room again before he whispered, "Yes."

"The difference between Washburn and me is that Washburn would pay to have you shot in the street. I'd do something quieter, easier to turn a blind eye to, like slip poison into your food." I shrugged. "You die either way."

Wilson shook his head. "No. I saw Washburn at your table. He meant business."

"That was just Washburn throwing a bluff." I made a gesture to indicate that it did not matter. "But you're right, this little war is going to get bloodier than hell—and you're on the wrong side. I'm giving you one chance to switch . . . or you become my first target. And I don't let unfinished work hang around long." I gave him a few seconds. "What'll it be?"

Wilson whispered again. "I'll come to your side, if I can keep it secret. I'll delay the cases Washburn wants and tell you what's going on in his camp."

I leaned into Wilson's face. "Judge, you can't stay neutral or play both sides. I've got writs I want approved . . . tonight."

Wilson sat back, a picture of cowardly alarm. "I can't. I won't." He looked between McAllen and me. "Can't we work something out? I'll do anything else."

I pretended to think through the alternatives. "Disappear. Tonight."

"Can I come back after the election?"

"No." I turned to McAllen. "If you see this man again, shoot him."

"With pleasure," McAllen said with a wicked grin.

"Where can I go? How can I make a living?"

I pretended to think. "Tell you what. You give me a letter of resignation, and I'll get you a letter of recommendation from the current governor. That should help you get a judgeship in another state. Telegraph me after you get to where you're going."

Wilson backed up his chair as if to leave.

"Stay put," I said. "I want that letter now." I motioned toward McAllen, who immediately went to the hotel lobby for writing materials.

With McAllen gone for the moment, Wilson started to get up, but I reached into my coat, and he sat back down. McAllen returned, set the inkwell down with a resounding snap, and tossed paper and pen in front of Wilson.

I merely said, "Write."

After a few minutes, the honorable judge Wilson handed me his resignation. I read it and then flipped my fingers in dismissal. Wilson bolted for the door without a word.

After he had left, I grinned at McAllen and said, "That was easy."

"He didn't wait for his lady friend," McAllen said with a chuckle.

I made a show of looking around and then gave McAllen a broad smile. "I don't think she's coming back."

"You'd make a good thespian."

"Too respectable. I prefer banking."

We walked back over to Bradshaw, and I threw the letter in front of him. "I regret to inform you that the Nevada circuit judge has found it necessary to resign. Do you think the governor can appoint a replacement?"

Bradshaw quickly read the letter. "I'll see him in the morning."

"Can you make it someone honest or at least corruptible to our side?"

"I prefer the latter." Bradshaw smiled, but I believed he was serious.

Sharp looked amused. "Shall we call it an evening or meander down to the saloon to demonstrate our fondness for violence?"

"After that bedroll last night, I can't wait to climb into a featherbed. But, Jeff, feel free to go kill someone if you like."

Bradshaw bristled. "Don't make light of this, boys. I meant what I said."

I got up to leave. "Don't worry. When it comes to it, we'll not hesitate."

Captain McAllen escorted me to my room. As we walked up the stairs, he said, "You forgot to mention that letter of recommendation to Bradshaw."

I kept climbing. "Why would I do that?"

Chapter 31

The next morning, I asked Captain McAllen to eat breakfast at another table. I had come to accept most of the new disruptions in my life, but I wanted a few private minutes with Mark Twain before the day began. I was reading Jeremiah's copy of *The Adventures of Tom Sawyer*, but I made a mental note to buy my own in Carson City. Twain had worked here as a reporter for a spell, so I felt confident I could find his book at one of the general stores.

Tom Sawyer was written in a fresh, natural style that somehow seemed uniquely American. I hoped it did not catch on, because my writing was much more literary, or at least what I believed New Yorkers thought of as literary. *Tom Sawyer* threw eastern conventions to the wind. The story engaged the reader with quick-paced action, spiced it with humor, and read so easy it seemed the writer had just taken down verbatim the narrative of a skillful storyteller.

The more I read, the more I became engrossed in the story and forgot about analyzing the style. I would read it again, but next time it would be my own copy, so I could make notations in the margins. This time, I would just let the story carry me along.

A glance at my pocket watch surprised me—I had

spent nearly two hours at the breakfast table. Reluctantly, I put the book down and then noticed McAllen staring intently at something or someone over my shoulder. When I turned to see what held his attention, I saw the two guards that had accompanied Washburn the prior evening. This was not good. Even with Captain McAllen and his men protecting me, I could not lose myself in a book. I needed to kill that habit, or I might get myself killed.

I stood, stretched, and then sauntered over toward Washburn's henchmen. McAllen leaped to his feet and moved quickly to catch up with me. The eyes of everyone in the restaurant followed my short walk, and I suddenly sensed a tension in the room that had probably been there the whole time I had been absorbed in *Tom Sawyer*.

As I approached, I noticed that their empty breakfast plates had been pushed away, and one of the men had turned his chair so that it faced the room instead of the table. "Gentlemen, I hope you enjoyed your breakfast?"

They sat silent, and the one facing the room tried a stern look meant to scare me into retreat. His three day's worth of black whiskers actually made him look scruffy, not mean. The other one finally spoke in a mocking manner. "Must be a good book."

"An excellent book. *Tom Sawyer*. When you learn to read, you should pick it up."

"You shit-eater; we can read."

"I wouldn't know it from the dumb expressions you've been wearing for the last hour."

The talker glanced at McAllen and then returned his attention to me. "Who you tryin' to buffalo? You never noticed us."

"I did. And I came over here to tell you never to sit at my back again . . . or you won't finish another meal."

"Fuck—"

I saw a flash of movement to my right and reached for my gun in a spasm of panic. With my gun leveled at the whiskered man, I risked a glance at his partner. McAllen's long-barreled Smith & Wesson pointed at a bloody mouth spitting teeth. Ramming my gun under the other one's chin, I reached down with my left hand and took his pistol. McAllen did not disarm his man.

McAllen smiled and said, "Now you can eat shit with that mouth. No chewing required."

The man tried to answer, but his mouth spewed only red spit and some odd noises.

"Don't try to speak," McAllen said. "Too late to apologize, and a threat will just get you dead. I only bash a man once. The next time I kill him." The only response was a pathetic gurgling. McAllen shifted his attention to the one under my gun. "You or your partner even look to cross our path, and I'll kill you both." When the man's face showed fear, McAllen added, "Now, help get your friend over to a dentist."

I holstered my own gun and spilled out the cartridges from the one I had taken. As the black-haired bodyguard helped the injured man to his feet, I dropped the empty pistol back into his holster. I saw his eyes measure the distance to the gun in his partner's holster, but the sound of McAllen cocking his weapon made it a fleeting thought. The two men stumbled out, and the room suddenly became noisy with animated conversation.

I walked back to my table, intending to pick up my book, when McAllen said, "Sit. Let's have a cup of coffee and talk a minute."

I did not need any more coffee, but I sat down anyway. After McAllen took a seat on the opposite side of the table, he said, "You were lost in that book."

"You're right."

McAllen nodded. "Good. Don't lie to me." He seemed to relax a bit and grinned. "But it was a fine lie to tell them fellas. From now on, order breakfast in your room."

"Of course," I said, realizing that my days in Pickhandle Gulch had caused me to forget the refinements of a decent hotel.

"All right." McAllen sounded friendlier than usual. "We sure didn't need to wait long for an opportunity to show our violent side." He looked around the room at all the whispering guests. "Bradshaw got what he wanted. Word will get all over town in less than an hour."

"That wasn't my intent."

"I know. Listen, you handled yourself real well there, but—if you don't mind—I'd like to give you some advice."

"Sure."

"Your man was still armed. He had a hide-out gun and a knife."

"You left your man with a gun."

"And I watched him close. A person might not pay enough attention to a man he thinks is disarmed."

"Meaning, get all their weapons or let it be?"

"And no more books in public. Stay alert."

"Anything else?"

"If you see either of those men again, they'll mean to kill you. Shoot first."

I nodded. I had been proud of the way I approached the two men, but I had intended only to challenge them verbally. McAllen went to direct physical violence. Last night, Bradshaw had recommended this kind of action, and McAllen had lost no time finding an opportunity to publicly show we could match Washburn's ferocity. I was also proud that I had pinned my man—only to find out he hid additional weapons. I had been lulled by old habits, habits that were harmless in my previous life but now might prove fatal. I vowed to do better.

"What're your plans for today?" McAllen asked.

"I'm going to try to find Bolton's lawyer. Put one

of your men with me, so you and Sharp can talk to that tobacconist."

"Sam'll go with you. We'll also ask if anyone saw Washburn and Sprague together."

"Your other two men?"

"Being sworn in as state officers at the capitol. Then they meet with Bradshaw to find out who they're to question."

"Let's meet for beer about two this afternoon. Figure out our next moves."

McAllen immediately said, "Here at the hotel. Stay away from the saloons."

Chapter 32

I asked the hotel clerk for the best lawyer in town. He directed me to a man named Jansen, who had an office across from the capitol. I then asked to see the chambermaid in my room, so I could give her some special instruction. After a brief wait, an exceptionally skinny girl arrived, whose cheap dress fell straight down from her narrow shoulders.

"You sent for me?" she said.

"I would like you to do me a favor. I'll pay handsomely."

"All right."

"I haven't told you what I want yet."

"Tell me . . . and then I'll tell you what handsomely means."

That took me aback, but I plunged ahead. "I want you to write a letter and sign it with another woman's name. Can you write?"

"You mean can I forge?"

I had to laugh. She may have been slight, but her wit had heft. "Yes, can you forge a letter?"

"I think the question is, will I forge a letter for you?"

"You're educated!"

"I teach politicians' children when I'm not cleaning chamber pots."

That surprised me. I was looking for a poor girl with rudimentary writing skills. It seemed that I had found a tutor. "Can't you get a secretarial position with one of the politicians in this town?"

"I'd rather work with their children."

Her bitter tone told me not to pursue that path, so I simply said, "All right, now tell me, what does handsomely mean?"

"Twenty dollars."

I whistled. "A lot of money." My instinct to barter showed I had not shaken off all my old habits. "Ten."

"How many women can you ask before rumors wreck your scheme? Ten dollars to write the note and ten dollars to keep my mouth shut." Her face showed absolutely no emotion. "That's twenty, in advance. Now, do you have a draft of the letter you want written?"

After she read my draft, she looked up at me with

an odd expression I couldn't fathom. "Will this harm the woman who supposedly wrote this letter?"

"No. I'm trying to help her. She's illiterate, or she would have written the letter herself. I need a feminine hand."

She gave me an empty stare. It was difficult to maintain direct eye contact. She evidently came to a decision and said, "Very well. May I see the twenty dollars?"

I handed her four five-dollar certificates, and she stuffed them in her apron pocket. The woman's demeanor made me curious, so I asked, "What do you intend to do with the money?"

"Put it with my other millions."

Chapter 33

Sam and I arrived at the lawyer's outer office without an appointment, so his assistant tried to brush us off. When the assistant further learned that I did not have business that required gaining the ear of some powerful government figure, nor did I want to file a claim that made other ore discoveries look small, he insisted I write a letter requesting an appointment, which he told me could be arranged within a week or so.

"I assume Mr. Jansen charges by the hour?"

"He does."

"I'll pay him two hours' worth for fifteen minutes

of his time. Tell him now, or I will barge into his office while my man here throws you to the floor and stomps your neck."

I meant this to be somewhat humorous, but the assistant jumped through the office door like he had suddenly encountered a coiled rattlesnake. This rough talk got results, but I reminded myself that if you picked the wrong target, you could get yourself shot instead of obeyed. I thought about apologizing to the assistant before I left the office, but I remembered that we were striving for a tough-as-nails image.

After a few minutes, the assistant partially opened the door and peeked around the edge to see if we still fouled his anteroom. His Adam's apple bobbed with an involuntary gulp, and he croaked, "Mr. Jansen will be with you gentlemen in just a few minutes. Please be patient." He ducked back into the office and tugged the door until we heard a solid click and the twist of a deadbolt.

Sam chuckled and said, "That little man sure scared easy."

"Must have been the nasty look you gave him."

"That, or word already got around town about your lack of cordiality at breakfast."

Sam made a good point. Gossip in Carson City probably moved faster than the news did by the telegraph, especially gossip about some new-comers who beat up a hired gunfighter. I hoped that our reputation would make Jansen cooperative, because all I had to convince him was a chamber-maid's scribbled note.

The office door opened, and a man who looked like a wealthy merchant hurried past us and out the door. In a moment, the assistant waved us in and warily took a side step around us to his chair in the lobby.

After we entered, Jansen kept his back to us while he worked at a Wooton rolltop desk that teemed with paper-stuffed cubbyholes. We remained standing and kept quiet. The lawyer continued pretending to ignore us as he scratched notes on the margins of a legal document. When he finally deigned to turn around, he looked exactly like what he was: a highly connected and prosperous lawyer. He was clean-shaven and wore a clean three-piece suit with a silk cravat that probably cost more than I had given the chambermaid to commit a felony.

He did not bother to extend a hand. "As you can see, gentlemen, I'm quite busy. Please be brief."

"My name is Steve Dancy. I'm the new owner and president of the Pickhandle Gulch Bank. I'm also a business associate of John Bolton and his family."

"You're also a gunman and a brute. I understand you threatened to break my assistant's neck."

"I'm afraid . . . actually I said my associate would stomp your assistant." I used a tone of voice meant to convey that the threat was not to be taken seriously. "Perhaps we could have gotten off to a better start." I reached into my suit-coat pocket and extracted a sealed envelope. Written in an obviously feminine hand, the outside of the envelope read, *Mister Claude Jansen, Esquire.* "These are instructions from Mrs. Bolton."

"The mother?" This question answered my question. John Bolton had used Jansen as his Carson City attorney. That meant I did not have to pay the chambermaid to address another envelope, and I suspected that each succeeding letter would cost more.

"No, Jennifer Bolton. The two women do not get along. I represent John's wife."

"Represent?"

"An agent, so to speak."

Jansen looked at me askance and then ripped open the envelope. The letter told him that I was acting on Jenny's behalf and that Jansen should provide me with a copy of her husband's will.

He studied it a minute and then said, "I didn't know she could write."

Jansen sounded wary, so his comment made me nervous. "John had hired a tutor for her, partly to keep her occupied and partly to put her in a room away from his mother."

I hoped Jansen had not spent a lot of time with Jenny when she had accompanied Bolton to Carson City. I felt the risk was low, because Bolton seemed to hang Jenny off his arm but exclude her from his business.

Jansen pulled on his chin. "Bolton sure hated his mother. I sometimes felt sorry for him, trying to keep peace in that house. Suppose that's why he spent so much time here."

"He was here a lot?"

"Far beyond what was necessary for his business interests . . . or senate duties. He told me his mother had pretty much run the ranch since his marriage. She must have been a strong woman."

"She *is* a strong woman."

"Yes, s'pose so." He pulled on his chin again. "I've never seen you in Carson City. Heard about you, of course, but in association with the Cutlers . . . and that nasty piece of business this morning." He looked up at me. "You say you had business interests with John?"

"Yes. Banking. But our stronger tie was political. I supported him for governor." I pretended to consider how much to divulge. "There was a bad incident with the Cutlers. I, uh, kind of helped John make things right."

Jansen sat straight up and bellowed, "That story 'bout Jenny was true? My god!"

"I prefer not to discuss it further, only to say that the Cutlers were under orders from Washburn."

"Goddamn that bastard." Jansen threw down the letter and then looked at me hard. "Were you a friend of John Bolton's?"

I felt this was a test. "I told you, I was a business and political ally of John's. I wouldn't characterize it as friendship."

"Jenny?"

"I barely know Jennifer Bolton, although I saw her at the ranch yesterday. She knows John trusted me with sensitive matters."

"I get your gist." Jansen seemed to be coming to a conclusion about me. "They were sensitive matters for Jenny as well. She must have appreciated your dispatching the Cutlers."

"We never discussed it, nor do I intend to."

Jansen leaned back and spoke in a friendlier manner. "Tell me something about yourself."

"I'm not the issue here. Jenny is."

"Are you here with Jeff Sharp?"

"Yes."

"And did you make a large deposit at Commerce Bank?"

"*That* is none of your business." I was peeved. "And further, I'm highly disappointed that you're aware of my business affairs. I may need to reconsider my relationship with Commerce."

"But it *is* my business. I'm on the board of directors. The size of your transaction did not go unnoticed."

I relaxed. I had made the deposit to gain credibility with the bank but had gotten the added benefit of increasing my stature with this lawyer. "Then you must know Bradshaw?"

"Of course."

"Last night he agreed to run for governor."

"I know. We had breakfast. He made me curious about you; otherwise you'd never have been admitted to my office." He smiled. "Peter isn't such a very good assistant. If you'd broken his neck, I'd have found another."

"I was joking."

Again the smile. "Peter does not have a sense of humor." With that he pushed back in his swivel chair and extracted two envelopes from one of the cubbyholes. "Please deliver these to Jennifer Bolton and her mother-in-law."

I accepted the envelopes. One was thick. "Any surprises?"

"For her? No. She gets the ranch and John's other assets. His mother, on the other hand, will fume. She gets ten thousand dollars and a one-way ticket to San Francisco." Jansen's smile now enlivened his entire face. "It's all in the envelopes."

"Thank you. I'll handle the mother."

"Jenny's hardly more than a child. John didn't expect this to be executed for years." The next question seemed to reflect honest concern. "Can she manage the biggest cattle ranch in Nevada?"

"I've met her foreman, and he seems a capable man. I also believe that there's more depth to Jenny than is obvious from the surface."

"I hope so. Ranch hands tend to be a hard lot."

I didn't know how to respond, so I put the

envelopes in my pocket and asked, "Would you accept a retainer to handle my legal affairs?"

"What type?"

"Do you get involved in criminal cases?"

"Are you in trouble?"

I laughed. "Not yet. But we're trying to build a case against Sprague and Washburn for Bolton's murder."

"One hundred dollars. Retainer only—I charge by the hour. And, just for your information, I play poker with the attorney general."

I took one hundred dollars out of my wallet and handed it across. "I'll be sending Captain McAllen of the Pinkertons to see you. Please consider him my agent in any dealings associated with Sprague or Washburn."

"Mrs. Bolton?"

"No, he'll represent my interests only for the criminal indictment."

"Very well. Anything else?"

"Does Bradshaw need legal services for his candidacy?"

"Already arranged. Bradshaw doesn't need financial support."

"One other thing. Can you recommend an assistant bank manager that can leave immediately for Pickhandle Gulch? I left things in the lurch, and I need someone right away."

"You want Peter?"

I laughed.

"I'm serious. He's better suited to banking than law."

I turned my head toward the closed door and thought about it. It was unlikely I would find someone with grit to run a bank, and with me in Carson City, the danger in Pickhandle should be minimal. Plus, I had promised Jeremiah. I turned back to Jansen. "Peter will do just fine. Sixty a month?"

"That should prove more than adequate."

I got up to leave and extended my hand. "I'd appreciate your support for a correspondence relationship between my bank and Commerce."

Jansen ignored my proffered hand. "No problem. The board will approve the arrangement at its next meeting. Peter's appointment will clinch it."

Jansen leaned back, as if the meeting were not over. "I have a question. I hope it's not too personal, but do you have a will?"

"Excuse me?"

"A last will and testament. A man of your means should have one. Especially since rumor has it that the man who shot Bolton wants to level his sights at you next."

Nonplussed, I sat back down. I had no will and did not know why it had never occurred to me to write one. I certainly had sufficient motivation. My closest relatives were uncles and aunts, all in New York and well fixed. I did not have the slightest idea who I wanted my estate to go to, and at first I felt irritated that Jansen made me think about it. Finally, I said, "Do you have time to write one up now?"

"I'll make the time. Perhaps your associate would prefer to wait outside? I'm sure Peter will be safe now that he's under your employ."

All three of us laughed, and then Sam said, "But Peter doesn't know."

"Yes, a formality we need to dispense with. Please ask him to step in."

In a minute, Peter came through the door with a backward glance toward where Sam probably stood in the outer office. "Yes, sir?"

"Peter, remember our discussion yesterday?"

"Yes, sir." He suddenly looked apprehensive instead of frightened.

"Well, an opportunity has come up for you to start a career in banking." Jansen stood for the first time. "I'd like you to meet Mr. Steve Dancy, president of the Pickhandle Gulch Bank."

Peter tentatively shook my extended hand. "I've heard about you."

"As has everyone else, I gather. But the stories you heard probably weren't in association with my bank."

Peter looked apprehensively at Jansen. "The position is with Mr. Dancy?"

"With Mr. Dancy and in Pickhandle Gulch. You shall be assistant bank manager."

"Oh no, sir. I want to stay in Carson City. I'm not fit for a mining encampment."

"Before you dismiss the idea, you should know that you'd be working with the Commerce Bank board to establish a correspondence relationship between the two banks. I'm sure that will be just the first step in a close working relationship." He waited for Peter to digest the implications. "Mr. Dancy is offering sixty a month."

Peter's eyes popped open. "In that case . . ."

When he hesitated to finish the sentence, I said, "Jeff Sharp has his operations in Belleville. He's promised to supply whatever assistance you may need."

I could see from his face that that clinched it. Sharp had a small army just a few miles away. After the briefest of moments, he shook my hand again, but this time with more purpose. "I would be honored to accept the position."

"Thank you. I would like you to leave immediately."

Peter looked shocked. "I don't even own a horse."

I thought quickly. "I'll equip you with a buckboard, a horse, and gear for the trail. Tell the livery to charge it to me at the St. Charles."

Peter grabbed my hand again and shook it enthusiastically. "I'll leave as soon as the gear is assembled."

"Great—and I apologize for my rudeness earlier."

"Think nothing of it, sir." Peter started to leave

the office with a bounce but then had a thought. "Are the buckboard and horse mine?"

"No, but you may have them at your disposal as long as you remain in my employ. When you get to Pickhandle, have the bank name painted on both sides."

"I presume you mean the buckboard, not the horse."

I turned to Jansen. "I thought you said Peter didn't have a sense of humor."

He grinned. "First I've seen of it." Jansen also shook Peter's hand. "This is a good move for you, Peter. You'll do right well in banking."

"Thank you, sir. Well, I have a lot to do, so if you gentlemen will excuse me . . ." With that, my new assistant bank manager scurried out the door.

"Now, let's talk about that will of yours," Jansen said.

By the time I got up to leave, we had been working for over an hour. After explaining what I wanted to do, Jansen had been bewildered at first, then intrigued, and finally amused.

As I opened the door to leave, he chuckled to himself and said, "Mr. Dancy, if Sprague kills you, I have an epitaph for your gravestone: "Here Lies Steve Dancy, Sore Loser."

Chapter 34

"Well, hell, it appears our little charade is over. You might as well wear your own clothes on our return to Pickhandle Gulch."

I had just sat down with McAllen and Sharp for our afternoon rendezvous. Before I could even order a beer, McAllen had made this odd pronouncement. I looked at Sam and jokingly asked, "Weren't you able to get that shirt laundered?"

"Picked it up this morning. Got the suit brushed and pressed as well. But I believe the captain doesn't think the precaution'll do much good anymore."

This puzzled me because Sam and I had been together since breakfast. How would he know what the captain was thinking? Had I missed something? I didn't want to appear stupid, so I resolved to remain silent until one of them volunteered to tell me what they were talking about.

McAllen was the one to speak up. "Did you see that man on the hotel porch, reading a newspaper?"

"Yes." As instructed, I had kept alert when we walked from Jansen's office to the hotel. The only person I spotted lingering had been reading a newspaper on the porch. He looked innocent enough, and the activity was certainly not unusual for a hotel guest.

"That was Bill Sprague."

"What?" I hesitated, but after thinking about it, I was sure I had not seen another man. "That was Sprague? Are you sure? The man I saw looked like a bookkeeper."

Sharp said, "That's him, all right."

Captain McAllen nodded and then added, "Rumor has it he once made his living totting up columns of numbers but changed professions when he discovered he had a natural knack for marksmanship. He brings a bookkeeper's methodical manner to long-range shooting."

I looked toward the door, but he had not followed us into the hotel. "Must take more than marksmanship. I can't image a man making his living by killing strangers for money. He must lack any conscience whatever."

Sharp actually looked worried. "When it comes to killin', he's about as detached a man as I've ever seen. Bet he thinks harder on killin' time than killin' a person." He motioned for a waiter to bring us a round of drinks. After he got an acknowledging nod, he said to me, "Don't let his looks fool ya—he's a nasty character. Story's told that he took a contract on a man's adulterous wife an' shot her twice, once through the heart an' again in the head. A needless extravagance with a .44-100."

"Ever married?" I asked.

"No . . . not to anyone's recollection." Sharp laughed. "But I get your drift. He might not like women much. Could be . . . but he's killed lots of men too, so maybe he hates all humankind—or just doesn't give a shit."

"Sounds like an odd man."

Captain McAllen said, "I heard a story about him. Don't know if it's true, but sounds 'bout right. Supposedly, Sprague once competed in a long-range shooting contest. Won it hands-down. But each time before he shot, he consulted this little notebook filled with numbers in tidy columns. The book contained his meticulous measurements for different ranges, wind conditions, and even different temperatures. This was years ago, when he supposedly still wore a green eyeshade to work. Not long after that contest, he put his talent out for hire. Now, I'm told, he carries those measurements in his head and uses his notebook to keep track of his money." McAllen took a swig of beer. "Yep, I'd say he's an odd duck."

I glanced toward the front door again. "Is there nothing we can do?"

McAllen shook his head. "He knows we can't arrest him. Can't do anything to him that won't get us in trouble with the law ourselves. That's why he can sit out there like a real gentleman, reading a newspaper."

"Captain's right," Sharp agreed. "The man's tauntin' us. If he wanted, he could keep an eye on us from inside any buildin' across the street."

"Did you have any luck with the cigarette butt or the hoofprint?" I asked.

Sharp explained that the tobacconist recognized the butt as the expensive tobacco brand that Sprague preferred, but they had found no one who had seen Washburn and Sprague together. McAllen said that his men's questioning of the citizenry was causing a buzz in town, and he thought they had made a good start on kindling a big scandal around Carson City First.

I told them how Sam and I had spent the morning. I relayed everything except my last will and testament. That, at least for the present, would remain my business and my business alone. One day, it might be their business, but I pushed that unpleasant possibility from my mind.

"Sprague's horse?" I asked.

McAllen lifted his beer glass. "Now that we know he's in town, we'll go over to the livery right after we finish these beers. I'll see if I can get the sheriff to go with us. I want another witness to see the missing nail in the right rear shoe."

"If you can't get the law, take Jansen. I hired him to help with legal issues."

McAllen nodded. "Jansen's better, anyway. People suspect the sheriff protects Sprague. Seems they like to eat dinner together."

"Even if the nail is missing, we're going to need more evidence," I mused.

Sharp smiled. "Sprague's right outside that door. Perhaps ya can ask him for a confession."

"The man doesn't look to be the talkative sort." I

turned to Captain McAllen. "You still think he's not a threat as long as we're in Carson City?"

"I don't think he'll do anything here . . . especially since he's made himself so brazenly obvious in front of the hotel. Besides, to my knowledge, he's never killed close-up." McAllen nodded his head toward the entrance to the hotel. "No, Sprague's here to get a good look at you."

"So we can't fool him with a change of clothes." I winked at Sam. "After my beer, I'm going to tell Chestnut the good news. He'll be—" I bolted upright and strode toward the door. I pulled my Remington .38 from beneath my suit coat and swore at myself for not carrying my .45.

Captain McAllen was quick at my heels. "Where are you going?"

"To get that confession Sharp suggested."

I felt his hand pull on my arm. "Stop. Sit back down and explain."

I jerked my arm away and said, "No time. Just back me up."

I stepped out of the hotel and turned toward Sprague. He still sat in the same chair, looking as if he didn't have a care in the world.

I took a half-step toward him and started to raise my gun, but before I had gotten far, I heard shots and felt a hand in the small of my back shove me with enormous force. I went down hard and slammed into the boardwalk with my cheek and knees. More shots. Wood splintered, glass shattered, and men screamed above the roar of gunfire. I rolled as fast as I could and found myself falling off the wooden walkway onto the dirt street. The shots came from somewhere else, but my fear centered on Sprague, so I lifted my head and gun over the boardwalk to shoot him. He was nowhere in sight.

Shots tore up the ground around me, and I realized they came from a building on the other side of the street. I twisted around prone and took aim but held my fire. My .38 probably wouldn't penetrate the wood front of the building, so I waited for a head to pop up in a window or door frame. Whoever was firing above me had no such limitation, and bullets tore up the wood around the building windows. A flash appeared in one of the windows, and I pulled my trigger twice. I don't know if I hit the man, but the shooting suddenly stopped, and everything grew still.

"Stay down," Captain McAllen yelled, but I was already on my feet. After the shooting stopped, the street became calm, and I saw only a blue haze wafting above the points of gunfire on either side of the road.

I glanced behind me and saw something that jolted my senses, but I pushed it from my mind: A man dressed in Pinkerton black lay wounded or dead in the front door of the hotel. McAllen scrambled down the steps and shoved down on my shoulder. I resisted and fell only to a shooting position on one knee and aimed my pistol at the now-quiet building across the street.

"Are you hit?" he screamed.

"No."

McAllen dropped to his knee and gave my face an odd look. Evidently satisfied, he leaped to his feet and raced to the right side of the building that hid the shooters. I noticed that another Pinkerton had already run to the left side. Once they had both arrived at the corners of the building, without hesitation they ran toward the door and swung inside with their guns at the ready.

I sensed movement behind me, and a quick glance confirmed that Sharp stood over my shoulder with a Winchester, a weapon I wished I held in my own hands. McAllen came back into the street, whipping his head left and right.

Sharp grabbed my elbow and tugged to indicate that I should stand. By the time I got to my feet, McAllen had reached my other side, and the three of us moved back toward the hotel. When I stepped back onto the porch, I saw that the Pinkerton crumpled in the doorway was Sam.

I heard another shot, and all three of us whirled and dropped closer to the boardwalk. In a second, the Pinkerton who had run into the building appeared from behind the structure and gave a hand signal to indicate that he had eliminated the danger.

We all turned our attention to Sam. He had been

hit in the stomach, and it looked like a bad wound.

McAllen stood and ordered, "Get him a doctor," before he ran across the street to his other man.

Sharp and I each grabbed an arm and a leg to carry him inside. As we lifted, Sam screamed.

"Where to?" I asked Sharp.

"Parlor." He turned to a bystander. "Get a doc!" he yelled.

The hotel was bedlam as dozens of people came out of hiding to find out what all the shooting had been about. Before we could get into the parlor, a room that stood off the central hall, nosy men surrounded us, making it difficult to move forward.

Sharp yelled, "We have an injured man here! Make room, goddamn it!" The sea of men parted enough for us to get Sam through the door, where we laid him on a couch.

The hotelkeeper raced over and exclaimed, "Move him into the back room! You're going to ruin that settee!"

I jerked my gun on him. "Back off, dammit!" The man stopped in his tracks. I jabbed my gun into his ribs. "Get a doctor. Now!"

He scurried away, white as a freshly laundered sheet. When I turned back to Sam, Sharp was already applying pressure to the wound with a handkerchief.

Someone nudged me, and I twisted my head to see a hand offering a flask. I nodded thanks, uncorked the flask, and gently placed it above

Sam's lower lip. He opened his mouth slightly, and I let a tiny trickle flow between his lips. It heartened me to see him swallow the liquor.

After Sam took another sip, I heard someone briskly command, "Make way. Make way." The doctor had arrived.

The doctor took a quick look and said, "All of you, git out of here."

A gruff-looking woman knelt by Sharp and said, "You too."

The doctor looked at the immobile crowd, which included Sharp and me. "If you people don't skedaddle, I'll personally file accessory-to-murder charges against the lot of you. Now, git!"

Sharp stood, and I helped him herd the people out of the room. Soon the only people left in the parlor were Sam, the doctor, and his assistant. I stepped out and quietly closed the door.

"Looks bad," I said, feeling frightened.

Instead of responding, Sharp grabbed the arm of a man in the crowded central hall. "George, keep people out of the parlor until a constable gets over here."

"Sure thing, Jeff." He took a position in front of the door, and Sharp led me out of the hotel.

After we got outside, Sharp turned to me and said, "Stand still." My cheek stung as he pulled something out of my face. He held up a two-inch wood splinter that I must have picked up when I smashed into the boardwalk outside. I rubbed my cheek, and my hand came away bloody. Now I knew what had grabbed McAllen's attention outside, and why he thought I might have been shot. I hadn't felt a thing.

After he confirmed that my wound was minor, Sharp said, "Let's find McAllen."

Captain McAllen and his two Pinkertons stood across the street talking to two lawmen. We started to join them but kept our distance when McAllen held the flat of his hand toward us.

In a couple of minutes, McAllen stepped off the porch and signaled us to follow him a few paces into the street. People milled around everywhere, so McAllen led us up a residential lane until we were out of earshot.

"Doctor say anything?" McAllen asked.

"No." Sharp answered. "Just shooed everyone out."

McAllen looked to see if his other two men were on guard. Satisfied, he said, "Steve, we were ambushed by the two men we encountered at breakfast. They're both dead."

"What happened to Sprague?" I asked.

"Rolled off the porch and ran, far as I know. I don't think he had any inkling, or he sure wouldn't have sat in the line of fire."

That made sense, but I was disappointed nonetheless. "Damn. If he hadn't moved so damned fast, I might have killed him."

Captain McAllen looked angry, and when he

spoke, I realized his anger was directed at me. "What the hell did you think you were doing? Why'd you charge out onto that porch?"

"Bookkeepers keep records. I wanted that book you said he keeps. It suddenly occurred to me that he might've made notations about his contracts . . . I'm sorry."

The muscles in McAllen's face relaxed only a bit. "Steve, that wasn't such a bad idea, but I hope you see what happens when you charge off without telling me what you're about to do."

I couldn't think of anything else to say, so I just muttered, "Captain, it won't happen again."

He waited just the right amount of time before saying, "See that it doesn't." His tone of voice scared me more than the Cutlers had.

Sharp put his hand on my shoulder. "If those two hadn't been waiting in ambush, it might've worked." He turned to McAllen. "If we run into Sprague again, we should search him."

"Steve Dancy!" The yell came from the hotel and caused us all to reach for guns, but it was only the doctor's assistant. When we approached the St. Charles, she said, "Your friend wants to talk to you."

I followed the assistant back into the hotel parlor and, as he stood, the doctor whispered, "Keep it quiet."

Someone had torn Sam's shirt off, and his skin looked pale from loss of blood. I knelt down beside the couch and leaned close to his face, and he whispered, "The bushwhackers?"

"Dead, both of them," I said.

"Good. They beat me to hell, at least." He grimaced in pain. "Steve, I need a favor." Another twitch, before he choked out the words. "Kill Washburn."

This surprised me, and before I could pull the words back, I asked, "Why?"

"Because he killed me."

"Sam, you'll get well. This is a good doctor."

"No bullshit. I know wounds." He was finding it hard to speak. "We're trail partners. You owe me."

"I do." I meant causing him to get shot, but I kept that to myself. "Don't worry, I'll take care of Washburn."

"Don't take care of him; gut-shoot him."

"All right. I'll do it. Anything else?"

"That brandy flask still around?"

I fed Sam sips of brandy until he died. It took over an hour.

Chapter 35

To my memory, I had not cried since I broke my leg at age twelve, but this day, it took a long while for my tears to dry and for me to get control enough to face people. By the time I opened the parlor door, the only person in the hall was the Pinkerton assigned to keep people out.

"Sam's dead," I said quietly.

The Pinkerton nodded and said, "The undertaker's outside on the porch. I'll get 'im."

I stepped across the hall into the restaurant and ordered a whiskey. After a few minutes, Jeff Sharp and Captain McAllen came in and sat at my table. I gulped the whiskey and gestured with my fingers for another drink. From the looks on their faces, I knew I didn't need to tell them that Sam had died.

When the barkeep set another full shot glass in front of me, McAllen said, "Take it easy. I need you sober."

"If you don't mind, I plan to take a bottle to my room."

"No. Time's a-wastin'. Sprague rode out of town in a hurry, probably afraid we'd come after him because of the shooting. He could be on his way to Virginia City, but I'm betting he's set out to pick a good ambush spot away from town. We need to leave now to catch him unawares."

"I'm more interested in Washburn."

"I'll not let you gun him down without provocation."

"That's none of your business."

"It is. I'm a lawman, of sorts."

I sipped the whiskey this time. "Sam deserves a little mourning . . . and some revenge."

"Not that way. There's a reason Pinkertons are supposed to remain nameless and faceless. I never should have let you get friendly with Sam. Bad for business."

"Business?"

"Yes, business. Part of my job is to protect the Pinkerton reputation. We don't accept clients set on murder."

I turned to Sharp. "What do you say?"

Sharp did not answer but called over to the barkeep for a beer. After he took a swallow, he said, "You're lettin' guilt cloud your thinkin'. I agree with the captain. We need to get on the road to the Bolton ranch before Sprague sets himself up for an ambush."

"You mean now? Right now?"

"Yep. Right now."

I took another slow sip to show I wouldn't be that hurried. "Did you get a look at his horse?"

McAllen answered. "Not before he bolted out of town, but the liveryman confirms the missing nail. We still need the bullet. Then we'll go to the law."

"Washburn?"

"He lit out for Virginia City with some other hired hands. Been gone since morning." McAllen scanned the restaurant and then added, "We'll not give chase. Have I made myself clear?"

"I want this to end," I said. McAllen continued to look stone-faced, so I glanced at Sharp. "I made a promise to Sam." Jeff gave no sign that he would join me in hunting down Washburn.

For a minute, I wondered if there were other men

I could hire, but I gave up the idea. These were the men I had made my pact with. They were good men, and I knew them. I swallowed the remaining whiskey in my glass and stood to leave. "All right, but I need to see Bradshaw before we go."

"Make it damn quick," Captain McAllen said.

Bradshaw's office was near the mint that converted Nevada silver into coins for the western United States. I guessed he wanted to be close to the power base in the state. It was a short walk, and when I asked to see him, his assistant did not hesitate to show me into his office. Instead of working at his rolltop desk, Bradshaw sat at a mahogany table he had situated in the center of the room.

He stood, extended his hand, and said, "My condolences. I understand you were friends with that Pinkerton."

"Not exactly friends, but I liked the man, and I think he returned the compliment."

"I'm glad you escaped unharmed." Then he gave me a quizzical look. "Your cheek?"

"Just a splinter. I'm fine."

We took seats on opposite sides of the table. "We're leaving for Bolton's ranch immediately. We'll retrieve the bullet and be back in a couple of days. Hopefully, it will be enough to at least tie Sprague up in court proceedings." I tried to get a measure on Bradshaw, but his face showed as little expression as when Washburn had taunted him.

"This gunplay hasn't given you pause, has it?"

"Pause, yes. Stopped me, no." Bradshaw took out a cigar and played with it for a moment. "If you had been killed, I might have reconsidered running for governor. But . . . I guess I'm still in. You taking all your Pinkertons with you?"

"Yes. Sprague's on the road, and we'll need them. Are there other men you can hire?"

"Already working on it. I've stationed men on the trail to Virginia City, so I'll have fair warning if Washburn or some of his ruffians return."

"Good." I pulled some papers from my pocket and pushed them across the table. "When the governor appoints a new judge, have these writs processed."

Bradshaw made no attempt to pick them up. "What are they?"

"Foreclosure on some mortgages. Washburn wrote me what I bet are bad checks against a Denver bank. I sent someone to Denver, and I'll wire him to get you word, one way or the other. Should be any day. The others are for the arrest of Sprague and Washburn. You might have to wait on them."

"Understood. But that's not why you came to see me."

"No. Can you get the mint to quit buying bullion from Washburn?"

"Under what pretense?"

"Disputed ownership. If you can get the charter

pulled for Carson City First, his Virginia City mort-gages may be in a questionable status. The judge might want to stop sale of all assets until he gets a handle on things."

"You think he's strapped for cash?"

"Gotta be. He's going through money fast."

"Well, I'd sure like to hamper his financing of Stevens's campaign." He lit his cigar. "I'll see what I can do."

"Thank you. I'll return as soon as I can bring other matters to a close at the ranch."

"What do you intend to do about Mrs. Bolton?" His knowledge surprised me at first, but then I real-ized Bradshaw made it his business to know every-thing going on in Carson City.

"I *intend* to escort John's sweet mother back to Carson City . . . even if I have to hogtie her and throw her in the back of a buckboard."

"Don't underestimate her. She's smarter than she looks, and she did a fine job of running that ranch when John was away."

"Are you suggesting that I leave her there to run the ranch for Jenny?"

"No! Heavens, no. That woman's a beast, and she'll kill Jenny within an hour of you leaving them alone. Get that woman back here and make sure she gets on a train to San Francisco."

"My intentions exactly."

I got up to leave, but before I got to the door, Bradshaw tapped the papers I had left him and asked, "You still think these arrests are the right solution?"

"No. I want a five-cent solution." He looked perplexed, so I added, "The price of a bullet."

Chapter 36

By the time I had returned to the hotel, McAllen had Chestnut and my belongings ready to go. As I swung into the saddle, I could feel the two whiskeys I'd drunk earlier. My melancholy clung close, so the others, sensing my mood, kept respectably quiet. I reined around and trotted down the road. Bystanders stopped in their tracks and watched the five of us leave town. A shooting frightens people, but it also makes them curious.

We rode in silence for many miles, and I spent the time trying to figure a way to get Washburn to do something stupid. I must have missed something. The man was smart but vain. He had more hired hands than me, but after my seduction of Bradshaw, I controlled more political levers within the state. I needed to get to him man-to-man; otherwise, this feud could go on for months.

I began to doubt that my political and business machinations could box Washburn in—at least not soon enough to avoid more bloodshed. When I had tried to play the game using New York rules, Washburn had proved himself a smart operator. If I had the time, I knew I could win in the end, but a quick solution would have to be a savage solution. Besides, I had made a promise to Sam.

I needed to quit running away from the code of the West. Men out here fought it out man-to-man with guns. Except for Washburn. That was my problem. He knew I was skilled with a handgun, and he was far too smart to be lured into a direct fight. I had to figure out a way to isolate him and then make him lose his temper, so he would draw on me. And I needed witnesses that he started the duel, because I had no intention of going to jail—or the gallows—for murder.

I used the end of my reins to lightly lash Chestnut into a gallop. I had to find a way to kill the son of a bitch. Dead, he couldn't meet payroll, and his hired guns would fade into the landscape faster than a pack of coyotes faced with a Winchester. But how to goad him into a fight? I had challenged him once, and he had walked away. Perhaps that had not really been a serious attempt, but it showed that Washburn kept calm in the face of provocation and would not be suckered into a fight where the odds did not stack up in his favor.

I had to make him want to kill me himself—it had to be personal. I needed to make him so angry that he lost control, or . . . maybe I could possess something that he felt he had to take away from me.

Then I had it. It all depended on capturing Sprague. Get Sprague, dead or alive, and I could force Washburn to fight—straight up.

"Slow down." McAllen had spurred his horse to catch up with me.

"I thought you were in a hurry."

"Slow down."

I started to protest, but he was right. No use lathering the horses. We might need them fresh if we encountered Sprague. I reined in and slowed Chestnut to a walk.

"What were you thinking?"

"I wasn't thinking."

"Bullshit."

"All right, I was thinking that Sprague is somewhere between us and the Bolton ranch. I was thinking that he left in a big hurry and is not provisioned, and he'll probably stop at the trading post at Fort Churchill. If we get there fast enough, maybe we can capture him. That's what I was thinking."

"Damn it." Captain McAllen whistled for one of his men. "That's my job, to think through our next step."

His man had pulled up beside us. "Ride hell-bent for the fort. Tell the commander that Sprague is wanted for a shooting in Carson City. Tell him to detain him. Got it?"

The man was already spurring his horse when he yelled, "Yep!"

We watched him ride away, and then McAllen signaled for his other man to ride up beside us. "Forge to the other side of the river and force anyone you see in the direction of the fort. Throw some shots if you have to but don't aim to kill."

"Yes, sir."

McAllen turned to me. "Good thinking, but you agreed to tell me what you're going to do. You said it wouldn't happen again."

"I was preoccupied."

"Preoccupation gets people dead."

"Let it go," Sharp said in my defense. "It's a good plan."

We rode for two more hours before we came into sight of the fort. Up ahead, I could see the Pinkerton slogging back to our side of the Carson River. The flat land between us and the fort presented little danger of ambush. When he rode up, we all stopped and faced him.

"I think Sprague was positioned about three miles back."

"Did you see him?" McAllen asked.

"I rode noisy and saw someone scurry away when I approached. The lay of the land gave a good sight line to this side of the river."

"Then let's hope our man is in the custody of our brave men in uniform," Sharp said.

"I coulda got off a shot, Captain. If I wanted to herd, I woulda been a cowboy."

"You did right. Better we get him alive."

I had a thought. "Will the soldiers turn Sprague over to you, Captain?"

"Shouldn't be a problem. I'm deputized in seven

states, including Nevada." McAllen gave me a rare smile. "One of the benefits of the Pinkerton reputation."

"I take your point," I said. "But we don't have a warrant."

McAllen patted his breast pocket. "I carry 'John Doe' warrants. Like I said, shouldn't be a problem."

"Then let's go find out if we've corralled our quarry."

From a distance, it looked like something had happened at the fort. We were about a half mile out, and I could see clusters of men gossiping outside and soldiers standing around. One soldier was leading a horse with a civilian saddle by the reins away from the trading post toward the gate of the compound. Then I saw a rider galloping toward us, and I soon identified him as the Pinkerton that McAllen had sent ahead.

"Sprague's in the stockade!" he yelled, before reaching us.

"Hot damn!" This came from Sharp.

We simultaneously spurred our horses and raced to the fort. Everyone else went for the gate, but I pulled up beside the soldier leading the horse. "Is that Bill Sprague's horse?"

"Don't rightly know his name, but it belongs to the man we arrested."

I swung down. "He stole something of mine. May I look in his saddlebag?"

He thought a second. "Go ahead 'n' look, but ya ain't takin' nothin' without the lieutenant's say-so."

"Fair enough. I just want to make sure you got the right man." I did a quick search, but the bags contained only a rolled-up duster and ammunition. Even the canteen was empty. Sprague had indeed left in a hurry.

"Find what yer lookin' for?"

"Nope, but he could've hid it along the way. We'll know soon enough. Thanks."

I walked Chestnut over to join the others at the gate. Everyone had dismounted, and I could hear Captain McAllen telling an officer about the shooting in Carson City. He did a masterful job of making it sound like Sprague might have been one of the assailants. The attack itself was not news, because riders who used the fort as a way station had spread the story ahead of us.

When McAllen finished, the lieutenant turned to me. "What were you doing in that man's bags?"

"Looking for evidence of another shooting. I'm sure you heard about the Bolton murder. We think this is the same man." I looked at McAllen and pointedly said, "The bag contained only a duster and ammunition."

McAllen nodded and then asked the lieutenant, "Have you searched the prisoner?"

"Only for weapons. He was unarmed, except for the rifle on his horse."

"May we see the prisoner?" I asked.

218

The lieutenant gave me a quizzical look. "Who are you?"

"A witness." I decided not to volunteer my name, due to the Cutler episode. "Captain McAllen asked me along to make sure we caught the right man."

The lieutenant seemed to think a minute. "All right. Leave your weapons with the guard."

We unhooked and threw our guns and knives on a table positioned between two guards. Fort Churchill looked large. A whitewashed adobe wall surrounded numerous buildings, corrals, and stables. Most of the buildings were also whitewashed adobe, which gave the fort a fresh, cool appearance.

We followed the officer to a small, squat structure in the middle of a yard. Two soldiers with Springfield rifles guarded one of several doors spaced about four feet apart. As we got closer, I noticed each wood door was reinforced with iron straps.

"Only Captain McAllen enters," the officer said.

"I need to see him as well," I said. "I'm the one who can identify him."

"All right. The rest of you wait here."

He told the guard to open the door, and we all watched him fumble with the keys. When the door swung open, I could see over McAllen's shoulder that the one-time bookkeeper sat on a cot. In the back wall, a high barred window provided some light. Sprague was dressed in the same charcoal city suit he had been wearing when I saw him that morning.

The lieutenant stood aside for McAllen to enter and then fell in behind me as I walked in. Sprague did not look intimidated. He continued to sit and stare at us as if we were a minor curiosity.

I stepped around McAllen and pretended to squint in the dark. "Stand up," I said, "so I can see you in the light."

After a long pause, Sprague slowly lifted a hand and put one finger in the middle of my chest and lightly pushed me until I took a half-step back. McAllen made a move, but I lifted a hand to halt him.

Sprague stood and said, "Excuse me, but I don't like to be crowded."

"That's a relief," I said. "I thought you might be marking a target."

The smile was sinister. "I couldn't possibly know what you—"

I slammed him against the wall with all my weight and jammed my left forearm into his throat. With my right hand, I reached into his breast pocket and immediately felt a small object. I did not resist when McAllen and the officer pulled me away. Sprague choked and wheezed and rubbed his neck. The lack of color in his face meant I had rammed him in the neck pretty hard. Good.

"Step back," the officer ordered.

"Yes, sir. I apologize." I held my hand down at my side as Sprague continued to sputter.

Captain McAllen asked, "Did you get the

journal?" He evidently did not want to disguise the fact that I had taken something from Sprague. On second thought, I realized an army lieutenant would make a good witness to Sprague having been in possession of the journal, so I held up the small black notebook I had lifted from Sprague's suit pocket.

No man's eyes ever went wider in recognition. "Give that back!" Sprague yelled.

"At your trial."

I turned to the Army officer. "That's the man. Congratulations. He may not look like it, but you've captured the most dangerous and wanted outlaw in Nevada. This will put Fort Churchill on the map and do your career considerable good."

The officer positively beamed, and my transgression was quickly forgotten. I tucked the little notebook into my front pants pocket and walked out of the cell into a suddenly more beautiful world.

Chapter 37

After we left the cell, McAllen and the lieutenant went off to negotiate the prisoner transfer. Jeff Sharp and I wandered over to an empty corral and rested our buttocks against the middle rail. We chatted for a bit, and when no one seemed to take notice of us, I pulled the notebook out of my pocket.

It was only about two inches by three inches and

very thin. The black leather cover looked expensive, like carefully tanned deerskin or perhaps calfskin. Sprague had tied the little book closed with a thin strip of black ribbon. Before I untied it, I decided that I wanted one of these for myself. When my journal wasn't close, a small notebook that I could carry in my pocket would come in handy.

Sharp fidgeted as I toyed with the notebook, so I tugged on the ribbon and opened the book to the first page. Sharp may have been nervous about the contents of the book, but I had no doubts. I had seen the look on Sprague's face when he first saw the notebook in my hand. That look was fear. Fear and chagrin—chagrin for making a mistake so huge that it might get him hanged.

Sharp looked over my shoulder and whistled. The page was filled with the tiniest and neatest writing I had ever seen. I flipped a few pages, and they all had the same format: three precise columns, two with numbers and one with letters. The first column was easy to identify as a list of dates, and the numbers in the last column had the two decimal positions used for monetary amounts. The middle column of letters was a cipher. I could not make sense of it until I noticed the dates were close together and the financial items small, many under a dollar. These were expenses. Sprague had meticulously recorded every cent he had spent and used initials or abbreviations in the middle column to represent the item he had purchased.

In the back of the book, I found the income side of the ledger. Perhaps it was the front, though, because I had to flip the book over to read the entries. The notebook had no obvious front—Sprague entered costs at one end and then turned it over and upside down to record income at the other end. I counted seventeen entries on the income side, the first dated seven years ago. The man seemed to have had a long career.

As I read down the rows of entries, I saw that the second to the last row displayed the initials SD—Steve Dancy would be my guess. The last initials were JB, which I assumed meant John Bolton. Both of these entries also had a dash mark and the letters SW next to them.

Every entry except the one with my initials had a little penciled dot in front of the line. It appeared that these tiny circles signified completed contracts. The contract amounts in the third column ran between five and twenty thousand dollars. Bolton hit the high mark of twenty thousand, while mine showed only ten thousand. My first reaction, admittedly ridiculous, was to feel resentful that Bolton commanded a higher price than me, but obviously the prominence of the victim would partially determine the size of the fee.

"Can you make out what it says?" Sharp asked.

"I think so." I pointed with my finger. "These are his contracts, but they're identified only by initials. Not the best evidence." I thought a minute. "If we can tie the deaths of people with these initials to the dates in this book, a reasonable jury ought to convict our friend."

"May I see?"

Sharp studied the entries intently for a few minutes. After he handed it back to me, he said, "I know two men, not countin' Bolton, whose deaths match initials in that book an' happened around the right time. My bet is that we can match up the rest of those entries with other murder victims."

"How were the two you know about killed?"

"Blown to smithereens . . . by a buffalo gun from long range." Sharp watched me tuck the little book back into my front pants pocket. "Be careful with that. It's important. That little book just might save your life."

"I know." I tapped the book in my pocket. "But the most important thing about this book is the absence of a little penciled circle next to my initials."

Sharp laughed. "Yep, guess so." He turned around and rested his forearms on the rail of the corral. "That book might hang Sprague, but what about Washburn?"

I turned around and assumed the same lazy posture as Sharp. "SW appears next to Bolton's and my initials, but if that convicts Washburn, it'll be a conviction based on the scantiest evidence in the history of this country."

"Then you're still in danger . . . unless Sprague testifies."

"He'll never testify against Washburn. Besides, I'm no longer looking to put Washburn in jail."

Sharp did not speak at first, but when he did, his soft tone surprised me. "Steve, be careful." He pushed away from the fence and looked toward the fort gate. "Let's get a beer at the tradin' post."

Chapter 38

Since it was so late in the day, we decided not to leave Fort Churchill until the next morning. The lieutenant graciously allowed us to use the guest quarters, which comprised nothing more than a barren room with two beds. Captain McAllen and his men slept outside, so Sharp and I each took a bed.

In the morning, the lieutenant invited us to join his unit for breakfast. In typical army fashion, they served large quantities of bad food washed down with an unending supply of extra-strong coffee.

After breakfast, we had a ceremony to officially transfer the prisoner to the custody of Captain McAllen and the Pinkertons. The army insisted on its little rituals. When the ceremony broke up, the lieutenant seemed relieved to be free of Sprague and eager to release his men from guard duty. One of the Pinkertons bound Sprague's hands in front, so he could grip the saddle horn, and then two soldiers lifted him onto his horse.

McAllen mounted his own horse and sidled up to

Sprague. "Please run. It's a hell of a lot easier to transport a prisoner strapped across the saddle."

Sprague looked at McAllen. "Captain, we both have obligations." He turned a nasty stare on me. "Perhaps you should allow me to complete mine before you proceed with yours." When he got no reply, he added, "No? Pity. Then I shall find another way. I always fulfill my contracts."

McAllen reined his horse around to bump Sprague's horse hard enough to almost knock the prisoner to the ground. "I hope you enjoyed your breakfast. I hear army food is a damn sight better than prison fare."

"I'll be eating my meals at the St. Charles Hotel before the first snowfall."

Captain McAllen did not respond; he merely wheeled his horse around and turned east along the Kit Carson Trail.

"That's the wrong direction," Sprague said. When McAllen ignored him, he yelled, "Goddamn it, where are we going?"

"This way," McAllen simply said.

"Damn you. Carson City's behind us."

"The Bolton ranch is ahead of us." McAllen turned in his saddle. "Our evidence goes well beyond that little book of yours. We're going to Bolton's to get the clincher. One of the hands saw you on the trail after you killed Bolton. He says he can identify your horse."

"Horseshit."

"This man could probably identify that as well. He's a renowned wrangler who knows horseflesh. His testimony, along with our other evidence, would have sealed your fate without that notebook. I'd say your hanging is only a matter of getting twelve men together."

I assumed Captain McAllen was taunting Sprague because he wanted him to believe we had a strong case and that his only salvation would be to testify against Washburn. I had other plans, but I had already decided not to share them with McAllen.

After we had ridden a few miles, Sprague asked Sharp, "How many politicians and judges do you own?"

"I own silver mines," Sharp said matter of factly.

"Pity." Sharp ignored him, so he added, "I own plenty. What I don't own, Washburn does." He rode silent for a minute. "I hope the trial's quick. I have a hunting date with our U.S. senator in three weeks."

"Worked often with SW, have you?" I asked. I wasn't above a little taunting of my own.

"Nope, never liked Smith & Wesson rifles. Heard they make a fine pistol, though."

"Your book lists Sean Washburn as your client."

Sprague turned in his saddle to give me a smug look. "I believe you're mistaken. Better take another look."

"Mr. Sprague," McAllen interrupted, "I wish

you'd keep your thoughts to yourself, or I shall be obliged to hit you across the mouth with my pistol barrel."

We rode on in silence.

About noon, we stopped along the river to rest the horses and grab a bite to eat. Once we dismounted, McAllen tied Sprague's ankles together and set him on a rock facing us at the river's edge. He could either try to swim with his feet and hands tied or attempt to hobble past us.

McAllen had taken possession of Sprague's rifle. After a less-than-satisfying noon meal of canned sardines spread on hardtack, I asked the captain if I could take a look at it.

I was working the action, when Sprague said, "That's the best rifle in the world."

"It's a fine rifle," I said, "but I'm not sure I'd rate it the best."

"The Paris Exposition did. They voted the Remington Creedmoor the finest rifle in the world."

Sprague looked so satisfied with himself that I couldn't help responding. "That was over ten years ago. A long time in the armaments business."

"Why don't you hand me over that rifle and some ammunition, and I'll show you shooting you wouldn't believe possible."

McAllen started to say something, but I held up my hand. He probably wanted to threaten Sprague again with a rap across the mouth, but I wanted to hear Sprague talk. The persnickety little man looked like a bookkeeper, which he had once been, yet he exuded confidence and menace like the killer he had become. Sprague hunted men for a living, and there was probably no more dangerous prey, yet he had been successful at it for years. It was as though we had captured some kind of wild beast, and we had a chance to study the animal's nature before we turned it over to a zoo.

"Is killing just a matter of being a good shot?" I asked.

"You would know better than me. I hear you kill pretty quick and easy." He smiled. "Does your conscience bother you?"

I decided to take the conversation in a different direction. "Tell me what you could hit."

Sprague made a show of looking around. "See that tree over there?" He smiled again. "Sorry, I can't point, but I mean the one hanging out over the river at the bend. I could shoot that branch off and drop it into the water."

I took a look. "Could you now? You think I should try it?"

"I'll bet you ten dollars you could never make that shot. I'll even give you three tries."

McAllen got up, and I gave him a nod to show I understood. He walked over to the water's edge so he could see beyond the bend in the river: the same view Sprague had from his rock. Before McAllen could speak, I said, "People on the other side?"

"Yep," McAllen said, as he kicked Sprague just hard enough to knock him off his rock and into the mud. "Now, Mr. Sprague, that would have been a pretty mean trick."

Lying on the ground, Sprague grinned wickedly. "If he'd made the shot, there'd have been no problem."

I got up and walked over to the two men. "A hundred-grain cartridge would have passed right through that branch and slammed into something on the other side of the river. Kick him again, Captain."

McAllen instantly obliged me.

Chapter 39

After our break for the noonday meal, we rode hard to arrive at the Bolton ranch before nightfall. As before, Captain McAllen rode up to the ranch house to announce our arrival, only this time, the elder Mrs. Bolton immediately waved us in from the porch. I suddenly felt nervous. Telling the resident baroness that she had to leave her home would not be easy. The first order of business, however, was to secure Sprague in something approximating a jail.

As we rode up, the nasty glare from Mrs. Bolton told me that the captain had explained about our prisoner. As I tied up at the hitch post, she commanded, "Follow me."

All of us surrounded Sprague, who was bound only at the hands, and followed her to the bunkhouse. She went around back and opened the door to a lean-to. Turning to her foreman, she demanded that he clear out what appeared to be a tack shed. In a few minutes, the space was empty, and another hand came over and threw an old mattress on the dirt floor.

McAllen stepped into the darkness and thoroughly inspected the lean-to. He tested the walls and ceiling, closed the door behind him and threw his shoulder against it, and then kicked around in the dirt to make sure no implements remained that could be used as a weapon or for escape.

Sprague said, "I want water and a decent meal." He peeked inside. "And a chamber pot."

"We'll water and feed your horse," Mrs. Bolton answered.

"I expect you to take care of my needs as well."

Mrs. Bolton bristled at Sprague's haughty attitude. "My foreman will shoot anyone who brings you anything. For all I care, you can wallow in your own shit and piss."

Sprague whirled on her corpulent form. "You should know, madam, that I've killed women before. You'd be wise to avoid earning my wrath."

"You damned piece of shit." She stepped toward him with venom in her eyes. "You threaten *me*? I might just kill you myself . . . before daybreak."

McAllen wedged himself between the two. My

first thought was that he was a brave man. McAllen untied Sprague's hands and shoved him into the windowless shed. Before he closed the door, Mrs. Bolton screamed, "Sleep light. I may come any time to slit your fucking throat."

The foreman quickly stepped over and snapped a weathered padlock through a rusted metal latch, and then McAllen tested the sturdiness of the closure.

"Don't worry, that'll keep the son of a bitch," Mrs. Bolton assured him. Then she yelled, "Kill my son, will ya? Pray you see light again!"

Captain McAllen stepped toward the foreman and held out his hand, palm up.

Mrs. Bolton was the one to speak. "What the hell do you want?"

"The key."

"That's my shed," she said.

"That's my prisoner," McAllen responded. When she continued to resist, he added, "His well-being is my responsibility, and I intend to deliver him in good condition to the authorities in Carson City." When she still just stared at him, he upped the ante. "And I want water and food brought immediately."

She stood arms akimbo. "No way in hell. You don't rule this ranch."

McAllen tipped his hat. "Then I must beg your leave." He turned to one of his men. "Bring the horses 'round."

I had seen this strategy before: do things the captain's way or watch his backside. The engagement held my interest. Would she submit, as I had, or remain stubborn? I did not need to wait long.

"No damn chamber pot."

"Agreed." McAllen gave her this victory.

She made a flippant gesture to her foreman, who reached into his pocket and handed over a key. I thought the confrontation over, when she said, "Hardtack and jerky only."

I was grateful to see McAllen ignore her taunt and give instructions to his men for guard duty. At the height of the argument, I had feared McAllen might leave, and I would be left alone with the shrew to reveal the contents of the Bolton will.

With the quarrel settled, we left the shed to tend to our horses. As we walked away, Sharp whispered, "We'll probably have to hogtie both of them for the return trip." McAllen lifted two fingers to halt any more quips.

After we had watered, fed, and groomed the horses, a ranch hand came over to tell us that we were all invited to the main house for supper. Now I could find out if the Bolton cook was the one to blame for this overweight family. I also felt relief that I didn't need to face Mrs. Bolton right away.

Before we washed up, McAllen and I inspected the wall behind where Bolton had been shot. There was a hole about waist high, and McAllen used his knife point to probe the wood until he extracted a bullet.

He held it up with two fingers to show me. "Looks like a .44 . . . and in pretty good shape."

I held out my hand, and he dropped the bullet into my open palm. I turned it a couple times and said, "It's a .44. Another small nail in his coffin." I had another thought. "That comment about him killing women, could that be construed as a confession?"

"Doubt it. His lawyer'll say it was an idle boast made in response to cruel provocation." McAllen thought. "Probably got a damn good lawyer too. What'd you think about his boast of owning judges and politicians?"

"As you said, the man has had an unusually long career. He may have bought some, but my real fear is that he's done dirty work for other prominent citizens. If so, then they sure wouldn't want him testifying in open court."

"That's my thinking," McAllen said. "Sharp told me about the entries in that book. Think we can tie any political types to the client initials?"

"I can't—don't know the people—but I'll bet Bradshaw can."

"Did you check for his initials?"

"Yep, first thing. He's clear. At least in that sense."

"We'll ask for his help, then." McAllen paused and then said something that may have been hard for him. "Steve, that was good thinking to go after that ledger."

"The trick may be to lead people to believe there are names and not just initials in the book. Probably scare the hell out of some muckamucks."

"I'll talk to Sharp. Don't talk to anyone else about the ledger. Just the three of us." After I nodded, McAllen held out his hand, and I dropped the bullet into his palm. He then said, "I'll take the book as well."

"You have your prisoner; I have the book. I want to study it and make a copy. When we get to Carson City, I think the original should go to Jansen."

McAllen looked like he wanted to argue, but instead he just dropped the bullet in his pocket and went to wash up for supper.

Chapter 40

When we entered the dining room, Mrs. Bolton was talking with her foreman. No Jenny. I noticed that the table was set for five, which meant that either Jenny or the foreman would not be joining us.

"Gentlemen, I've set a fine whiskey and glasses on the sideboard," she said. "Please fix yourself a drink. Mr. Dancy and I have a little private business before we eat." As the rest of the men went to the sideboard, she said pointedly, "Please join me in the parlor, Mr. Dancy."

Evidently, I was wrong. No last meal for the condemned. I took a deep breath as I followed her out of the room and into the parlor. Following her backside, I could not take my eyes off her bouncing buttocks.

"Where's Jenny?" I immediately asked, upon entering the parlor.

"Finishing her packing. She'll be ready to go at first light." She held out her hand. "May I have the document?"

"Yes, but I'm afraid I was too late."

The veneer of pleasantness disappeared. "What the hell do you mean?"

"John's attorney, Mr. Jansen, had already delivered John's last will and testament over to a magistrate."

"You bastard! You lied to me."

"Mrs. Bolton, I told you about the risk in timing. News traveled fast. John was a prominent citizen."

"Prominent citizen? You ass. John was one of the most powerful men in Nevada. Soon, my son would have been *the* most powerful."

"Probably, but I'm afraid that now he's dead." I reached into my pocket and pulled out the thick envelope. "And he left clear instructions that have already been filed with the court." I extended the envelope toward her. "This is for you."

She just stood there, as if touching the document would make it real. I became convinced that she had had arguments with her son, and he had thrown his intentions in her face. I walked over to where she stood and held it out to her.

"What does it say?" she asked, still refusing to accept the envelope.

"Read it yourself."

She hesitated another moment and then ripped it out of my hand and tore it open with a vengeance. Large-denomination bills spilled out all over the floor. "Money?" She looked perplexed. "Is this some kinda fucking bribe?"

"Read the will."

"And what the hell is *this*?" She stooped over and picked up a train ticket. After a glance, she collapsed into her easy chair. "San Francisco. My God!"

She sat, stunned, for a moment and then screamed, "You bastard! You bastard! You stole my ranch." She jumped to her feet. "Well, you won't get away with it. I'll fight you till my dying breath." Shaking a finger in my face, she snarled. "No one—not you, not anyone—will take this ranch from me."

"Your son already did."

"We'll see about that." She raced to the fireplace, struck a match, and touched the flame to the unread will. While she twisted the document to keep the flame from burning her wrist, she started cackling so violently I feared she might be losing her mind. "That little whore took my son, but by God, she won't get my home."

"That does no good," I said, evenly. "There are at least two more copies . . . and don't burn the money. I understand San Francisco is an expensive town."

"I'm not going to San Francisco."

"You won't enjoy the bunkhouse."

She took a menacing step toward me. "That whore can't run this ranch. Jenny's just a child. She doesn't have the balls to handle these men." She waved toward the door and snarled, "They work for me. They're my men, and I own 'em."

"Do you think you've earned their loyalty? That they'll mutiny for *you*? Back you? I don't think so. The hands work for who pays them." I let that sink in a bit and then added, "Jenny has control of the bank accounts and title to all the property. You don't have the money to pay them."

Her smirk looked wicked. She bent down and gathered up the bills on the floor and thrust the wad of currency in my face. "I have this."

"Yes, you could buy a small army with that but only for a short time. Jenny can outlast you . . . and my Pinkertons will protect her."

She sneered. "I notice you have one less than last trip."

I had tried to be a gentleman and absorb her abuse, but her venom had touched a sensitive spot. "Did it ever occur to you that your son didn't run *to* Jenny, but *away* from you?" Her face told me I had pierced her shell and hurt her deeply. "You're a reprehensible human being. John meant to hurt you. This is his vengeance from the grave, and he did a tight legal job of it." I watched her face turn from rage to something that could almost draw pity. Almost.

"You're through here," I said.

She walked over to the window and turned her back on me. She stood at the window for many minutes, looking, I presume, at a view of her ranch that she had studied many times. As I watched, her shoulders slowly slumped, and when she turned back toward the room, she had completely wilted.

"What's to become of me?" she asked softly.

"I'll escort you to Carson City in the morning. That ticket will take you to San Francisco."

For the first time, she looked at the money, rifling it like a bank clerk. "This is only ten thousand. It's not enough for the rest of my life."

"Ten thousand is a great deal of money . . . if you're careful." A thought struck me. "You may take only personal items, like jewelry. Your bags will be searched in the morning."

"You—" But the wind had gone out of her.

"Call Jenny in."

She said no, but her voice sounded despondent, not belligerent.

"Then I'll traipse through the house until I find her myself."

We stood our ground and stared at each other for the longest time. Finally, she walked to the door and called the foreman into the parlor.

"Joe, please ask Jenny to join us."

Chapter 41

When Jenny walked into the parlor, she was dressed in a formfitting green dress with a high neck. The material had a slight sheen like silk, and the color accented her emerald eyes. Her hair was neatly tied in a bun, and she wore a single strand of pearls. Altogether, she looked more like a grown woman than at any other time.

Her eyes held steady, but the sparkle seemed dimmed. Despite her standoffish manner, I found her just as enchanting as when she effervesced and squealed with merriment.

"Mrs. Bolton, Mr. Dancy." As she spoke, she nodded at both of us, but then she gave Mrs. Bolton a queer stare. I am sure she noticed that the haughty manner was gone and that Mrs. Bolton's facial expression and posture radiated defeat.

Defeat? I had to keep in mind that this tigress could revive in a heartbeat and revert to her natural instincts for cannibalism and thuggery.

I turned to Jenny. "Mrs. Bolton has something to tell you."

I wanted to further humiliate the baroness by forcing her to tell Jenny about the will. The ferocity that returned to her eyes told me I had been right. To at least some degree, she had been playing possum, her mind calculating the grit of her enemies. Just as I had to fight Washburn with his weapons of choice, I had to utterly subdue the old witch or face her again after she refreshed her resolve.

After giving me the evil eye, Mrs. Bolton smiled sweetly and said, "Jenny, my dear, it seems John has bequeathed the ranch to you."

"And?" I said.

She whirled on me. "And what?"

"And what else? Tell her."

It took all my willpower to withstand her glare without comment. She turned on Jenny and stepped toward her until her face was inches away.

"You get it all. Everything. I get a few lousy dollars and a train ticket out of here."

Jenny looked stolid. "When does this occur?"

"Now," I answered. "In the morning, I'll escort Mrs. Bolton to Carson City and put her on a train to San Francisco."

I pulled the thin envelope from my pocket and handed it to Jenny. "This is your copy of John's will."

She used her fingernail to open the envelope and looked at it. Then she extended the document out to me and asked me to read it to her.

Mrs. Bolton started to sit down in her easy chair, but I interrupted her. "I don't think we'll be needing you any longer, Mrs. Bolton, and I know you need time to pack your things. Your presence will not be required at dinner, so we won't detain you any longer."

"I want to hear you read the will."

"Read your own copy."

"You know damn well—" She stopped, then tossed her head regally and curtsied. "Very well. I shall leave you two parasites to pick over my son's carcass. Good night."

And with that, she lifted her chin, held up her skirt with both hands, and strode out of the parlor. I thought I had finally escaped her wrath, until I heard the door slam like a clap of thunder.

After the echo had died away, I said, "Shall we sit?"

Jenny glanced around uncertainly, walked over to the easy chair, and flared her skirt as she assumed the seat belonging to the lady of the house. "Please read me the will."

"Do you read?" I asked.

"No."

With no further comment from her, I began to read. After I finished, Jenny sat silent for several minutes. Then with no comment to me, she went to the door and called for Joe, the foreman. Before he entered, she had resituated herself in the easy chair.

Joe came in looking as apprehensive as any man I had ever seen. His eyes flitted between us, and he chose a standing position in the middle of the room.

"Yes, ma'am?" He looked confused, but the slamming of the door and the sight of Jenny in Mrs. Bolton's chair must have told him that there had been a sea change.

Without preamble, Jenny said, "Joe, I am now the owner of the Bolton Ranch. Mr. Dancy, let Joe read the will."

I handed the document to the foreman, and he read with a rapidity that confirmed his literacy. After he finished, he asked, "Any orders, ma'am?"

"Yes. I want you to fire Cliff and Pete. Tonight. I don't want them on the ranch when I get up in the morning. Understood?"

"Yes, ma'am."

"I know that leaves us shorthanded, but drifters come by nearly every week. Use your judgment to hire two more hands."

"Yes, ma'am. Anything else?"

"Yes. I'm increasing your pay ten dollars a month . . . starting the first of this month. Give me your recommendations on the other hands."

"Thank you, ma'am. I do appreciate it."

"Joe, I'll be looking for your help to run this ranch."

"You'll have it, ma'am." He spoke without hesitation.

"Thank you. That'll be all. After you finish with Cliff and Pete, you can rejoin us for dinner."

"Very good, ma'am. And thank you again."

The foreman was almost out the door when Jenny interrupted his departure. "Joe, one more thing. I'm going to have a lawyer draft a document that'll give you 10 percent of the profits from the next roundup."

He looked flabbergasted. "That's exceedingly generous of you."

"Not at all. You'll earn every dollar. Now, you have an unpleasant task, so you better get to it."

"Yes, ma'am. Thank you, ma'am."

After the foreman left, the room grew silent. At first, I did not want to interrupt her musing, but eventually I had to ask. "Cliff and Pete?"

Jenny acted like someone jerked away from hard thinking. "They took advantage of my exile by Mrs. Bolton."

"Joe?"

"He did nothing to stop it, but he had the good manners to make himself scarce during the ordeal. He's a good foreman, and I need help."

"I think you handled the situation wisely."

"I'm not looking for your approval."

Her face remained blank and her voice flat, but I felt a pain that her words alone should not have inflicted. I merely muttered, "No offense intended."

She shifted around in her seat to face me more directly. "Please excuse me. This has come on so quickly, I'm still trying to get used to it." There was the barest of smiles. "It appears that I am in your debt."

"No, ma'am. What I did was for my own purposes."

"And what purposes might those be?"

"To capture Sprague and save my own skin. Carrying the two envelopes didn't add to my burdens."

"We both know my debt to you goes far beyond that."

"A simple 'thank you' will do. I'm certainly not looking for the remuneration you spoke of during my last visit."

"Good, because I withdraw that offer. I am now a woman of means, and I can repay my debts with other currency."

"I'm a rich man. I don't need or expect anything from you."

"Oh, I presume you expect a lot." There was a nasty edge to her voice. My face must have shown something, because she blanched and then seemed to soften. After a moment she said, "You must excuse my bitterness. You do have my gratitude."

When I said nothing, she stood and extended her hand. "Thank you, Mr. Dancy."

Chapter 42

Jenny asked me to join the others because she needed a few minutes alone. When I stepped into the dining room, Sharp met me with a glass of whiskey and a low whistle. I took a big gulp and asked, "How much did you hear?"

"Only the banshee wail." Sharp made a show of rubbing his ears with the heels of both hands. "It hurt our ears an' pierced our souls." He put a comradely hand on my shoulder. "We never expected to see you alive again."

"At times I thought I might never escape the room whole."

"Who says ya did? She probably put a curse on ya. Tomorrow, you'll wake up as a toad."

I laughed. "Well, she threw curses at me, that's for sure. That woman can curse with the best field hand." I walked over to the sideboard to get a second measure of whiskey. "But I suspect she thinks spending my life as a toad too light a sentence."

McAllen remained all business. "She coming with us in the morning?"

"Yes. I didn't give her a choice."

McAllen looked irritated. "I want her ready early. First light. And get one of her ranch hands to drive the buckboard."

"Captain, that won't be my call, but I'll talk to Jenny. She fired two of her men, so she's short-handed."

I didn't want to explain why Jenny had fired them, but neither asked. McAllen gave me a dismissive look and said, "If you can't get a ranch hand to accompany us, then you drive the team. She's your responsibility. Mine's Sprague." He looked at the empty doorway. "When's this meal gonna get started?

I was ready to snap at McAllen but simply said, "Jenny and Joe have a few tasks. They'll be along shortly."

I realized that my encounter with Mrs. Bolton

had been lengthy and that both men had had plenty of time to sample the fine whiskey. A couple of drinks had made Sharp playful and McAllen testy. I wondered if the captain ever truly relaxed.

Sharp said, "Captain, with a buckboard, we can truss Sprague up hand and foot. He'll be easier to handle."

"I already thought of that," McAllen said, "but even so, I don't want one of my men with his back to Sprague."

"Threaten to unleash Mrs. Bolton on him if he misbehaves," Sharp said lightly.

While Sharp and I laughed, McAllen just looked at us, stone-faced. After our little moment of gaiety had subsided, he said, "Take it easy on the whiskey. We need to have our wits about us in the morning."

During the wait, Sharp and I talked quietly, while McAllen impatiently paced the room, sipping his whiskey. With relief, I saw Jenny and Joe enter the room after another half hour had passed.

"I apologize, gentlemen. We had some business we needed to attend to before we could join you. Please sit. Joe, would you tell Frenchie to serve dinner. I'm sure our guests are famished."

Famished and a bit drunk. But we didn't have to wait long. Frenchie appeared immediately to serve soup. As we devoured the tasty beef barley broth, Frenchie placed heaping bowls and platters all around the table. He had probably been pacing in the kitchen, worried that his meal would spoil.

With Mrs. Bolton upstairs, dinner was a comfortable affair. Wine flowed freely, and the food was excellent and plentiful. Jenny's mood lightened considerably. She even laughed a bit at some humorous stories Jeff told. The foreman spent the meal saying *ma'am* this and *ma'am* that. Some of the spark came back to Jenny's green eyes, and I suspected she was starting to get used to her new position.

After we had been sitting around awhile, digesting our meal, Jenny went to the sideboard, opened the door, and withdrew an expensive decanter. She held it aloft. "Brandy, gentlemen?"

As Jenny poured each of us a glass, she told us we could light our tobacco. She obviously had no intention of leaving our presence, so we lit up and filled the room with smoke. One sip told me this was John Bolton's private stock, used for special occasions. I could not think of a more special occasion. Jenny and I were each free of our nemeses— or at least we would be as soon as we delivered the two of them to Carson City.

With the whiskey, wine, and brandy, the mood turned celebratory, and Mrs. Bolton must have heard the noise of our party. She would be furious in the morning.

When there was a pause in the bantering, Jenny asked, "What's Sprague like?"

"Cold," McAllen said. "Cold as death."

"Will he hang?"

"We have some good evidence," I said, "but to be honest, a good lawyer might get him off."

Jenny straightened her posture. "I might be able to help hang him."

"Oh, really? Please tell us how?" Captain McAllen looked more amused than intrigued.

"I'll need to see him." She pushed back her chair. "Joe, get a lantern."

"No." McAllen did not move. "Sit down."

"Mr. McAllen, I should think you'd want this man dealt with permanent." Jenny put on a coy smile. "Or do people like Sprague provide your employment?"

"Bad men are common enough. I've no need to worry about my employment."

"Then let me see him. If I'm right, I can identify him and seal his fate."

McAllen looked dubious. "I thought you didn't see who shot your husband."

"I didn't, but I saw Washburn point out my husband to a man."

"That seems unlikely," McAllen said.

"Are you calling me a liar?"

"Of course not. But perhaps you could explain the circumstances."

Jenny's next action showed she had learned a thing or two from Mrs. Bolton. Her green eyes became ice as she gave McAllen a glare that would freeze a small pond.

"After we left Pickhandle Gulch, we went directly

to Carson City. My husband had business to discuss with other politicians about his governor's race. When we left the statehouse grounds, I saw Washburn across the street, pointing his finger at us. Another man standing beside him nodded."

"That hardly seems like conclusive evidence," McAllen said.

"If you don't need testimony that Sprague knew what my husband looked like, then I apologize for interrupting with a woman's trifling." She took a sip of brandy. "I suppose a connection between Washburn and Sprague would not be of much value either."

Sharp and I laughed at the baffled look on McAllen's face. Jenny had matured fast and, in fact, continued to grow right in front of our eyes. McAllen flicked his angry eyes between us. People probably did not laugh at him, drunk or sober.

McAllen turned back to Jenny and softened his glare only a little. "Excuse me, ma'am, but you aren't intending to travel with us tomorrow are you?"

"Heavens, no. In fact, I don't intend to be up by the time you leave. I shall say my farewells to you fine gentlemen this evening. Why'd you think I was going with you? I have to learn how to run a ranch."

"With all that talk about Sprague, I thought you wanted to testify."

"I'll testify if it puts my husband's killer on the

gallows, but you can send a rider for me once the trial date's set. That is, if there's any reason for me to testify."

"You were right, ma'am. I apologize for my ill temper. There'd be plenty reason for you to testify if you saw Washburn point out your husband to Sprague."

"I said I saw Washburn point out my husband to another man. Until I see him, I have no idea whether that man was Sprague."

McAllen stood and unhooked his gun. "Joe, I think we'll be needing that lantern. Any of you who intend to join us should leave your guns and knives in the house."

"Why?" I asked.

"Sprague's dangerous. Do as I say."

"Not that dangerous unarmed."

"Put a weapon within his reach, and he could get dangerous with one swift grab."

"I don't think he's that comfortable with handguns," I said off-handedly.

"This is not a debate. If you want to carry your gun, stay in the house, but if you intend to join us, unhook. Am I clear?"

McAllen remained too testy for me to argue with, so without a word, I unbuckled my gun and hung it over the back of my chair. I wanted to see firsthand if Jenny could identify Sprague. Or perhaps I just wanted to spend every remaining moment with her.

Sharp remained seated and armed. "If you gentlemen don't mind, I'll wait here with another glass of this fine brandy. I'll see enough of Sprague on the trail tomorrow."

Joe stepped back into the dining room with a lit lantern. "Ready."

Jenny stood and smiled demurely. "Gentlemen, please excuse me. I need to step to my room for a moment. I shan't be long."

After she left, McAllen whispered to me, "Never argue with me in front of others."

When I responded, I did not bother to whisper. "Perhaps I made an ill-conceived comment, but I did not argue with you. And may I remind you that you work for me?"

"I accepted responsibilities beyond your purview when I took custody of Sprague. I'll decide how to best handle the prisoner."

"In that case, Captain, take it easy on the brandy. I need you to have your wits about you in the morning."

For the briefest moment, I was happy McAllen was unarmed.

Chapter 43

The night was pitch dark, so the three of us kept close to Joe and his lantern as we walked to the shed. In an unnecessary gesture, Captain McAllen held Jenny's elbow and guided her across her own property.

When we arrived at the backside of the bunkhouse, the Pinkerton on guard said, " 'Night, Captain."

"Open the shed, please," McAllen ordered, flipping him the key.

"Sir?"

"We have a potential witness here. Open the shed so she can get a look at our man."

"Yes, sir." The Pinkerton stepped forward and fiddled with the lock until it snapped open. Before opening the door, he asked, "What would you like me to do, Captain?"

McAllen talked loud enough for Sprague to hear inside. "Stand back, at your post. If Sprague comes through this door, shoot him. Clear?"

"Yes, sir."

"Dancy, you and Joe go in first, give an 'all clear' call, and then Mrs. Bolton and I will follow you into the shed."

I suppressed a "yes, sir." Until tonight, McAllen had been brisk but polite. I looked at him still holding Jenny's elbow and decided perhaps I was not the only one infatuated with her. She was always pretty, and with some of her animation returned, she had begun to regain her power to captivate. Did McAllen's ill temper disguise the fact that this enchantress had ensnared him as well? And whom was he trying to fool? Others or himself?

I pulled the shed door open, standing to the side,

so Joe's lantern could light the interior. Sprague sat on the mattress, eating something from a tin plate—something other than jerky and hardtack. Evidently word about the dethroning of Baroness Bolton had reached the bunkhouse, and someone had been thoughtful enough to bring the prisoner a plate of beans—and a single candle to light his elegant meal.

"Who brought you beans?" I asked.

Sprague barely looked up. "If you didn't bring thumbscrews, I'll never tell ya."

Joe swung the lantern around to search the corners of the shed. After his search, he said to me, "No thumbscrews, but I got a rusty old vise that might do the trick."

"Bring it on in, if you want me to squeal." Sprague said this around a mouthful of beans.

"Captain, things look tame in here," I said loudly enough to be heard outside.

Joe and I squeezed around to where Sprague sat to allow McAllen and Jenny enough room inside the tight quarters. Joe stood at the head of the bed and held the lantern high so Jenny could see Sprague's face, and I bent at the knees so as not to throw a shadow.

When they entered, McAllen still held Jenny's elbow in a protective manner. I started to get angry as I watched McAllen play the guardian role, when suddenly I felt a tug and found myself lying in Sprague's lap. He had my hair in one hand, pulling my head back, and held something sharp at my throat. How would he have gotten a knife, and how did he find someone at this ranch to help him?

"Nobody move!" Sprague yelled.

"Now what good will that do you?" McAllen asked the question with as little emotion as if he were asking directions in a new town.

"Tell your man outside to sit easy." Sprague shifted under me, and I could tell he was positioning himself to stand while still holding me hostage. "Pull my horse around to the door here, and make sure my rifle's in the scabbard. Tell your man to move quickly."

"He already has his orders," McAllen said. "You heard 'em. You step through this door . . . he kills you."

"If you don't give him new orders, then I'll complete my contract on this greenhorn, right here and right now."

"With a fork?"

Knowing what was at my throat, I felt less terrified. Surely, Sprague could not seriously injure me with a table fork. I slowly lifted my arm to drive my elbow into his ribs when I felt a pinching pain in my neck—and then the pain became sharp and throbbing. Before the thought entered my mind, I had dropped my arm.

"That's foolish," McAllen said. "I'm not going to let you go because of a little blood."

"It will gush in a minute. I studied to be a doctor

before I went into bookkeeping. This fork is pressed against his carotid artery. One more little shove with this fork, and he'll spurt blood all the way across this fucking shed. I'll twist his neck back and forth and splatter all of you like I was holding a fire hose."

"And how long do you think you'll live after that?" It bothered me more than a little that McAllen's voice sounded less confident.

"You're taking me back to hang me. What difference does a week or two make?" When he didn't get an answer, he said, "I'll tell you the difference. This way I die having never failed a contract. I'll go out with a perfect record. You know I'm ruthless enough, so get me my horse. Now."

"I can't do that. I'm responsible for your custody. I have a reputation as well."

"Doesn't that put you in a pretty pickle? Lose a Pinkerton client or lose your prisoner. In the matter of pride and honor, you lose either way, and I win."

I felt a different type of twinge and recognized that Sprague had twisted the fork to get my attention. I sensed that his back was against the wall, and he was using it for support as he slowly scooted up to his feet, dragging me with him. For a second, I feared I would not be able to get my feet beneath me, and he would ram the fork home. Then desperation gave my legs a spurt of energy, and I managed to ascend with Sprague.

"Decide," Sprague said.

"How do you know I won't shoot you when you let go of Dancy to mount your horse?"

"No more stalling. You're unarmed. When I get to the door, you tell your man I want to see him throw his rifle and gun as far as he can. Give the orders, or we'll just call it a night here and now."

McAllen looked livid, but he gave instructions to the Pinkerton outside to comply with Sprague's demands. I was trying to figure out if there was any way I could gain some advantage over Sprague, when Jenny stepped from the shadows into the light.

"This has gone far enough," she said. "Captain McAllen, do not interfere with Bill Sprague's escape." She took another step toward Sprague and met his eyes. "Sir, you have done me a great service. My husband was a depraved pig. Now I am rid of him and rich to boot. You may go . . . and you have my word that no one will follow you until morning."

"You can't control the Pinkertons."

"But I can set you free," she said.

Bang!

In the small, enclosed space, the gun's report was magnified to earsplitting intensity. I automatically twisted away from the noise, ignoring the fork in my neck. Before I could grasp what was happening, another gunshot ruptured the tiny shed.

As I hit the wall with my shoulder, I craned my neck around to see if Jenny had been hit, but the shed was dark. Joe had evidently flinched and turned away from the gunfire, unconsciously lowering the lantern. As he recovered and raised the light again, I saw a smoking derringer in Jenny's hand. McAllen had instinctively moved to stand in front of the door and block the only path of escape.

I took in Sprague next. Blood seeped from a chest wound, and a bloodless hole had appeared where his left eye used to be. As I watched, he slid to the floor, leaving two swaths of blood on the wall behind him, one from each of the two places where large-caliber bullets had left his body.

I heard someone say, "Shit!" and realized that it was me.

McAllen reached around Jenny and took the gun from her hand. "This work out 'bout the way you expected, ma'am?"

She took a long look at Sprague on the ground before she spoke. "I only said what I did so I could get close to him."

McAllen cocked his head, "To me or to Sprague?"

Jenny turned to look the captain in the face. "Excuse me?"

"Why did you bring a gun into the shed against my specific orders?"

"I forgot I had it hidden in my dress." She looked back down at the body. "Lucky for us, I suppose."

"I doubt that luck had anything to do with it." McAllen's voice had a nasty edge.

Jenny lifted her chin. "What are you implying?"

Instead of responding, McAllen stormed out of the shed. I touched Jenny's shoulder and gently pushed her toward the door. As we stepped into the night, I noticed McAllen had marched on toward the house without pause. I stopped Jenny and said, "Thank you."

"You're welcome." She gave me a genuinely sweet smile and said, "I believe we're even now." And with that, she marched toward the house. Befuddled, I had no choice but to follow.

As we approached the porch, McAllen came out of the house wearing his gun. He stepped down the three steps and held out the derringer to Jenny. "I believe this is yours."

"Yes, thank you."

"You always carry a derringer?" he asked.

"Since my sojourn in the bunkhouse, yes. It makes me feel safe."

"And now you've revenged your husband, and the ranch hands know you're a man killer. You've pretty much taken charge."

"I only did what I thought was necessary."

"Necessary for what?" I suddenly wished I had my own gun, because McAllen looked crazed. "I could have handled the situation and kept both men alive."

"It looked to me like Sprague was in control." There was now an edge in her voice. "Mr. Dancy has done me numerous services. I could not let him die in front of me like my husband."

"Your husband?" McAllen shouted. "Like you cared a hoot for him."

"Mr. McAllen, leave this ranch immediately and take that carcass with you. I'll not have you denigrate John. Whatever you may think, he was the first person to treat me well, and I cared for him. Now get off my ranch."

"With pleasure. I was on my way to do just that."

He immediately marched away toward the shed and yelled for one of the men to gather up and saddle the horses.

"Captain!" I yelled. "What about Mrs. Bolton?"

"You escort her in the morning. I'll leave one man to go with you."

Jenny started toward the house, and I stopped her with a couple of fingers on her forearm. "Can I speak to you alone for just a moment?"

She looked ready to ignore my request but then walked to the corner of the house and stood still until I followed.

"There's a new moon, and they've been drinking far too much to ride in the dark. This has been traumatic for all of us. McAllen takes his reputation a bit too seriously and said things I'm sure he'll regret in the morning. Let them stay in the bunkhouse, and we'll leave at first light."

"McAllen's ridden in the dark before . . . and drunk too, I suppose."

"Perhaps, but if we leave this way, the wounds will fester."

Her face softened a bit, and she craned her neck to get a look at my own wound. Noticing her attention, I put my hand to my neck and could feel dampness. "Come in the house, and I'll bandage that."

As we walked into the house, she said, "Joe, tell Captain McAllen that if he prefers, he may stay in the bunkhouse and leave in the morning."

"Yes, ma'am." And he scurried away.

While I sat at the kitchen table, she examined my neck wound and said it didn't need stitches. I enjoyed her attention as she expertly bandaged the cut. I put my hand to my neck. The bandage felt secure. When she stepped back to appraise her work, I asked, "Where did you learn how to do that?"

"Brothers. Three rowdy ones."

I wanted to ask about her family but instead asked, "Are you all right?"

She looked at me queerly and then said, "Of course."

"I just thought—" I let it go.

"He was going to kill you," she said. "Released or not. As he said, he had a contract."

I suddenly knew she was right. It had been close. Even closer than with the Cutlers. I nodded and asked, "Can you handle things after we leave?"

"I had good teachers. John built this ranch from a middling homestead. He took me everywhere, and although he didn't mean to, he showed me how to run his enterprises. His mother taught me toughness."

A nasty voice suddenly came from the door. "Is that little gun of yours empty, dearie?"

We whirled to see Mrs. Bolton standing in the doorway, holding a shotgun.

Chapter 44

My hand automatically went to my side, but my gun still hung on a chair in the dining room. Mrs. Bolton saw my futile movement and cackled in a way that made my stomach tighten.

I heard Jenny beside me speak in a calm voice. "You won't shoot me."

She raised the shotgun. "Why shouldn't I? Because you killed the murderer of my son? That don't buy you redemption for stealing everything from me. I have nothing."

"Because you won't kill your grandchild."

Mrs. Bolton's face flashed many emotions but settled on incredulity. With a sneer, she said, "How do you know its John's?"

"Because I'm nearly three months pregnant."

Her eyes immediately went to Jenny's midsection. "I don't believe you."

I didn't know whether to believe her either. My mind raced. Pregnant? What did this mean? Did this dampen my infatuation? What were my expectations, anyway? I had never contemplated marriage, and I certainly had never envisioned a family. What did I want? A tryst? I had never thought it through, but obviously I needed to figure out why I had let my life get mixed up with hers.

Jenny, on the other hand, remained composed. "Is it so hard to imagine?" she asked. "John and I had a complete marriage."

"What took so long?" Mrs. Bolton continued to hold the shotgun in a threatening manner but seemed to aim at some point between us.

"I don't know. Certainly not from lack of trying. John was a gentleman, but insistent . . . and I met my obligations."

"You met your obligations? You bitch. A woman should love her man, not see it as an obligation. You're nothing but a commonplace whore."

"I was young when my father sold me. He said it was my duty. No one ever spoke to me of love."

"John adored you. You should have returned his affection."

"I gave John what he wanted. I don't know why it took two years, but now I'm carrying John's baby . . . your blood."

"Damn you!" Mrs. Bolton slammed the shotgun barrel against the doorjamb so hard I was surprised it didn't go off. She swung the barrel back in our direction. "Why should I care? You'll never let me see it."

"Because it's all that's left of John. And . . . maybe we can work something out."

Mrs. Bolton was interested. It showed in her face. "Like what?"

"You can visit the ranch two weeks a year. When he's old enough, he can visit you in San Francisco . . . if he wants to. His decision."

"He?"

"A feeling."

This girl that I seemed obsessed with was pregnant. She also intended to live on a ranch in the middle of the barren state of Nevada. I had to come to my senses. While I tried to deal with my shock, Mrs. Bolton showed where her son had come by his skill at bartering.

"I want five thousand dollars a year as a stipend."

"Why should I give you money?"

"So you can have leverage over me. To keep sweet grandma's visits cordial and something your child will look forward to."

Jenny did not hesitate. "I agree."

"Payable in advance. Now, before I leave."

"Any other demands?"

She lowered the shotgun barrel a few inches. "Write the draft now."

Without a word, Jenny went to a small fold-down writing table in the corner and withdrew a bank draft. She scribbled for only a moment and handed it to me. Something that approximated a signature appeared below the number 5,000. "Please write the rest," she requested.

I moved to the writing table and finished the

draft. When I stood back up, I handed the draft to Jenny and turned toward Mrs. Bolton. "Put the shotgun aside first."

"How do I know I can trust you?"

Jenny continued to sound even. "Do you want to see your grandchild?"

Mrs. Bolton looked torn, but eventually her stern expression melted into her too-sweet smile, and she leaned the shotgun against the wall. "I'm not sure I coulda shot you, anyways."

When she stepped forward to accept the draft, I walked around behind her and took the shotgun. She said she was not sure she could shoot us, but I was sure. That woman had the devil in her.

After she snatched the check from Jenny's hand, she said, "Are you really pregnant?"

After a theatrical pause, Jenny said, "Yes."

Then I saw a genuine smile on Mrs. Bolton's face. "And I can visit once a year."

"You may . . . as long as you behave."

"The five thousand?"

"At the end of each visit."

"How do I know you'll continue paying?"

"I'll continue to pay only as long as my child wants to see his grandmother." She paused. "I think you understand."

After a moment, Mrs. Bolton said, "I understand." Then she pointedly looked at me. "Did you know I have a grand house in San Francisco?"

"No."

"It's in my name. John bought it to get rid of me a couple of months a year." She turned to Jenny. "It's in my name, and you can't take it away from me."

"Nor will I keep you from your grandchild if you behave as a grandmother should. I know we can never be friends, but whether we like it or not, we have something that binds us."

"Indeed, we do. Whether we like it or not, we're stuck together." After she examined the draft more carefully, she added, "McAllen told me about you dispatching that murdering son of a bitch." She put the draft in her dress pocket. "Thank you."

Turning to me, Mrs. Bolton said, "I'll be ready in the morning." Just before she walked out of the room, she looked at me pointedly and said, "I love San Francisco."

After she left, I said, "That was quick thinking."

"I had thought it all out in advance. Even the amount I would offer to pay her each year."

I was confused. "But she came up with the number."

"I know her."

"You thought she would do this?"

She shrugged. "Or something like it."

I began to see Jenny as a different person than I had imagined. I had guessed she was smart, but I had never thought she could be so calculating. I began to suspect there were depths I had still not seen. I had to ask. "Are you pleased to be with child?"

266

"I'm not pregnant."

She threw the answer out so casually that I was shocked. "You're not?"

"No. I'll write her after she's in San Francisco. She'll not get another dime from me."

"My God. You planned all this in advance?"

She said offhandedly, "I've lived with that woman for two years. As I said, I know her."

She stepped toward me and examined my bandage once more and then added, "I think that looks like it will hold. If you'll excuse me, I'm very tired." She extended her hand. "I won't be up when you leave, so goodbye—and again, thank you. I trust you will keep my confidence during the ride."

"Of course. How is she to travel?"

"Joe's been told to have her buggy ready at first light."

"McAllen wants you to send a hand to bring the buggy back."

"No. You drive and leave it at the livery. I'll send someone to pick it up later."

I hesitated. "Can I make a suggestion?"

"Of course."

"I was thinking if you sent a hand, he could bring back a tutor. Someone to teach you to read and write and figure."

Jenny's face lit up with the wild exuberance I had seen on that first day at Jeremiah's. "Yes. Do you have someone in mind?"

"A woman. Very smart and savvy." I grinned. "You'll like her."

"Mr. Dancy, that would again put me in your debt. Someone will be ready to drive the buggy in the morning. Thank you, and good night."

Having been dismissed, I picked my hat off the kitchen table and started for the dining room to retrieve my gun. Just before I left, I asked, "Was Sprague the man you saw with Washburn?"

"I never saw that man before in my life."

Chapter 45

When I stepped off the porch, there was just enough light for me to see McAllen step into his stirrup and swing into his saddle. I quickened my pace and came up alongside him. "Why are you leaving?"

"I already told you. Jeff and one of my men will help you bring that hag to Carson City. We'll meet up when you get there."

"Captain McAllen, you're still in my employ."

"We'll discuss that when you get to town." Without waiting for a response, he spurred his horse, and they all rode off, leading a horse with Sprague's body draped across the saddle.

With nothing else to do, I walked over to the bunkhouse to find my bed. As soon as I stepped inside, Jeff Sharp got off a bunk and came over to me. He jerked a thumb at the door I had just come through and said, "Let's get a smoke."

I saw my gear on a bunk and went over to grab my pipe and tobacco. The bunkhouse was a single large room with about a dozen beds. Five men sat playing poker at one of the two tables by the door, and a couple of other hands lay on their bunks reading. I looked around before joining Sharp and saw that one bed was off by itself in the corner with a chair and writing table. The foreman evidently did not have a separate room or cabin.

As I surveyed the large common room, I wondered how many other men had had the courtesy to make themselves scarce during Jenny's ordeal. No wonder she had developed a hard edge so quickly.

I was grateful Sharp wanted to talk, because I did not want to think about what I had learned or about my feelings. My previous relationships had all been in New York, with proper young women appropriate to my family's station and my age. My extended family had shown disappointment when I abruptly broke off from each of the women with little or no explanation.

I had never put the reason into words, even to myself: I had become bored. Any of those women would have trapped me in New York and in a social circle that scared me. My obligations to family and even my businesses seemed to be overwhelmed by wanderlust and desire to experience new adventures. I had long ago realized that my journal and book deal were just a convenient excuse to leave home and escape the pressures to settle down and establish a family.

When I first saw Jenny, she epitomized the untamed nature that had lured me away from everything stable and secure. My infatuation and lust had been irrational, compulsive, and indefatigable. Until tonight. Thinking Jenny pregnant and anchored in Nevada dampened my ardor for the first time. She had suddenly become like every other woman that had ever been in my life: a commitment, not just to a person but also to a place.

Place? I knew I didn't want to be tethered to New York City, but I sure didn't want to be tied to Nevada either—especially to a ranch in the middle of nowhere. And Jenny came with both. I knew nothing about ranching and had no desire to learn. Too much work, too little freedom. I shook the thoughts from my head and stepped out into a clear, dark night.

Sharp must have had an affinity for horses, because I found him leaning his arms across the top rail of the corral, smoking a cigarette. I leaned my back against the rail, facing away from him while I packed and stamped my pipe. After getting a good draw, I turned around and said, "Nice night."

"Not for travel."

"What has McAllen so riled?"

"He believes Jenny went to the shed intent on killin' Sprague."

"That's ridiculous." And then I immediately wondered if it was.

"I'm not so sure. McAllen says she had no gun during dinner. Remember, she excused herself to go upstairs before we went to the shed."

I thought through the implications of that statement. If true, it meant that I had only accepted Jenny's surface connivances and that she was far more mean-spirited than I imagined.

"Perhaps he's wrong," I said, without heart.

"Not likely. It's his business."

"But she couldn't have planned Sprague's attempt to escape."

"McAllen thinks that was just luck. She intended to just shoot him." Sharp flicked his butt over his shoulder. "He even thinks that story about Washburn pointin' out her husband was a lie."

That statement jolted me, especially after the way Jenny had so nonchalantly said she had never seen him before. Could she have gone to the shed with the intent of murder?

"That makes no sense. We already had him in custody. and he was probably going to hang."

"She knows Carson City politics. Hell, she probably picked up so much in tow with her husband that she has a better grasp than even Bradshaw. Sprague coulda got off, an' she knows it."

"But then she might have been tried for murder."

"A pretty, distraught girl defended by Jansen with all his connections would never be convicted . . . probably never even tried."

"But why? She didn't love her husband. I heard her say so in the house."

"Got me." Sharp rolled another cigarette. "Maybe because she couldn't get to Washburn, she went about settlin' the score in the only way she could."

"Killing's hard for most people."

"Not if you hate enough, Steve."

We stood there with our own thoughts for several minutes. Jenny was like an onion. Removing each layer just exposed another. If McAllen was right, she was not only conniving but also capable of killing face-to-face. I took a deep breath and decided to focus on Washburn. Then I remembered the smile she had given me when I mentioned a tutor. Damn.

Finally, I asked, "Will McAllen resign?"

"Don't know. His pride is hurt because he's lost a man an' a prisoner. In his mind, he made stupid mistakes." Sharp gave me a look. "All that man has is his pride."

"He shouldn't take it so hard. She had us all fooled."

"But it's his job. He feels especially foolish because he allowed himself to get smitten an' took his eye off his obligations."

"What?"

Sharp laughed. "Did you think you were the only one?"

"I—" In truth, McAllen's attentions toward Jenny had bothered me, but I had thought it was only my imagination. "He told you this?"

"Naw, but it was there to see. Just like you look love-struck whenever she's around."

"That obvious, huh?"

"Some things a man can't hide. They just happen to 'im." Sharp gave me a pat on the shoulder. "Don't fret. We've all succumbed, one time or other."

"But I do fret. Not because I'm struck with Jenny, but because Jenny is not the girl I had supposed."

"They never are, but I gotta admit, this one's a bigger puzzle than most."

I cleaned out the bowl of my pipe with my knife and said, "Can you help me with McAllen?"

"I'll talk to him. This ain't over yet."

I stuck my pipe, stem first, in my front pocket. "No."

I looked up at a huge sky dappled with so many stars that it reminded me of the sparkles in the Long Island sand on a sunny day. Did that thought mean I was homesick? I hoped not. I wasn't ready to go back east yet.

I pushed myself off the rail and said, "Let's get some sleep."

Chapter 46

Sharp gave a low whistle. We rode about a hundred feet in front of Mrs. Bolton's buggy, and I had just finished explaining the pregnancy ruse to Sharp. "That's scary," he said. After a moment, he asked, "How old are you?"

The question surprised me. "Thirty-one."

"Thirty-one. Well, you've done a lot. Been involved in some rough deals, I gather. But at her age, tell me what you had done?"

I thought a minute. "I had won a bird-hunting contest and negotiated my first business deal. I had bought four bicycles in New York City and sold them on Long Island. But my father helped. Oh, I hadn't had a woman yet." I smiled. "Close, though."

"Where do you think Jenny'll be at thirty-one?"

I surprised myself with the first answer that popped into my head—married to a forty-five-year-old man. Instead, I said, "From what I've seen, probably running the state of Nevada."

"The state may not be big enough to contain her." Sharp laughed.

I glanced back at the buggy, uneasy about showing levity in front of Mrs. Bolton. It was an irrational dread. I felt like we were two kids in the back of the class, giggling behind our hands because we were afraid of the schoolmarm.

Just as I dismissed the concern, Mrs. Bolton yelled, "Mr. Dancy, come here!"

I reined Chestnut around and trotted back to her buggy. Pulling up alongside, I said, "Yes, ma'am."

"Ride ahead and reserve me the suite at the St. Charles Hotel."

"No. I'll see you to Carson City myself. Besides, it's already occupied."

"I'll be fine with these men. Ride ahead and tell the hotelkeeper to throw out whoever's in there. That's my room. I always stay in the suite."

I had expected anything but this. The person she wanted the hotelkeeper to throw out, of course, was me. "I'm sure they'll find an adequate room for you. You're only staying one night."

"If it's anything other than the suite, it will not be adequate."

This was not worth it.

"I have the suite. I'll vacate it for you."

"You? What's a gunfighter doing in a suite in the finest hotel in Carson City?"

"Moving," I answered, as I spurred my horse to catch up with Sharp.

When I caught up, I rode in silence because I was angry with myself for giving in to her preposterous demand. Then it occurred to me that somehow she had found out that I had the suite. Damn her.

After a few minutes, I asked Sharp, "What are Washburn's interests in Virginia City?"

"A mine, two saloons, an' I don't know how many whorehouses."

"When he's there, where does he stay?"

"He has a place above the Comstock Lode Saloon. What are you thinkin'?"

"I want to catch him unawares."

"Virginia City makes Pickhandle Gulch look tame. It has a large police force, but it's still rowdy as hell. I don't suggest ya challenge him there. Too dangerous."

"Does he feel safe in Virginia City?"

"Yep. In fact, he has fewer bodyguards when he's in his own saloon, but the Comstock's always filled with people beholden to him."

"He can't make payroll after he's dead."

"Maybe not, but the police could arrest ya."

"Not if it's self-defense."

"You're underestimatin' Washburn. He's too clever to be goaded into a fight, especially when he knows about your skill."

I didn't respond immediately but then asked, "What's he do when he's in town?"

"Sees to his holdin's, breaks in new whores, hosts shootin' contests."

"Shooting contests?"

"Yep, out behind the Comstock Lode Saloon. He has a gallery set up an' gives five-to-one odds that nobody can beat him."

"Good?"

"Never been beat to my knowledge, but the

suckers keep comin' for the fun of it an' the chance to win five dollars on a one-dollar bet. He makes quite a show of it."

"He must have seen a Bill Cody show."

"One with Bill Hickok in the cast, no doubt. He wears the long hair . . . and that two-pistol cross-draw like Wild Bill."

"You knew Hickok?"

"Sure, in New York. Couple of westerners caught in the big city. We drank a few nights away, pinin' for the big sky."

"What was he like?"

"Unhappy. When I knew him, he worked for Buffalo Bill an' hated it. He was only in New York a few weeks. Then he went on the road with the troupe, an' I never saw him again."

"Did you see the Cody show?"

"Yep. Had to see if it was as bad as Hickok said. It was."

"I loved it. Probably why I'm out here."

"You bought that bunkum?"

"Not the show, but I bought the mystique and adventure of the frontier."

"Disappointed?"

"Not a bit."

Sharp started to say something, but I held up my hand and said, "If you don't mind, I need to think awhile."

We rode in silence for nearly an hour. I had most of it figured out, but the particulars would depend on events. If I read Washburn right, it should work. After going over it one more time in my head, I said, "Jeff, I need a favor."

"I think you're on the wrong path, but I'll come with ya to Virginia City."

"No, I need you to go ahead of me. Is it safe for you there?"

"Always has been."

"I insist you take two Pinkertons with you."

"All right." The quick response surprised me, but then I remembered that although Sharp could handle himself, he was careful. I explained the plan to him.

After I finished, he asked, "When are ya goin' to go?"

"Couple of days. I need to see Mrs. Bolton safely onto the train and give your part of the plan time to ferment."

"I'll leave tomorrow. Don't dally. Instead of fermenting, your plan may rot."

"One other thing. McAllen can't know."

"Figured as much, but what's his role?"

I told him.

Chapter 47

"Last time, you had a bigger room." The chambermaid had lost none of her insolence.

"I temporarily gave up my suite for someone."

"That would be Mrs. Bolton."

"How do you know that?"

"Mr. Dancy, I work at this hotel."

"Do you know Mrs. Bolton?"

A long pause. "Of course. She's a frequent guest."

"But you don't like her?"

"Do you have another letter for me to forge?"

"No. Please sit."

"I don't sit in guests' rooms. How can I be of service?"

This woman was exasperating. "Do you know Jennifer Bolton, Mrs. Bolton's daughter-in-law?"

"Yes."

"Do you like *her*?"

Another long pause. "Why should that matter?"

"Because she needs a tutor."

"Dollar a lesson. A lesson lasts two hours," was her immediate answer.

"Not here. At her ranch in Mason Valley."

"*Her* ranch?"

"You must have heard about her husband being killed. He bequeathed the ranch to her. It's a big operation, and she needs to learn how to read and write and how to keep books. She has a man here with a buggy, and she asked me to find her a tutor. Are you interested?"

"Does she know you're asking *me*?"

"No. Not you specifically." Her tone puzzled me. "Why?"

"We're friends." She looked away. "Sort of."

Then she squared her narrow shoulders and gazed directly at me. "Her husband paid me to play cards with her and occasionally to escort her to the stores or to do other errands. The answer to your question is yes, I like her, but I won't take the job."

"Why not?"

"It's hard enough to be in the same hotel with Mrs. Bolton. I refuse to be in the same house."

I laughed. "I don't blame you, but I'm escorting her to the train station in the morning. She's going to live in San Francisco."

The chambermaid smiled for the first time. "I'm not sure that's far enough away." Then a thought struck her. "Will she come back or visit?"

I ignored her question. "Did Jenny ever talk about her?"

She looked wary. "We shared a few confidences."

"Then you know Jenny hates her. Jenny has almost all of John's assets, and she won't allow her back . . . ever."

She thought that over. "I live in Carson City. Staying at her ranch would be an imposition."

"She'll make it worth your while."

"How much? What's the pay?"

This was a problem. I had not discussed pay with Jenny, and I already knew this girl was a shrewd bargainer. I decided to take a chance and not try to be clever. "What would it take for you to accept the position?"

Again, without hesitation: "Forty a month, plus room and board. In the main house, with no other duties."

Shrewd—hell, greedy was more like it. I would bet forty a month was more than Joe earned, even after his raise. "I have a question first. If you and Jenny are sort-of-friends, why didn't she mention you when we talked about me sending her back a tutor?"

"She thinks I'm just an uneducated chambermaid. I never told her I taught the children of politicians."

"I was under the impression you were her hired companion over an extended period."

"I was. Whenever Mr. Bolton came to town."

"And yet you never told her you were educated. That doesn't sound like you were sort-of-friends and shared confidences." I gave her as hard a look as I could muster. "Just tell me the truth. I'll not send her someone who lies."

She shuffled her feet and looked uncomfortable for the first time since I had met her. "Mr. Bolton told me he would fire me if she ever found out. He knew she would insist on lessons, and he wanted her . . . well he didn't want her able to fend for herself."

She looked down, embarrassed. "I know that's not what you do for a sort-of-friend, but I needed the money." She lifted her chin. "I did help her, though. She attended meetings with her husband,

and afterward I'd tell her who the people were and explain what I could. She's smart. She asked good questions and showed an appetite to learn. She wanted the gossip too: lovers, drinking and gambling habits, payoffs, everything. She just kept asking questions. I never taught her the three Rs, but I told her lots of things about how this town and this state work."

"You knew?"

"I'm a chambermaid in the most exclusive hotel in Carson City, and I'm in politicians' homes almost every day." She shrugged. "I have ears."

I was stunned. Perhaps Jenny *would* one day rule this state. "So she had another teacher," I mused.

"Another? What are you talking about?"

"She learned a lot from trailing after her husband, more than he ever knew. And whether you like her or not, Mrs. Bolton taught her how a woman can run a bunch of rough-and-ready cowhands."

Her face displayed revelation, and then she muttered almost to herself, "Yep, Jenny would soak it all up like a sponge." She gave me a clear-eyed look and spoke directly to me. "Jenny's clever. Clever enough to keep her smarts to herself."

"When I met her, she seemed innocent and unaffected. Was it all just an act?"

"Are you in love with her?"

This was another clever woman. Heaven help the men when these two got together. "I don't know."

"If you love her, tell her."

"I don't know which Jenny I'm attracted to."

"The real Jenny's a much more engaging woman. Perhaps too much of a woman for someone attracted to the bouncing princess with the winsome smile."

That hurt. And I knew why. It might be true. Now it was my turn to shuffle, and I took the coward's way out. "Forty dollars is unacceptable. Thirty."

"Done."

I had been had. Damn.

"All right, I'll write Jenny a letter and tell her about our agreement . . . and that you are not to empty chamber pots. If everything you've told me is true, there shouldn't be any problem. Can you leave tomorrow?"

"Yes." Then she gave me a coy smile. "And how do you suppose she will read the letter?"

"Her foreman can read." Why did the women in this state rile me so? "Thank you. A buggy will be in front of the hotel at seven. Be ready." I decided to motivate her. "I'll be in the lobby with Mrs. Bolton at seven-thirty."

Without comment she moved to leave, but just before she opened the door, I said, "Just a minute. Why didn't you tell me you knew Jenny when I asked you to forge that letter?"

"Because I didn't want you to know. None of your business. If you used it to harm her, I would have told Jansen that I actually wrote it."

"That might have gotten you in trouble."

"I've been in trouble before. Now if you'll excuse me, I have other duties to attend to."

After she left, I plopped into a chair. I told myself I didn't have any more time to think about Jenny or her tutor. I had an appointment in Virginia City. If it didn't go well, none of my feelings would mean a damn thing.

Chapter 48

The next morning, I sat in the hotel lobby, fidgeting. Mrs. Bolton was late. I was just about to go to my suite to get her when she entered the lobby with the élan of royalty. Damn her, she had no luggage and no porter followed on her heels.

"Where are your trunks?" I asked.

She smiled sweetly. "In my room. Would you be a dear and go fetch them?"

Damn her. "You're late. The train leaves in less than an hour."

Her too-sweet smile again. "Then I suppose you ought to hurry."

Damn, damn, damn her. I sprinted to the desk and demanded that a porter be sent immediately to my suite, and then I bounded up the stairs. When I opened the door, I gasped. Everything she owned was strewn around the room.

Well, this crude attempt to delay her departure wasn't going to work. I started shoving all her clothes into her trunks willy-nilly. By the time the porter arrived, I had two pieces of baggage jammed full and instructed him to hurry and stuff a third.

By the time we manhandled the trunks downstairs, we had only a half hour until departure. Luckily, I had a rented carriage positioned at the front of the hotel. I waved at the porter to load the baggage and walked over to Mrs. Bolton, who sat on a settee as though she had all the time in the world.

"Why weren't your bags packed?" I demanded.

She sat in a relaxed pose. "I couldn't decide what to wear. San Francisco is such a stylish town. I do hope you were careful. I have such beautiful things. I'd hate to see them ruined."

"We treated your clothes respectfully," I lied.

She cocked her head at me in doubt, and I had a fear that she would insist on an inspection, but she merely said, "I knew you would. You've always conducted yourself as a gentleman."

I hoped she would wake every neighbor within miles when she opened the trunks in San Francisco. I suddenly realized she must have more mischief on her mind. There was no way I was going to let her win, nor would I allow her to squat in my suite for even one more night.

"Get up; we're leaving. Now."

She defiantly remained seated. "Relax, Mr. Dancy. It's only a ten-minute buggy ride."

"The train leaves in thirty minutes, and it takes

time to load trunks. You'll be on that train, even if I have to truss you up. You decide right now whether your trunks accompany you."

"Oh, very well. You needn't get so riled." She extended her hand for me to assist her up.

I resisted jerking her to her feet and played the gentleman. After I got her to her feet, I stepped behind her and gave her a nudge with one finger in the back.

She whirled on me. "You bastard!" she screamed. "You can't poke me like some damn cow. How dare you?"

I had expected her to make a scene inside the hotel, and I was ready.

"Shut up!" I yelled, to show I was not going to be embarrassed by a rowdy scene. "You *are* an old cow. If you don't climb on that buggy right now, I'll knock you cold and throw you on."

The venom returned to her eyes in an instant. "One day—"

"Save your breath." I pushed her with my boot in her derrière. I meant it to be somewhat playful, but when my boot pressed her right cheek, it seemed to sink to the bootstraps. I only wanted to show her that I couldn't be intimidated by a tantrum, but I pushed too hard and sent her staggering forward. Expecting a stream of curses from her, I instead heard a rousing round of applause. It startled both of us that we had a large audience. Even the hotel staff clapped at her humiliation. Mrs. Bolton clearly had been tagged as the villainess in our little theatrics.

"Now go, before you're the laughingstock of Carson City."

It worked. She started walking toward the door. Thank God she could be embarrassed. Just when I thought she would go quietly, she whirled on the spectators. "You people haven't seen the last of me." She made a show of looking at each face. "I'll remember all of you, each and every one. You'll rue this day."

"Come on; get going. Nobody's paid attention to a witch's curse since the Salem trials." I pushed her shoulder. "Go."

She went, but if looks could kill, she was armed with 100-grain ammunition. When she arrived at the buggy, she threw me her sweet smile and waited for my arm to assist her. Nothing could deflate her for long.

After I climbed aboard, I told the driver, "A two-dollar tip if you get us to the train station quick."

His whip snapped before I finished the sentence, and the horse bolted. As we trotted away, I heard a yell from the hotel porch, "Go, ya damn bitch!" Obviously, she had not made many friends during her visits to Carson City.

When we arrived at the train station, Mrs. Bolton turned to me and demanded, "I need something from one of my trunks."

"Too bad. Get it in San Francisco."

I had anticipated this as well. She knew I hadn't folded her clothes, and she wanted another opportunity to throw the kind of fit that might delay her departure.

I handed the driver a five-dollar bill, far more than the fare plus a two-dollar tip. "Get these trunks loaded onto the baggage car. Then stand guard. You can earn another five if you keep her away from those trucks."

"Yes, sir," he said with enthusiasm.

I turned to Mrs. Bolton. "Time to board, ma'am."

"Why won't you let me in my trunks? My clothes better all be in there and in good repair."

"They're all packed, and I assure you, none are damaged, but I want you in your seat. You don't have time to rummage through your luggage."

We had a contest of wills for the next few seconds. Would I need to get rough? Could I? I thought about another day with her and decided I could do whatever it took to get her on that train. It must have shown in my face because she suddenly leaped out of the buggy like a woman half her age and half her weight.

As I took her elbow to escort her to the railcar, she said, "I apologize. I'm afraid I'm still angry at my son and took it out on you."

"Let's just get you aboard."

She stopped and turned her big face on me. "You don't believe me, do you?"

"I'll believe you if you willingly step up those stairs and into the car."

With a smile that almost looked genuine, she boarded the train and started across the grated platform toward the door. Then she stopped, and I almost cursed out loud. She turned and placed one foot on a lower step and signaled for me to come closer. When I approached the car, she leaned down and motioned me even closer. We each edged closer until our heads almost touched.

"Please, Mr. Dancy, don't let Sean Washburn kill you." Then she gave me her candied smile and whispered in my ear, "I want that pleasure all to myself."

Chapter 49

McAllen sat down, and his demeanor told me this would not be an easy meeting. Sharp and I had agreed to meet with him for a late breakfast to discuss his Pinkerton contract. I had already seen the chambermaid off to the ranch and Mrs. Bolton onto the morning train. It suddenly occurred to me that I had never asked the chambermaid her name.

McAllen interrupted my thoughts. "Not too private."

I looked around the sparsely populated hotel dining room. "It'll be fine, unless you start yelling."

"I never yell." McAllen's tone was all business.

"Nor do you have much of a sense of humor."

McAllen bristled but merely said, "I've telegraphed my office and explained what happened. They responded that our continuing relationship was at my sole discretion."

Now I bristled. "They must think highly of you."

"They trust my judgment." He was arranging his napkin on his lap, when his head snapped up. "You telegraphed them as well, didn't you?"

"Yes."

"That was a mistake."

I tried to be nonchalant. "And unsuccessful."

"They value my continued services more than your contract."

"Then you have smart bosses." I gave Sharp a *please help* glance, but he looked amused at my predicament.

"Captain, I still need your services, probably for a week or two longer. I know you're unhappy with the course of events, but you have a contract with me."

"The contract's fulfilled. Sprague's dead, and you no longer need protective services."

"Washburn's my real enemy, and he's still around."

"He's in Virginia City and will probably stay put for a while. If you're still scared, hire other men. There's plenty about. I've already telegraphed my men in Pickhandle Gulch to ride out today and meet up with me here."

"I want you and your team, not men I don't know. There's no one else of your caliber." The flattery had no apparent effect. "Captain, I need professionals."

"Why? You don't listen to 'em."

I wasn't going to listen this time either. When McAllen discovered that I was misleading him about my plans, I probably would be unable to hire McAllen or any Pinkertons again.

I decided I needed him despite the consequences. "Captain, I want your services for tasks other than protecting me. I saw Jansen last night. We think we can get a warrant issued against Washburn. I want your team to arrest him, but only if he leaves Virginia City."

"How're you gonna get a warrant?"

"New circuit judge. The warrant will be issued from Pickhandle Gulch."

"On what evidence? His initials in a book?"

"We don't have enough for a trial, but an arrest warrant will keep him bottled up, afraid to leave a town where he owns the police."

McAllen turned thoughtful. A good sign. "Are you asking me to arrest him or just discourage him from leaving Virginia City?"

"I want it known around Carson City that you and your men intend to arrest Washburn on sight. Don't go into Virginia City. We just want him holed up in his saloon to buy us time . . . enough for an election."

"I've lost a man and a prisoner in this engagement. My instincts tell me to say no."

We all waited while a waitress served coffee. After he took a sip, McAllen asked harshly, "Will there be any further trips to the Bolton ranch?"

"No."

"Will Jennifer Bolton visit Carson City?"

"I don't control her, but no, not to my knowledge. If she does, you needn't have any dealings with her."

For a moment, McAllen looked ready to spew some vulgar epithets, but instead he simply said, "I ain't gonna argue about that girl, but if I see she's got a hand in any of this, our contract is terminated."

"Agreed." McAllen stared at me until I blinked. "Any other conditions, Captain?"

"Sam's bonus."

That was an easy condition to meet. I reached for my bankroll and handed over one hundred dollars. McAllen counted it, seemed to examine the bills, and then handed them back to me.

"Did I miscount?" I asked.

"No." He blinked several times. I thought it odd that he appeared to be blinking back tears. "Sam bequeathed his bonus to you. But he insisted I get it from you and then hand it back."

"Shit."

I could see Sharp swallow hard. "I think ya should feel honored."

"I do." I held up the bills. "I've even got something special in mind for this money."

McAllen said, "I'm only considering giving you another chance because of Sam. What else do you want besides us looking mean and ready to arrest Washburn?"

"Jeff has business in Virginia City. I want two of your men to accompany him. He doesn't need to get anywhere close to Washburn, but I want some protection for him, just in case."

McAllen looked at Sharp. "What kind of business?"

"Mining."

McAllen looked at both of us and seemed to come to a decision. "All right." He gave Sharp a hard look. "Don't leave until my two men arrive from Pickhandle."

"I need to leave in the mornin'. I can't delay my business anymore."

"Nothing's happening here," I said. "Let your men already here go with Sharp. It's only a couple of days, and you can keep an eye out for me."

"You mean keep an eye on you. Promise you won't leave town?"

"Yes," I said. "Does this mean you'll continue in my employ?"

"Will you stay away from Jenny Bolton if she comes to town?"

"Yes."

McAllen looked a little surprised. "You're not gonna defend that girl?"

"No." I played with my coffee cup and then looked McAllen in the eyes. "I'm not sure about her. I'm beginning to suspect you might be right about her intentions in the shed."

McAllen nodded. "Then my team will continue to work with you." McAllen took a sip of coffee and gave me a rare smile. "I like you, Steve, but sometimes you're a damn fool."

I returned the smile. "Fools need even more protection."

Sharp raised his hand. "Let's order food."

I reached out and lowered Sharp's hand. "One more thing. When your men are in Virginia City, I want them to spread the news that there's a warrant for Washburn. Also have them complain that they aren't allowed to bother him while he remains in Virginia City. Have them grumble about their orders."

"I understand," McAllen said. Then, "You think Bradshaw can win?"

"Bradshaw is doing such a good job smearing Stevens, I'll be surprised if Stevens doesn't withdraw from the race. Washburn must be furious."

"Will he sit still?" McAllen asked.

Sharp leaned forward. "I'm going to spread the story that Sprague's little black book contained names instead of initials. Make him think we have a stronger case. I'll also start a rumor that he'll be indicted for corruption associated with the First Carson City Bank. He'll spend at least a few days figuring out a response. After that, it depends on whether we can actually get an indictment."

"Where's that book?" McAllen asked.

"With Jansen," I lied.

McAllen nodded and then said, "Remember, you stay close by me."

"Chestnut's getting new shoes, and the blacksmith can't get around to it until tomorrow."

"Don't go down to the livery. I'll check on your horse. Stay close to the hotel unless I'm with you. Understand?"

"You don't trust me?"

McAllen grinned. "Sometimes you do foolish things."

Chapter 50

I looked in the mirror and snuggled a bowler hat on my head. I liked what I saw. My dark New York suit draped off my shoulders perfectly, and my shirt looked crisp and white. I picked up my gun belt and slung it around my waist, cinching it comfortably tight.

I pulled my Colt to check the load and then enjoyed the heft for a minute before slipping it back into the holster. The last thing I did was pick up the little black book and secure it in my inside breast pocket. I was ready.

It had been three days since the meeting with McAllen, and I had kept busy closing an important business deal. Sharp had left for Virginia City with two guards almost immediately after our breakfast, and yesterday the two Pinkertons from Pickhandle arrived. McAllen ordered them to march up and down the streets asking people if they had seen Sean Washburn. Everybody in Carson City knew they meant to arrest him. Hopefully, everyone in the state knew.

McAllen had made himself obvious around town and had hired a man to ride out to Virginia City to eavesdrop in the saloons, so we could have an early warning if some unsavory characters rode out toward Carson City. The newspapers and the senate continued to rail against the sinister doings of Carson City First Bank, with hints that Stevens and Washburn were in cahoots with shysters. Bradshaw had certainly demonstrated that he could pull the levers of power.

That morning, I had received a telegram from Sharp, saying that Washburn was still in Virginia City. More importantly, the telegram informed me that Washburn was staying at the Comstock Lode Saloon and that Sharp's own business was near completion.

These messages were codes in case McAllen saw the telegram. Mention of the Comstock Lode Saloon meant Washburn was still hosting his shooting contests, and the reference to Sharp completing his business meant that the rumors he was spreading had reached Washburn. Both were crucial to my plans. The shooting contest would help me escape the law, and the rumors would, hopefully, protect me from Washburn's henchmen. It seemed that everything in Virginia City was ready and waiting for me.

One part of Sharp's telegram bothered me. He said Washburn appeared unconcerned. Was he a good actor, or did he have plans of his own? I didn't know, but by the end of the day, it shouldn't matter.

All of this was sideshow. I had deceived McAllen about the book and lied to him about staying close by him in Carson City. I grabbed my lapels and tugged them taut. The curtain was about to go up on the main act.

Since I did not own this hotel, I was able to exit by an unbarred back door. I had told McAllen I wanted to finish *Tom Sawyer* in my suite so he would not look for me until dinner. I left the hotel, walked west until I reached a residential street that paralleled Carson Street, and continued toward the train station. There was a short spur that connected Virginia City to the Carson City main rail line. It was used mainly to transport ore and mining materials between the two towns, but it also had a passenger car.

I had walked out of the hotel only twenty minutes before the train was supposed to leave because I didn't want to hang around the station and be spotted by a Pinkerton. I arrived with only five minutes remaining before the scheduled departure, and I was pleased to see that the train was in the station. No delays. With a quick ticket purchase, I was on board before anyone noticed me.

The freight train took nearly an hour to travel the twenty miles to Virginia City. When I walked out of the rail station, the city visually fell away down a steep, stony mountain, and the steeply terraced roads provided good sight lines of much of the town.

The vibrancy startled me. Virginia City was bigger and more frantic than I had imagined. The town streets cut horizontally across the hills, and I could see hundreds of people milling around. Someone with little imagination had named the streets after the letters in the alphabet, and a simple inquiry informed me that the Comstock Lode Saloon was on C Street. I found it with little trouble, but I didn't want to go in yet. I looked around, spotted a café across the street, and hurried over before I was recognized.

I took a seat at a tiny table and ordered a meal I had no desire to eat. Timing was everything. The shooting contest had to have begun before I made an appearance. My plan suddenly seemed a bit shaky. It depended on Washburn taking action on the spur of the moment, and the man had not shown himself to be rash.

I had been in the café for less than an hour, when I heard gunshots. I grabbed a waitress by the elbow. "Who's shooting?"

"Don't worry," she said. "The men just like to practice behind the saloon across the street."

"They practice shooting in town?"

For some reason, this made her laugh. "Oh, you'll be surprised what they do in this town. New?"

"Just arrived." I started to get up and threw two dollars on the table. "That should take care of my check."

"You want change?"

"Keep it," I said as I hurried out the door.

The Comstock Lode Saloon was as outrageous as the rest of the town. About two hundred men squeezed into the huge main room, some gambling, some playing pool, others dancing with saloon girls, and everybody drinking. A three-piece band played in a corner, and a woman danced seductively on a platform by herself. If her dance was meant to encourage men to take harlots upstairs, she was doing her job superbly.

I ambled up to a bar crowded with dozens of other men and eventually was able to order a beer. When the bartender brought my brew, I asked, "What's all the shooting about?"

"It's a contest."

"Can anyone compete?"

He looked me up and down in my eastern suit and starched white shirt and chuckled. "It costs at least one dollar to get a turn. Maybe more if there's a lot of takers."

"Can I just wander back?"

"Sure." Without further instructions, he left me to serve the endless stream of shouting miners that lined the bar.

I picked up my beer and walked toward the rear of the saloon. A burly man stood by the back door, so I said, "I heard anyone with a dollar can join the fun."

Without a word, he opened the door.

Outside, about a dozen men watched another man get ready to shoot. They all had their backs to the door, so nobody noticed me. Hay bales had been stacked along the rear of the lot to provide a shield, and I supposed the neighbors appreciated the courtesy. In front of the hay, an elevated board held up six brown whiskey bottles, the obvious targets for the shooting contest. Under the raw-lumber board, deep piles of glass shards covered the barren dirt. The bottles stood about twenty feet from a row of three bricks on the ground that evidently marked the shooting line.

I moved closer to the spectators, but nobody threw me a glance. This was evidently not a quick-draw contest, because the shooter had his gun out and took careful aim before his first shot. In rapid fire, he shot at the six bottles, hiting only three. A boy of about fourteen immediately ran out to replace the three broken bottles.

Washburn emerged from amongst the crowd and patted the shooter on the shoulder. "Nice try. I surely don't know if I can beat that."

This drew a round of laughter, and Washburn stepped up to the brick line. He looked dapper in his trademark gray suit, accented with a gray bowtie and even gray boots. He steadied his hand at about his belt buckle and then in a flash, he drew and fired six rapid shots. Five of the six bottles exploded. Everybody hooted and hollered and whistled.

When the men settled down, Washburn said, "Well, hell, must be losing my touch. Someone else better challenge me while my aim's off."

I needed the advantage of surprise, so I tried to step quickly around the spectators to make my challenge. Damn. Someone else grabbed the shooting position first. I quickly slipped behind another onlooker and glanced around with growing apprehension. I was in Washburn's terrain, and I was surrounded by his admirers. The rowdy crowd looked mean and more than a little drunk. If things did not go exactly as I had planned, I was not going to leave this yard alive.

The new contestant had drunk too many beers and didn't hit another bottle after his first shot. Washburn good-naturedly slapped the man on the back and raised his gun high in the air. "How 'bout it?" he yelled. "Should I give the man a chance and shoot left-handed?"

Everybody yelled and whooped, and Washburn deftly flipped his six-shooter to his other hand. He paused theatrically and then whirled to blast four of the bottles in the blink of an eye. He was good—possibly better than me.

I needed to get this over with, or my nerves might fail. As Washburn reloaded, I elbowed my way forward to the front of the crowd.

"Mr. Washburn, I'd like a try."

Chapter 51

When Washburn spotted me, he raised an eyebrow but kept his composure. "Mr. Dancy. Well, I'll be." He made a sweeping motion with his arm. "Gentlemen, may I introduce you to the killer of the infamous Cutler brothers?"

He grabbed my left shoulder and turned me toward the crowd. "Mr. Steve Dancy killed two ruffians at the same time in the streets of Pickhandle Gulch and became known throughout the land." Washburn patted me on the back. "Shows how easy it is to build a reputation in this wilderness. All ya gotta do is kill a couple of inbred jackasses, and men in these parts start thinkin' you're a gunfighter."

Everyone laughed as if Washburn had said something funny. He reveled in the attention for a few moments and then stood back and appeared to appraise me. "Are you a gunfighter, Mr. Dancy?"

I merely reached into my pocket and pulled out Sam's hundred dollars and held it up for everyone to see. "I heard that you give five-to-one odds."

Washburn eyed the bankroll and then yelled, "Clyde, take this man's money!"

The sheriff of Pickhandle Gulch immediately emerged from the surrounding men and grabbed the bills out of my hand. "With pleasure, Sean."

"Sheriff, don't you have duties back in Pickhandle?" I asked, mildly.

"I'll get back soon enough . . . leastways, sooner than you."

"You'd better hurry if you want your four thousand dollars. I could take the offer off the table at any time."

"Go to hell." But I could see from his nervous glance at Washburn that he hadn't told his boss about my offer to buy his half of the Grand Hotel.

I turned back to Washburn and casually said, "I'd like to see the five hundred dollars before I shoot."

Washburn put on a huge grin. "Ya don't trust me? Why, you've hurt my feelin's." Again, all of his camp followers laughed uproariously. I was not in sympathetic company.

"I intend to hurt more than just your feelings," I said loud enough for everyone to hear.

"Well, Mr. Dancy, I'm more than happy to take your hundred dollars, but we frown on gunfightin' here. I'm a businessman and town father in Virginia City. Despite my desire to accommodate you, I need to keep my good reputation with our police chief."

"You misunderstood. I mean to see you hang."

"Hang? It ain't no crime to kill bottles. Hell, been doin' it for years." More laughter.

"But it's a capital crime to pay one man to murder another."

"Well, that would be a dastardly thing to do."

"Cowardly as well."

"Whoa! That's not polite, but I'll let it pass because I'm sure you're talkin' about someone else."

"Let me see." I reached into my inside coat pocket, pulled out the little black book, and flipped it to a random page. "Sean Washburn? Yes, I believe I have that right."

For the first time, Washburn flinched. It was fleeting, but I caught it. He recognized the notebook as the one Sharp had been talking about all over town.

"These are Sprague's accounts," I said. "He wrote down everything, including his two contracts with you."

"Bullshit!"

"Bullshit?" I smiled. "You and I know it's the truth."

"I know no such thing. Prove it to me. Show me the book." Washburn reached his hand out for the journal.

I returned the book to my pocket. "You can see it at your trial."

Washburn gazed across his audience. "He won't show it, 'cuz he's lyin'."

"Am I?" I pulled it out and opened it again. "Two

contracts between Bill Sprague and Sean Washburn. One completed for twenty thousand dollars and another for ten thousand dollars . . . uncompleted, I might add." I snapped the book closed and slid it back into my pocket.

The consternation on Washburn's face was more than fleeting this time. The use of numbers that only he and Sprague had known proved that I had Sprague's records.

"Why are ya here?" Washburn asked, sounding genuinely perplexed.

"To win five hundred dollars. You got it?"

"Yep." Then his tone turned nasty for the first time. "No thanks to you. But I have sources ya can't hamper." He waved over his shoulder. "Clyde, show him."

Clyde stepped around Washburn and opened a cloth purse filled with coins and paper money. "You want to count it?"

"How much do you think is in there, Sheriff?" I asked.

"Close to a thousand."

"Then I'll trust you." I turned to Washburn. "What are the rules?"

"Shoot the first bottle any way ya want, but ya gotta shoot at the next five in rapid fire. Clyde here'll call it if ya fire too slow."

"No problem. And you?"

"I like to show off a bit." Everybody laughed but this time more from nervous relief. "You saw. But the same rules apply to me, I guess."

"What if we both hit the same number of bottles?"

"Keep goin' until one of us misses, but don't worry—that ain't gonna happen."

"Who goes first?"

"The challenger always goes first."

"All right." I stepped up to the brick boundary and smoothly drew my Colt. I barely hesitated. Six speedy shots blew the bottles to smithereens—all six bottles. When I reholstered, the air was filled with smoke and pieces of flying glass.

"Fine shootin'," Washburn said after the echoes died away.

I waved my hand toward the boy replacing the bottles. "Your turn."

"I will. But only after you give me that book." He held his hand out and smiled.

Shit. I looked around at the other men, but I could see no support. Nobody moved, nobody spoke, and if anyone was breathing, they kept that quiet as well. I took a step toward Washburn. "No."

"Oh, I think you will. Yer gun's empty."

I glanced around again, but I would receive no help from any of these men. Had I miscalculated? I turned to Washburn and was embarrassed by the slight quiver in my voice. "You wouldn't dare kill me in front of witnesses."

He shrugged. "You're right. Just maim ya bad. Now give me that book, or I'll take it while ya squirm in pain at my feet. Yer choice."

I hesitated several seconds and then moved forward another step, until I was in his face. "No."

He went for his gun.

I swept my left arm to knock his gun hand away and drew a pocket pistol from my shoulder holster. Three blasts ruptured the silence. His missed. I put two bullets in his belly.

Chapter 52

"Everybody stay calm!" I yelled.

Washburn yelled from the ground, "Kill 'im," but it was more of a cry of agony than an order.

The men looked uneasy and confused. No one spoke and no one moved.

"Washburn's dead, or soon will be," I shouted. "Those of you on his payroll are now on mine."

"No!" Washburn's utterance was little more than a croak.

"Think. I pay well. Ask the men in Pickhandle Gulch."

Indecision gripped the men around me. I held my gun level, pointing at no one specific. My shooting in the contest helped. I pointed at Washburn.

"No more money is coming from that man. I own the mortgages on all Washburn property. I can pay. Nothing's changed but your boss." I could tell from the faces that I had given them an excuse for inaction.

I looked down at Washburn. Both hands gripped

his gut, and he had his knees pulled up to his chest. His pain had caused him to lose awareness of everything around him, and his groans of suffering almost drew my pity. Almost.

I was about to walk away when Washburn regained enough alertness to ask, "What was in that black book?"

I pulled the book out and held it up so he could see it.

"Nothing." I flipped the book at him, and it hit him in his tearstained face.

His expression of defeat made the gauntlet ahead worthwhile. I still had to pass through the saloon to escape. I sensed no danger from the men around me, so I holstered my pocket pistol and reloaded my Colt.

Looking toward the door, I saw the burly man who had let me into the yard. I gave him a hard stare, and he just stepped to the side to give me clear passage. I let the Colt hang to my side and walked up the steps and through the saloon without incident. Reaching the boardwalk outside, I retraced my steps toward the train station.

As my luck would have it that day, the train was in the station.

Chapter 53

The prior evening I had gone from the Carson City train station directly to my hotel room. I couldn't remember ever having been more tired. I slept the night away soundly but woke up famished because I had skipped supper.

By the time I made it to the hotel dining room, Sharp and McAllen had already finished their breakfast and were nursing cups of coffee.

I sat down and bid them a cheerful, "Good morning."

"We were waiting for you," McAllen said.

Somehow I dreaded this encounter more than the one with Washburn. "Captain, I apologize for misleading you."

"I said you do foolish things sometimes." McAllen didn't seem angry. "Sometimes you do things smart. You handled this well."

I was relieved. "No hard feelings?"

"Toward you? No." He nodded his head at Sharp. "I've given Jeff a piece of my mind, though. I'm used to being misled by clients, but I have a different standard for friends."

His tone said that whatever had transpired prior to my arrival had been worked out between them. Sharp had preceded me to Virginia City, not only to enlarge the stories about Sprague's book and his pending arrest, but also to spread rumors that I had

Washburn's enterprises under siege and was about to take over his operations. It had worked well enough to get me out of town safely.

"He did me a service." I looked at Sharp. "One I'll be eternally grateful for."

Sharp flipped his hand. "Forget it. By the way, McAllen's exchanged telegraphs with the police chief in Virginia City. No charges. Almost twenty witnesses said it was self-defense."

I smiled. "Then I don't have to run like the dickens." I raised my hand at the waitress. "I'm so hungry, I may eat till noon."

"Plannin' a short meal?" Sharp asked. "Ya slept the mornin' away."

My easy laughter came from relief.

After I'd ordered a hearty breakfast, Sharp asked, "What are your plans after noon?"

"First, I need to see Bradshaw and complete the sale of the Pickhandle Gulch Bank to First Commerce."

"You're selling?"

"I'm not going back to Pickhandle," I said. After the waitress brought my coffee, and I had the first sip of the day, I added, "Commerce Bank will control all of Washburn's assets. They'll need a manager."

"Not interested," Sharp said. "I only run what I own."

"So you're going back to Belleville?"

"Not right away."

My breakfast arrived, so conversation stopped

until the food had been distributed. While I started digging in, Sharp explained. "Do you remember when you and McAllen caught up with me in Jeremiah's store?"

"Yes."

"I was readin' purchase contracts for minin' claims in Leadville. I worked on the deal while I was in Virginia City."

"Where's Leadville?" I asked, swallowing a huge mouthful.

"In the Rocky Mountains. Colorado. My agent did most of the barterin'. Now I got a few more details to nail down, an' I'll leave to inspect it."

"Train?"

"No. I'm goin' by way of Durango. Other minin' business." Sharp mused for a moment. "Why don't ya come with me? Appreciate the good company, and it don't look to me like ya got anything holdin' ya here."

He said this last with a lilt at the end of the sentence that meant it was really a question.

I did my own musing. "Could we stop at the Bolton ranch? Then I'll know."

"Sure." That was his only comment, but I heard disappointment in the tone.

A thought suddenly struck me. "If you don't mind, can Dr. Dooley join us?"

"He leavin' Pickhandle?"

"Yes, he sent me a telegram a few days ago. Seems he's done with wild mining towns. He secured a position at a consumption clinic in Glenwood Springs. If he hasn't left already, we can pick him up on our way to Colorado."

"Always wanted to travel with my own doctor. Never know when it might come in handy."

"I'll send him a telegraph." I hesitated. "You'll pick him up then, even if I don't join you?"

Sharp smiled. "Yep, don't worry. Any other news from Pickhandle?"

"No more from Doc, but Bradshaw told me he has convinced Richard to run for the state senate. If he wins, he's going to move to Carson City and open a print shop. Bradshaw has fixed it so he'll get plenty of business from the mint as long as he doesn't open a competing newspaper. I suppose Jeremiah's rooted in Pickhandle."

Sharp nodded. "Glad to hear they all survived this mess."

"I'll be leaving with my team tomorrow," McAllen said. When I heard you'd gone to Virginia City, I knew it was over . . . one way or the other."

"Only one way. If he had killed me, you'd still be in it up to your neck. I wrote a will with Jansen. Sharp was the executor, and my entire fortune— quite substantial, I might add—was to be used to destroy Washburn."

"Vengeful bastard, aren't ya?" McAllen laughed for the first time in my memory.

I reminded myself to write a new will. I had other unfinished legal work as well. I stood to make a decent profit selling the bank and withheld the hotel from the deal. I needed clear title, but I believed I would have no further trouble with the sheriff.

As soon as that little administrative task was complete, I would deed 25 percent of the Grand Hotel to each of my whist partners. Since Jeremiah was staying, he could run the establishment for the lot of us. I still thought the hotel was misnamed. From now on it would be called Hotel Whist, and there would be a permanent whist table set up in the lobby.

I pulled a thick envelope out of my pocket and shoved it toward McAllen. "Here's the rest of your pay, including bonuses for you and your men."

McAllen took the envelope and put it in his pocket without counting. "Thanks."

"Thank you, Captain. You were thoroughly professional, and I appreciate it. I'll send a telegram to your office this afternoon." When he made no response, I asked, "Did Sam have family?"

"The Pinkertons were his family."

I nodded. Finished with my meal and having a lot of work to complete during the remainder of the day, I got up to leave.

McAllen said, "Washburn lasted three hours."

I nodded again. "I should have shot him only once. He would have lasted a couple more."

With that I went to my room to freshen up before seeing Jansen and Bradshaw.

Chapter 54

The following day, I rode out of Carson City before first light. Sharp intended to leave later in the morning, and I wanted to be ahead of him by several hours. Chestnut made the trip with ease, but I had seldom been more anxious.

As I reined up in front of the main house at Bolton ranch, operations seemed to be back to normal, and everything had the appearance of a working ranch. After I hitched Chestnut, Joe sauntered over from the corral area to bid me welcome.

"Ya here to see Jenny?" he asked, after the preliminaries.

"Yes. She around?"

"Over in the barn. Just delivered a calf. She's gonna make a good rancher. Want me to let her know you're here?"

"If you don't mind, I'll go over with you to the barn. Like to see that new calf."

As we walked together, Joe said, "We heard about the doings in Virginia City. Think all the trouble's over?"

"Troubles never seem over, but that particular brand seems done."

"Glad to hear it." After a pause, "An' glad to see ya whole."

"Thanks. Glad to be whole."

When we walked in, Jenny was a mess: blood all

over from the waist down, with a streak across her face where she had swiped at herself. She beamed. Despite her dishevelment, I had never seen a more beautiful or happy woman.

She came toward me and said, "Nothing makes a day better than a new life." She gave me an appraising look and added, "How're you faring?"

"Me? I'm fine. My business is at an end."

"So I gather. Well done, I might add."

"Thank you." Her buoyant mood encouraged me. "I came here to talk to you."

"Go on up to the house, and I'll be there shortly. Ask Jenny to get you something cold to drink."

"Jenny?"

"The tutor you sent me." Her unaffected smile seemed to convey affection. At least, that was my hope. "I guess I owe you a lot. Her coming here made me brave enough to face my new world."

"She has the same name as you?" I was still confused.

"Yep. The hands call her Teach to distinguish us."

"Two Jennys?" I shook my head. "One's hard enough to handle."

This made Joe laugh. "Ya got that right. This second one's a handful as well. Come on. I'll take ya up to the house."

With everyone's spirits so high, I harbored good expectations as we walked to the house. In the background, I heard Jenny yell instructions about the new calf to one of the hands. She obviously knew her way around animals.

"Good afternoon, Teach," I said to the newly transformed chambermaid.

"Mr. Dancy, a pleasure."

Joe gave me a pat on the back and left for the corral. The new Jenny directed me into the familiar parlor and returned shortly with two glasses of lemonade.

After taking an appreciative swallow, I said, "Looks like you've settled in right smartly."

"I've found a home. At least for the time being." She looked a touch embarrassed. "This may be presumptuous, but you saved two lives when you sent me here. Thank you."

"I'm sure both of you would have done just fine without me."

"Probably true, but you made us happy with our lives. I'm safe and needed and nourished. And Jenny has someone she can talk to. A friend. Someone she can end the day with."

Suddenly, I felt wary. The happiness at this ranch had nothing to do with the end to the Washburn affair or my showing up. My self-absorption had caused me to completely misjudge the situation.

Jenny, or Teach, regaled me with the details of her pupil's rapid progress. It seemed Jenny devoured her lessons like a starving lioness. I was grateful to see my Jenny finally bounce into the room, looking bright as a newly bloomed daisy.

Her face was scrubbed rosy, her eyes twinkled green, and her yellow dress made the sun look pale.

"Mr. Dancy, you can't imagine my surprise and delight when I saw my only friend in the world ride up in that buggy. Thank you, thank you, thank you."

I was less enthused with my good deed. "You're more than welcome, but I was wondering if I could speak to you alone."

This made both women giggle. Without a word, the ex-chambermaid left the room and softly closed the door.

After a few moments of embarrassed silence, I realized Jenny was waiting for me to say something. "I hear your lessons are going well."

"You could have said that with her in the room."

"I'm stalling."

"John used to say, if you got something difficult to say, it's best to say it right out."

"Then I'll test the soundness of his advice. I came here to see if there was any opportunity for us."

"I thought you invested in banking, not cattle." She wore an overly puzzled expression.

"No. Not business, I meant—" I stopped because the look on her face said she was playing with me. I cleared my throat. "I mean personally. I know you've been through a lot lately; we both have, but since that first time I saw you, I—"

She held up a hand to stop me. "I surmised as

much, but I can't let you continue." All humor and even the exuberance had left her face. "This has been difficult, and I'm not—"

She looked down at her lap. "Mr. Dancy, you're right. I have been through a lot. My husband's been murdered, I killed a man, and foul-smelling men have raped me. My husband watched some, and my mother-in-law engineered the others." She lifted her chin. "I'll survive. In time, I might heal. But right now, I need a friend, not a lover."

"Excuse me, I wasn't proposing anything . . . anything like that now. I just needed to know if I courted, would I be received?"

"Mr. Dancy, I suspect you're a good man. I know your actions have generally been well-intentioned, but I don't know you, and I don't have the energy to get to know you."

The air seemed to have been squeezed out of my chest. "Energy follows desire," I offered weakly.

"Right now, my desire is book learning . . . with my tutor. I'm sorry."

Was there something more? Something between the words? I wasn't sure, but I was extremely grateful to hear Sharp's voice outside the open window.

I stood and peeked around the curtains. "That's Jeff Sharp. We're going to Colorado for a spell. It was a pleasure seeing you again . . . and I'm especially pleased to see you happy again."

"Again?" She actually looked startled by the term.

"A poor choice of words, perhaps. Anyway, we must be going." I stepped toward her and held out my hand. Her shake befitted a rancher.

Just before I opened the door, she said, "Write occasionally."

"I will." But I didn't know if I meant it. With that I turned my back on Jenny and joined Sharp.

We rode out of Mason Valley with the sun at our backs. Sharp had been mistaken when he said I would be good company.

Without prompting, he said, "Ya both need time." I did not respond. "Ya get a flat rejection?"

"To my way of thinking."

"Men in love don't think straight." When I again did not respond, Sharp surprised me by asking, "Did ya tell her ya loved her?"

"No." I rode a few strides, wondering if I did. I must, because her dismissal sure hurt.

"Why not? Women like to hear that, and it's a sight easier to say when it's true."

"Because sometimes I do foolish things."

For several miles we kept our thoughts to ourselves. Eventually, Sharp turned in his saddle and leaned his hand on the horn. "Steve, go back."

"I can't. At least, not now."

I kept my head and Chestnut facing east.

Center Point Publishing
600 Brooks Road ● PO Box 1
Thorndike ME 04986-0001 USA

(207) 568-3717

**US & Canada:
1 800 929-9108**
www.centerpointlargeprint.com